TEASING THE TYRANT

BWWM Rock Star Romance

JAMILA JASPER

Copyright © 2021 by Jamila Jasper

ISBN: 9798483075721

All rights reserved.

No part of this book may be reproduced in any form or by any electronic or mechanical means, including information storage and retrieval systems, without written permission from the author, except for the use of brief quotations in a book review.

❦ Created with Vellum

This is a book dedicated to growth, change and healing from our trauma and imperfect pasts.

Thank you to everyone who has been a part of my journey.

Thank you to everyone who taught me the value of hard work, to appreciate creativity and to take risks.

Thank you to everyone who taught me pride in myself, my writing and more.

Thank you to my readers who challenge me, support me and encourage me. You have helped me through so much more than you can ever know.

I will carry this gratitude for life. — J

For my Patreon family.

Sydney, Phia, Sharon, Charlotte, Assiatu, Regina, Romanda, Catherine, Gaynor, BF, Tasha, Henri, Sara, skkent, Rosalyn, Danielle, Deborah, Kirsten, Ana, Taylor, Charlene Louanna, Michelle, Tamika, Lauren, RoHyde, Natasha, Shekynah, Cassie, Dreama, Nick, Gennifer, Rayna, Jaleda, Anton, Kimvodkna, Jatonn, Anoushka, Audrey, Valeria, Courtney, Donna, Jenetha, Ayana, Kristy, FreyaJo, Grace, Kisha, Stephanie E., Amber, Denice, Marty, LaKisha, Latoya, Natasha, Monifa, Alisa, Daveena, Desiree, Gerry, Kimberly, Stephanie M., Tarah, Yolanda, Kristy, Gary, Janet, Kathy, Phyllis, Susan

[Join the Patreon Community.](#)

THE COMPLETED SERIES

Pretty Little Monster

Teasing The Tyrant

Seducing The Sadist

Each story can be read as a standalone tale.

DESCRIPTION

Rain has 237 photographs of Nashville's hotshot rock star Mickey Ford in compromising positions.
Perfect blackmail and perfect content for her growing blog.
One blackmailing mishap and she reveals her true identity to the <u>**mentally disturbed but insanely hot**</u> rock star.
Now Mickey has the woman who ruined his life in his clutches.
And he wants more than revenge... *he's out for blood.*

PROLOGUE

I've made mistakes.

Big freaking mistakes.

I shaved my first Barbie's head.

I called my mom a bitch once and I have the scar above my left eyebrow to prove it.

I've even failed exams.

No mistake I made was bigger than messing with Mickey Ford,

Back then, all I could think about was getting away from Keith, the toxic fuckboy who moved into my house the second he heard my cousin was *the* Meg Nigel.

Back then, I thought I knew everything about everyone.

Back then, I was so stupid.

But do you blame me? I was only 18...

He had everything I *didn't* and more.

I didn't know what would happen because of me.

I didn't know that I would end up killing Mickey Ford.

1

I'M THE BIGGEST LOSER YOU'LL EVER MEET

RAIN WILSON

The last thing I want to do on Saturday night is hide out in my apartment from my cousin Meg and her best friend, Angie. Alone. Whatever, I'm always alone.

Why am I hiding out? Right. It's mostly because Angie's also my boss and I just betrayed her by selling secrets about her famous baby daddy to a celebrity gossip blog.

I betrayed my cousin, too.

My boss is pretty cool, but she's scary as hell and her man is ten times scarier. He's in the band *Rebel Blood* — super popular, super country rock stars who inspire middle America to wave their stupid confederate flags and feel all "patriotic". Yuck. They don't really talk about that stuff in their music, but their fans *suck*. A lot.

Everyone in the country *loves* Rebel Blood because they're all young, extremely hot, and really country for rock stars. They're all walking 70s revivals in the flesh. Tall. Handsome.

American. They're all old-school sexy, which works for some people, I guess.

These guys are too hot for me. I would never date a guy that's too hot. It's just like... yuck. I'm simple. I'm basic. Give me a bald guy with a beer gut any day. Ugh. Who am I kidding?

Keith has a beer gut — and he's freaking out about balding. He has the weirdest haircut too, like he's trying to hide it. I don't know how to break it to my boyfriend that everyone knows he's balding and that ratty little ponytail isn't making a difference.

I could never be with a guy in a band like *Rebel Blood*... Guys in my lane are guys like Keith. I prefer to be realistic, unlike their stupid little fans who write fan fiction about banging Seb Jefferson. I read a *crazy* fan fiction once where some girl imagined having all three guys at once.

Yikes. The fan fiction stopped when Seb Jefferson got engaged to my boss. The tabloids are still going bananas over the 'mystery girl'. Is she a model? Is she a celebrity? Everyone's dying to know and the truth is ten times crazier than the rumors.

I'm not jealous or anything, but I want to know Angie's secret for snagging a tall, rich, and sexy man. Platinum blond hair and eyes like Seb Jefferson's would be a plus, but I don't want to aim too high. Famous people are obviously all completely fucked up, but still...

Angie's the only other woman I know as dark-skinned as I am. Well, Angie is darker than me, but still. She has the world's most desirable fiancé. My mom always told me I was too dark to find a good man. Angie proved her wrong. Meg also thinks my mom's wrong, but Meg... she just doesn't get it.

My cousin thinks the world just opens up for me and I can just get a man better than Keith, but she doesn't understand.

When I was twelve, I told my mom I had a crush on a white boy in my class and she just laughed at me. She said I needed to just be grateful that *any* man would put up with my black ass, especially the way I spend time in the sun.

I tore up the drawing I was going to give to him and I stopped having crushes on white boys. Forever.

Sigh. My mom might be dumb as hell, but she's probably right. Plus, Keith's beer gut is sexy. In its own way. At least it covers up the "Put Mouth Here" tattoo above his crotch.

Meg just thinks I'm a loser who needs to "stay off the internet" and "put myself out there more". She's not even wrong.

I *am* a loser. But this job at Angie's bar isn't making me any less of a loser. My coworker Elijah hates my guts and I never know what to say when people at work make conversation. They all went to Vanderbilt or University of Tennessee and they talk about college stuff.

I only pretend to know what they're talking about when they say 'hegemony' or 'equity' or any of those words. I don't want to get caught being 'problematic'.

I only learned about that stuff on social media and honestly? I don't really get it. Say the wrong thing and they'll call me toxic. I'll never forget what happened to Sara after her first day at the bar...

She was immediately "canceled" and had to quit because she said that the homeless man outside made her uncomfortable. Elijah called her classist. Marissa said her privilege was showing. And I kept quiet to stay out of trouble because that same homeless guy pinched my ass one day after the lunch shift.

I learned to keep my mouth shut at work when I didn't know what was happening. But then everyone hates me for being quiet. Black girls aren't meant to be quiet, so they get confused that I'm not sassy or entertaining enough, like it's my job to entertain people because I'm black.

Work sucks. But whatever. My new apartment is at least a great place to hide out. Maybe if I went to college, I'd have friends. Elijah has tons of friends from Vanderbilt, even if he's annoying about going there and *always* brings up his stupid student loans.

I'll never go to college. I'm too poor to afford it and too dumb to get a scholarship. My mom laughed when I asked for help to get financial aid.

Keith would never let me go to college, anyway. He says that college girls get bad ideas. Keith isn't the best boyfriend, but he always comes back to me. That's loyalty. Even after cheating, going back to his baby mama, and all that stuff... he just comes back. Always.

I'm not like Meg. I'm not smart enough to claw my way out of the hood. I can't even find an apartment that doesn't have roaches. I've just learned to live with them. I caught myself talking to a roach in the shower once about *90 Day Fiancé*. I think that was rock bottom. Who am I kidding? My whole life is rock bottom.

The only thing that will get me out of my dismal life is the story I just sold to *Celebz Leaked* — the gossip blog that nearly ruined my boss's life.

The person behind *Celebz Leaked* only goes by a screen name.

The Tyrant

The Tyrant doesn't want to let me out of my contract. **The Tyrant knows** because of Meg, I can get in anywhere in Nashville's social scene, especially with Meg's new contacts to *Rebel Blood*.

The Tyrant knows my phone passcode, my social security number and where I went to high school. **The Tyrant** knows that I have access to important people because of my cousin — that makes me important. Useful.

I was losing my usefulness until 2 years ago. Meg moving back to Nashville was the best thing to happen to me because damn, my cousin is connected.

I can't tell anyone who **The Tyrant** is or I will die.

I don't know who scares me more: Keith or **The Tyrant**. I want to escape both of them forever, but I'm totally trapped. The worst part is knowing that I can't hide in this apartment forever or even for long.

I ought to tell someone that I know who it is now. I know **The Tyrant**'s true identity. If I even *think* the name to anyone else, **The Tyrant** will know I told and then **The Tyrant** will slit my throat. This is not some Gen Z joke, okay. *The Tyrant will literally slit my throat.*

JAMILA JASPER

●○○○○ CRICKET LTE 3:45 AM   5% ⬜

‹ Messages   **The Tyrant**   Details

> I've covered up a murder before.

📷 iMessage   Send

> I've covered up a murder before.

> Don't forget no one will actually care that you're dead.

> Rain Wilson.

Don't forget, no one will actually *care that you're dead, Rain.*

Sorry, Meg, but I choose my life over saving Mickey Ford any day. He's a scumbag, just like Sebastian Jefferson and the rest of *Rebel Blood*.

They're gross white, redneck-American celebrities who profit off our outrage by doing offensive things on purpose. I hate them more than anything. Their records are *so* stupid.

Love songs are just what guys like Keith use to trap you.

I don't even care about getting my stupid Limited Edition *Rebel Blood* vinyl records back from Keith. I only started collecting them because Mickey Ford's ex used to post them all to her social media. I don't even like *Rebel Blood*, but I followed her and all the band members in case there was any good tea.

Keith sends me another text. Ugh. He is so thirsty. My mama told me that a 34-year-old man would be good for me and that Keith would mature soon but he hasn't matured at all. I'm 18, he's 36, and I'm ten times more grown than he is.

If I even talk to Keith, he'll find some way to get back together with me… or *worse…* move into my damn apartment again.

Meg *tried* to warn me about these "hobo-sexuals" but I thought she was a bitter thirty-something woman jealous of my youth. She never liked the fact that Keith was so much older, but I shouldn't have judged her.

Sorry, girl! In my defense, Meg *is* bitter. At least she was until she left the life of single ladies for the freaky-dick ex-con she's pretending not to be in love with. She's lucky. I tried to get a boyfriend, but all I got was a Keith...

There's a loud thud at my door and I realize that I've failed at hiding. I'm not even surprised because I fail at literally everything. I don't want to open the door. My new place is only a studio (and it has even bigger roaches) but it's mine, and I don't want to let anyone in. I pull the blanket over my head and tell myself that the brushing on the back of my neck is my hair and not *another* cockroach.

When I hear the voice on the other side of the door, I know there's no way I can hide forever. It's **The Tyrant**. I climb out of bed and throw on a hoodie as The **Tyrant** pounds again.

"I know you're in there..."

Why is no one else scared of looking into The **Tyrant's** eyes? Their eyes always scare me. I never liked eyes that weren't brown. They always made me uncomfortable. I don't know how Angie does it with Seb.

I'd freeze right up with those redneck-demon eyes staring at me. I've just never seen it for these white boys.

I throw the door open with a scowl. I know The **Tyrant** has absolute power over me, but I *have* to act tough.

"What do you want?" I snap, rolling my head as much as possible.

There's no point in me asking how **The Tyrant** even found me. It's what **The Tyrant** does.

"You were right. He's in Ithaca. I have our team on it and honestly, Rain. It's going to be huge."

"What do you mean it's going to be huge?"

"You got his location and we have a story and will prove once and for all that Mickey Ford's a fucking fairy. Let's see how his fans like him once they know the truth."

I roll my eyes as dramatically as I can afford to do without pissing The **Tyrant** off. **The Tyrant's** use of the slur disgusts me almost as much as the passion behind it.

"It's 2021. No one cares if people are gay anymore."

The smug words fall out of **The Tyrant's** mouth next, "They might care if he's been lying about having AIDS."

"He doesn't have AIDS," I say, as if **The Tyrant** gives a damn about the truth.

"All we need is an *element* of truth. And anyway, Mickey Ford can make this problem go away."

2

THE WORLD'S BIGGEST FUCK UP

MICKEY FORD

I don't know what's wrong with me. I don't know why I can't stop. I wasn't born this way. I wasn't always like this. Believe it or not, I used to say that I'd never touch liquor after what I saw it do to my daddy. After what it did to my family. He went to jail, my mama turned to church and in the end, daddy got out of jail and left her for a man. That didn't make me drink.

I was carrying along fine, really.

Then something happened. I saw something. Then more stuff happened.

I spent the next three days wandering around my house. Numb. Then, I drank. Seb was high as a kite when he offered me my first bump.

"We're rich, Mick. Who gives a fuck? Do the drugs. Fuck the women. The world is ours."

Yeah, Sebastian. The world is ours. Next thing you know, I'm losing it. Robbed on 14th Street — $20,000 gone from my wallet. Scammed by a stripper (pretending to be an aspiring singer) for $100,000. Spending $10,000 a week on blow. Spending $30,000 a week on my LA 'friends'.

All of it careened into this mess. Mickey fucking Ford hiding out in his Finger Lakes mansion, staring at a screen and wondering who the fuck could have found out… everything.

Me. The girl. My nudes.

Damn. Seb was right. It's stupid to take pictures of my junk. I can't help that sometimes I just want to take a picture.

It's hard to describe, but it's just an urge. I've been trying to find a plantain bigger than it and… it just doesn't work.

Earl Wayne Jr. thinks its proof I'm an idiot. I think it's proof that he ain't as well hung as he thinks. I have yet to find the right plantain…

Anyway, my bigger-than-a-plantain dick ain't the biggest problem. At least not when it comes to the blackmail showing up on my screen and even in my physical mailbox.

It's not just the dick stuff. Under my clothes, I have tattoos that Vogue definitely doesn't know about. Tattoos that could end my career, even if Lord knows our fans don't give a damn about what ink I've got going on.

TEASING THE TYRANT

MiCkEy,
I WiLl fuCk up
your liFE if yOU
Do Not OBEY.
I hAve YOur nAkEd
picTures.
NIce taTtoo, fAg.
KiLl YouRSeLf
befoRE CElebz
LeAKeD geTs you.
it'S oVeR.
XO t

At first, I thought Tati (my ex) sent the note. I texted her to ask and she sent me a picture of her new boyfriend. Yeah, I wasn't trying to get back together with the singer (she cheated on me). I just wanted to know… who has these pictures?

The next note came, proving once and for all, Tati has nothing to do with this. She doesn't know about what happened. No one does… not even my best friend Sebastian Jefferson.

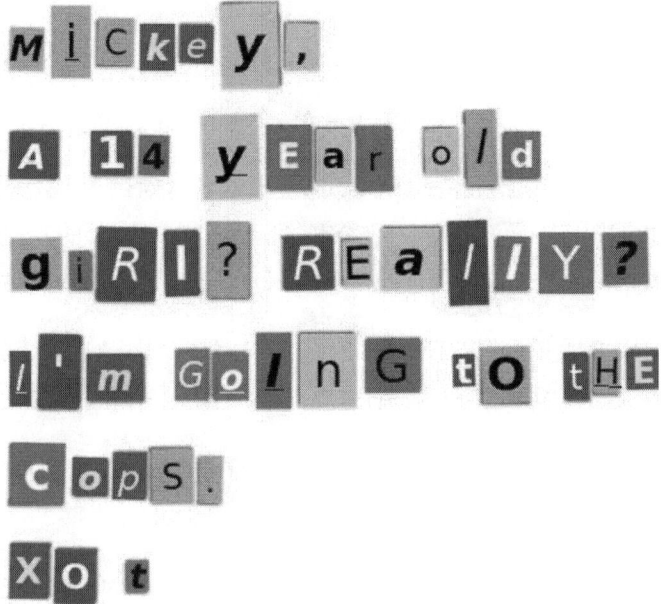

Mickey,
A 14 year old girl? Really?
I'm going to the cops.
xo t

The next note shows up a week after the first, and my blood runs cold. Seb has his own problems. I can't tell him what's happening, but each pasted note points to a riddle that I can't solve. I ain't ever been the type to solve puzzles really good. Kara, our band's second guitar, likes to remind me I'm stupid.

Hell, my siblings like to remind me I'm stupid. Especially my sister, Shelby Ford, who doesn't have a lick of time for sinful rock-and-roll.

The notes got worse, though. Much worse.

I knew after that note, I should call Seb. But Seb just found out that he's the proud father to a spunky little girl with gorgeous dark curls and a smile that's as broad and mischievous as her father's. I can't bring danger into Seb's life.

I have to trust the other members of Rebel Blood. Sweet Kara and loud-mouthed Earl Wayne Jr. I don't want to put them in danger by telling them the details, but it's time I come clean about the stalker. The notes and everything else.

Earl might know what to do. He's been through something like this before. Not exactly the same, but Earl has *interesting* taste in women. Blackmailers are some of the most normal ex-girlfriends left in the giant man's wake.

Earl's not just as tall as I am, he's broad and built like someone who started milking cows when he was as tall as my knee, though we all know that Earl never milked a cow in his life or did any of the country shit he writes about in his songs. He's a rich boy and fortunately for me, rich boys know blackmail pretty damn good.

Earl wanders into my house, looking around for bottles and glass pipes, spoons, scorched pieces of tinfoil, powder and lighters. He glances at my hand for scorched fingers, but he won't find a sign of anything.

"I flew up as soon as I could."

"I know you have to go back down tonight. I just needed to talk to someone. Where's Kara?"

"You know you can always reach out to me, right?"

"You have enough on your plate with Devonté and LaShawn."

Earl's cheeks flush. He protects that side of his life from us as best he can, but we spend so much time together that it's hard not to know details about Earl's life that he tries to hide. We've known each other for too long. We're like brothers in a proper sense. We didn't exactly choose this band. They threw us together and made us... a product.

Earl took it easier than all of us. He was a product from the start. Prep school educated at Northfield Mount Hermon up north, and then Duke University before he joined Rebel Blood. So, he's older than me and Seb. And hopefully wiser.

"You're my brother," Earl says in a deep, booming voice. "You don't have to run to Seb with everything. I want to help."

"Blackmail," I tell him. "Can you help with blackmail?"

"Fuck's sake, Mick. Who did you piss off?"

Yeah, when you're the world's biggest fuck-up, everyone assumes you're the problem, even when you're being blackmailed.

"It doesn't matter. They're asking for money and... I think my sister's in trouble."

Earl kissed my big sister Shelby years ago and even if she slapped him across the face after, I think he still has a soft spot for my religious West Virginian sister who would rather die than date a rock-n-roller.

"Shelby?" Earl asks eagerly. "How's it been with her and Randy?"

"Still married, Earl. But she's in trouble. And so am I."

I explain everything that I can to him and Earl listens intently. He ain't doubting a thing I said. He's just slow to consider, protective, but slow to act. He strokes his chin.

"Any idea who it could be?"

"Would that make a damned difference? I don't have $55k. Seb's helping me with my expenses until the next album, but... I'm the world's biggest fuck up."

Earl sighs.

"Let me guess, you just closed on the Nashville property even if we all told you it's much too expensive and you don't need 10 acres just for yourself?"

"Shut up, Earl..."

Earl pulls out his hip flask and takes a reluctant drink, throwing a severe glare in my direction.

"I can give you the money."

He could have given me the money before Rebel Blood. Earl's family owns one of the largest plantations in Georgia. And Louisiana. And Virginia. You get the point. They're stinking rich.

"It's not just about the money, Earl. I'm fucked."

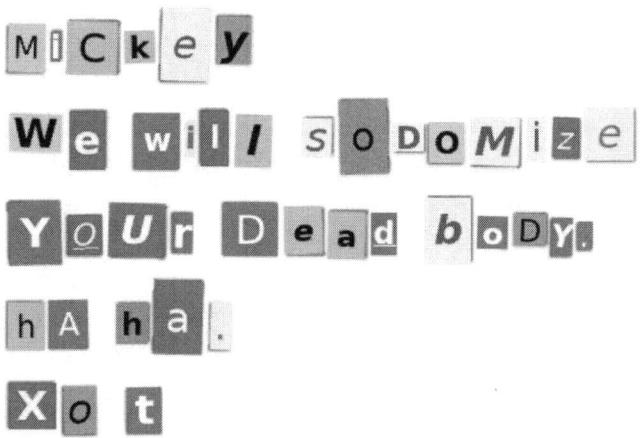

"And you can't think of anyone you might have pissed off?"

"No! Not like this."

"Tati?"

"Tati wouldn't do this. Tati couldn't."

He doesn't know the content of the notes. So he's not sure if this is my wishful thinking or reality. My ex-girlfriend and I don't care enough about each other to go through a mess like this.

"Have you tried asking Seb's team? Since the Celebz Leaked situation all those years ago, he has Daisy and Charlene working his brand image."

"Yeah, and that damned blog has picked me as its next target," Mickey grumbles. "I don't need internet people. I need real help."

Earl nods, taking off his hat and fixing his hair before adjusting the Stetson again.

"Actual help. Listen, I'll help Shelby. You call Seb's people. Charlene and Daisy can help you out."

"What about the threats on my life? The money?"

"They gave you an account number, right? It's simple. All we have to do is trace the account."

"Any fucking clue how to do that?"

Earl and I both stare at each other for a few moments and he shakes his head. Shit. We're right back where we started, aren't we?

"I'm a fuckup," I groan.

"Maybe," Earl says. "Depends on what you did."

It's not what I did that's the problem. It's what I didn't do. And now my entire world is going to come crumbling down.

When he sees that I'm going properly pale, Earl strides over and puts a semi-comforting hand on my back.

"Chin up, Mick. It's a stalker. They ain't going to make good on these threats."

Right. No one would actually try to kill me. Earl's correct. That would be insane.

3

MY LAST SHRED OF DIGNITY

RAIN WILSON

Making Mickey Ford go away? Why would anyone want that? It's a gossip blog. That means you need people to gossip about, including loathsome people like Mickey Ford.

I fold my arms incredulously and keep staring, hoping that one of my roach friends will carry me out of this hellish conversation.

None of this explains why **The Tyrant** came here. None of this explains how **The Tyrant** found me. My heart races as I vainly hope **The Tyrant** will reconsider.

"So you're *not* going to leak the story then?"

"Not before giving that racist fag a chance to make it go away."

I guess The **Tyrant** doesn't see the irony in calling someone a racist in the same breath you call them a slur. **The Tyrant** only lets the mask slip around minions, anyway.

Everyone on the internet thinks **The Tyrant** is the monarch of the social justice warriors. With over 300,000 followers fawning over the anonymous account, **The Tyrant** is probably monarch of something. Insanity? Self-interest?

I try to appeal to a moral sense that doesn't exist. "Is it worth it to possibly ruin some guy's life for a little money?"

I have no love for Mickey Ford or anyone who celebrates anything, even a little racist, but calling him all those words doesn't feel right. Maybe it's because I'm only eighteen. **The Tyrant's** older.

"Mickey Ford is a racist. How could you defend him?"

"I'm not defending him. I mean… he can't help if his fans are racist, right?"

"This is right-wing garbage, Rain," **The Tyrant** warns.

"What the hell does this have to do with being right wing? *He's a person.*"

Okay, celebrities might not really be people, but now that I've met Seb Jefferson, I'm starting to think I might be wrong about that.

The Tyrant spends so much time online. My attitude is finally getting to be too much for **The Tyrant** and my blackmailer's voice drops until it's low and terrifying. I still have to pretend **The Tyrant** doesn't scare me.

"I just didn't take you for a race traitor."

"A race traitor? He's just a stupid celebrity, and I already gave you what you wanted. I just don't see the point of you coming here. I don't have anything else."

"You know the point. The point is… I can *find* you. Something big is coming and I don't want you getting cold feet or snitching to Meg Nigel. If you tell her, I will *burn* you."

I believe **The Tyrant**. I've watched **The Tyrant** do it to all my fellow minions. I'm not the only teenage idiot feeding info to Celebz Leaked. We all started off innocently enough. Then slowly, we'd spend more and more time 'researching' and 'helping' until the internet became our everything.

The Tyrant direct messaged me on social media and was *nice*. *At first*. All The **Tyrant** did was ask for my help and I thought, why not? **The Tyrant** wants to help black people everywhere gain *freedom*. At least that's what I thought when **The Tyrant** added me to the group chat.

Then everything changed. **The Tyrant** wanted us on the phone all the time. **The Tyrant** threatened us. Our little black girl group chat was my online leash and personal torture chamber. Slowly, it became about blackmail, cruelty and online torment.

JAMILA JASPER

●○○○○ CRICKET LTE 10:05 AM   75% ⬛▮

⟨ Messages   Details

> I need you all to expose @KellyDoukas_ as a racist. Make up whatever lie you have to, invent footage, use photo editing. I want that bitch gone by Monday or I'll send all of the shit @LaShawna told me to her brother. What happens next is up to you.

 iMessage

The Tyrant was cruel. Critical. I didn't know why I couldn't just make myself turn my phone off or delete my stupid account. I guess I just didn't have any other friends. I guess I thought we were doing something *real* by taking down the man. You know, the *Rebel Blood* assholes, D-List celebrities, social media models and people like that.

Then it became about so much more than taking down *Rebel Blood*. It became about the power of taking anyone down just because we could. **The Tyrant** laughed in the group chat the night the singer/sing writer Charlotte Potter made her suicide attempt.

And then... just when I thought I could delete Twitter and get free from **The Tyrant's** clutches, the ghost from the internet found me. In real life. In Nashville, of all places. Nothing ever happens in this city, and then **The Tyrant** found me and my online torture chamber became real life.

Celebz Leaked became more than a stupid gossip blog I contributed to secretly. It became my universe. I want freedom from the black hole.

"I'm staying out of trouble. My cousin can't possibly find me," I tell **The Tyrant**, hoping this conversation can just end. It's getting harder to hide my fear the longer I have to look into **The Tyrant's** dead eyes.

"You stupid bitch," **The Tyrant** hisses — an overreaction if you ask me — "Meg already knows where to find you. Find another way to keep your mouth shut and keep your phone on. I might need more information and even if I don't... I still own you."

I half expect a hand around my throat or something worse.

"I thought you said I was done? I'm finished. Seriously. I just… it's nothing personal. I just don't want to do this anymore."

I mean it. I pretend like I'm above it when I talk to Meg, but I know it's wrong to hurt other people. I know just because I have a fucked up life, it doesn't give me the right.

The pitch of **The Tyrant's** voice changes the way it always does when **The Tyrant** makes threats. I know it's not official, but every time we have an encounter, I look up "traits of sociopaths". **The Tyrant** checks off every single box.

The Tyrant taunts me with slow speech, "Nothing personal? I guess it wasn't personal when you were distributing child pornography."

The Tyrant gags as if I'm the most disgusting thing in the world.

The Tyrant lingers on the criminal act, and my stomach lurches. The dumb smirk on **The Tyrant's** face makes me regret thinking we had anything in common at all. *Not all skin folk are kinfolk.*

I'd been *so* stupid. And sixteen.

I filmed myself doing unspeakable things. I didn't think I was doing anything wrong. I was just curious. Horny. And really fucking stupid.

I read about sex online. Girls online talked about how empowering it was to get naked on camera. I almost started one of those accounts where you get naked so creepy guys can jack off to your twerking or whatever. But I couldn't bring myself to do it. I mean, what if Meg found out?

I didn't think there was anything wrong with doing it all alone, though, and touching myself. Now that I'm 18, it's totally gross to me. *Just why, Rain!?*

I sent the video to Keith after one spicy night shift at Moe's.

He told me that if I was going to make him wait until I turned eighteen, I might as well make it worth his while. He was my boyfriend, so I thought he wouldn't tell anyone or show anyone. Plus, this was empowering, right?

I don't know how **The Tyrant** got it.

But my world shattered. Empowering my ass. Now this horrifying monster can show up where I live and tell me exactly what to do.

I'm too scared to tell anyone.

Meg is a lawyer, and she is my rich cousin from the good side of the family. I'm just the hood cousin who can't keep a job or a man or her coochie inside her pants.

Meg is just... *better*. Her parents sent her to private school, and she was always the center of attention. She has money, a banging body, a great office and men going nuts for her. Men will go through prison for her. Now that's love. Meg doesn't know how hard it is to live up to her. She's like... effortlessly perfect.

Seriously. It's like if Beyoncé's cousin was a slug. I'm the slug in this analogy.

If she finds out that I took a video of myself masturbating, I'll be lower than dirt to her. Meg would never do something that stupid. She was probably studying for the LSATs when she was sixteen, not trying to impress her married boss from Moe's. (Yes, that's where I met Keith.)

Meg already thinks I screw everything up.

Try living at the beck and call of a crazed social media psychopath for two years, and you'd be fucked up too.

It's why I keep taking Keith back. He knows my darkest secret. He has that video. If I break up with him for good, they could join forces. I don't want to tease **The Tyrant**.

"I don't care if you don't want to do this anymore," **The Tyrant** snarls. "You are my property, Rain Wilson. Worse than that, you're a dirty whore. Dirty whores don't deserve freedom. I need more dirt by next Friday, which is more than generous."

"I'm not doing it," I say flatly.

"Rain... I have so much more dirt on you than you can even imagine. If you know what's good for you... you'll keep your head out of your ass and do what I say. Okay? This is not a discussion."

The Tyrant kisses my cheek before leaving. It's another power play.

Maybe I have more in common with the *Rebel Blood* boys than I thought. I don't control my life.

I text the only person I can think to text, but I doubt she'll reply after what I did to her. She'll know who and what I'm talking about. She's the only one who left our stupid group chat cult before it ruined her life.

How did you get out?

My ex-BFF doesn't reply. She's probably at Vanderbilt getting laid and laughing about how much of an idiot I am. I'm fucked. I'm just totally fucked. This can't get any worse. It can't…

@Celebz_Leaked
Sup Leakerz,
Paparazzi chased MICKEY FORD off the highway in **BUM FUCK NEW YORK**. Watch our footage of his 2020 Ferrari Portofino FLIPPING over the highway railing

and getting dragged beneath a big Mack truck HERE.
 #VICTORY
>>>CLICK HERE FOR MICKEY FORD DEATH VIDEO<<<
Jk Jk… We all HATE *Rebel Blood* here at Celebz Leaked, but as you all know… white men *never* die.
Not even Mickey Ford.
Celebz Leaked is offering a substantial financial reward to anyone with information about Mickey Ford's hospital location.
I want to see the bruise pictures LEAKED.

PROOF REQUIRED BEFORE PAYMENT.
Rich boys get wrecked. We will never apologize for speaking our TRUTH no matter what the haters say about us.
Fuck *Rebel Blood*. Fuck white men. Fuck America.
— CL

4
I'VE LOST MY HUMANITY

MICKEY FORD

My heart monitor wakes me up. *Dum. Dum. Dum. Da. Dee. Dum. Dum. Dum. Da. Dee Dee.* I'm *so* bored, but I can't move. My fingers tap a rhythm on the side of my bed. They're all talking around me. Blink once if you can understand. Blink twice if you're afraid you'll need a woman to wipe your ass every day for the rest of your life.

Maybe I wouldn't mind if it were a pretty woman, but the nurses here are more sturdy than pretty. Sturdy ain't bad in a wife, but it ain't great in a sexy nurse fantasy.

Oh yeah. It's a fantasy, right? So it's fine if I imagine a colored girl. Sorry, I mean African American. The last time I said colored in front of Angie Victor, I thought she was going to wring my neck.

Yeah, I wouldn't mind one as dark as Seb's girl, but I don't know what I'd do with a girl like her. I heard they were wilder, but I never asked Seb. In my fantasy, the nurse touches me with her hands and I can't stop looking at the brown skin touching my pink flesh.

She'd be really nice too. Angie's real nice when she ain't biting Seb's head off for being an idiot. A nice dark-skinned nurse would be perfect…

Fuck. Why am I getting myself hard when all I can do with my hands is tap my fingers to the beat of Seb's last song? I shouldn't be here. I should be dead. That's what I was trying to do. There are two ways out of drug addiction and I didn't want to choose this. I wanted to choose death over sobriety… I wanted to choose death over the secrets coming out.

I tried to go to Seb's people for help, but… it didn't work. Charlene, Daisy, and the rest of Seb Jefferson's crew disappeared. Fired because of information leaked to the press. I don't know who the fuck is blackmailing me. I don't want to know anymore. I just want… an end.

Fuck being famous.

Twelve hours later.

Do da dee do do

Do da dee do do

No one here but me and the dark. I can see the blackmail notes etched on the back of my mind. Shelby didn't want to move, but thank God Earl made her.

She's in danger.

And so is that 14-year-old girl. Of course, she's 19 now. But that doesn't change what happened five years ago.

I never spoke to her again after what happened.

Three days later...

Sebastian's here. I can smell his rage across the room. I can hear his steel-toed boots tapping impatiently on the floor. Where's his woman? She normally calms him down, but I can hear him spitting like a rattlesnake at everyone who walks into the room.

"Anyone on this staff so much as makes a peep against their NDA, I want them *dead*."

Half the time, I hear him arguing with Brent on the phone over my condition and the album timeline. All Brent gives a fuck about is the goddamn album.

"Brent can have a fucking album when he can tell me what the fuck happened to Mick 5 years ago," Seb snarls into the phone. Yeah, I'm technically unconscious, but I can hear him. He's probably talking to Kara, and he's right about Brent.

Oh yes, Brent knows. Our fucking manager knows exactly what happened five years ago. I can recall everything that happened that night with perfect clarity.

Fourteen. That was my little brother's age. I got lots of siblings.

Closing my eyes feels nice. Another nurse approaches my bed. This one is sturdier than the last and her breasts are twice the size of my head. She puts something in my arm. I want to ask her if she's giving me the good stuff, but my lips don't move.

Five days later...

The nurses wake me up and tell me that Sebastian Jefferson and his fiancée are coming with their daughter. That little girl looks nothing like Seb's ugly mug, thank goodness.

She's like her mama, with a round face and big dark eyes. I wonder how Seb feels staring into his baby's face. I wonder if he cares about the complexion on her. I wouldn't care. But I'll never have kids. I'm pretty sure I had a vasectomy, but I was high as a kite, so I don't remember.

The thing is, if I have to see Callie and Angie, Seb's going to be here to scream at me. *I told your ass to quit drinking.* Fuck. I wish I could get out of bed and get out of this. I bet there's a bar in the hospital. Fuck, that would be nice.

They're all talking like this is the worst thing in the world. No. The worst thing in the world is I'm still alive and because of that, everyone I know and love is in danger. I'm not worth putting all 11 brothers and sisters of mine through hell.

I'm barely even human, just a face and fingers pressed to a bass guitar. I'm a brand. I'm... a total fuckup. Seb has no problem telling me as much, although bless him, he tries to be gentle.

He starts all his lectures with the fact that he wants me to stop drinking. I quit soda. Doesn't that count for something?

I don't want Seb's rage. I want to tell him something important. I want to tell him why I got in my car and sped down the highway. I want to ask him where I am too. Then, I'll ask for a drink. Then a gram. Seb can get me a gram. I know he's clean, but he's still got to know dealers. Earl can help. Earl will definitely help.

Earl's back in Nashville. I *can't* be in Nashville. Can I? I was in Ithaca. The pretty countryside reminds me of home, but no one knows who I am in Ithaca, so I like it better than heading back to West Virginia. I like privacy, probably more than Seb.

Seb throws the door open and stares at me with a concerned look on his face. Don't get all mad, Seb...

"You son of a gun," Seb snarls. "I thought you'd fucking died on me."

Seb crosses the room as fast as his 6'6" body can carry him. Then he holds me. Seb ain't an emotional motherfucker, but I must have put the fear of God in him because his blue eyes are bloodshot like he's been drinking and he holds me like I'm fragile. I feel fragile in that giant motherfucker's arms.

I choose to drink over eating and I've lost so much weight that I'm rail thin, just like Seb was before he got clean. He's got muscles now.

"I'm fine," I groan. "I'm fine."

"Angie's brought Callie to see you."

"Uncle Mickey!"

Callie scrambles away from her mama and runs over to the bed.

"Callie, you can't jump on him!" Angie says.

"Mickey!" Callie yells before leaping on me. I grunt as she hits my chest, but Sebastian's little princess commands just as much attention as her father.

I give the kid a hug and she sticks out a tiny brown stuffed fox.

"We got this for you."

"Callie, come here," Angie says. "You can't go jumping all over him."

"Okay," Calypso says before scrambling down.

"Thanks, kid. This is cute…"

I groan and let out a foul word, which makes Calypso giggle and Angie scowl. Seb keeps looking at me with that terrified paternal look in his eye. Only a few weeks of knowing about his daughter and he's a different man. Ten times more responsible than before. I know he ain't going back to drugs. We made it. We're fucking famous, we're rich. Untouchable. We shouldn't have to do this shit anymore.

Seb touches my shoulder, but I interrupt him before he can give me a lecture.

"Where am I? No one's talking to me."

Seb's face regains its stern expression. His dark brows knit together over eyes nearly as blue as mine. His are ice, mine are cobalt.

He murmurs, "It's better if no one knows where you are right now. Do you know how you ended up here?"

"I was drinking. I had to tell you something. There were people after me… Trying to get… their stuff back… That's about it."

His lips purse into a line so thin it's nearly invisible.

"Mickey, once you get out of here, you're going to jail."

"What?"

"You crashed into a truck and caused a seven car pileup on Route-81 South, 10 miles away from Binghamton. Two other people are in the hospital. One of them is in critical condition. One of them's a *child*, Mickey. You almost... *killed a child.*"

Angie claps her hands over Calypso's ears and then leads her away, talking about how Seb didn't mean "killed" he meant "thrilled". Unfortunately, Seb's dead serious and the color's gone from my face. The fact that Seb's here and not my lawyer or Brent means that nobody knows the truth about what happened yet — at least not the press.

The world probably doesn't even know if I'm alive or not. It's like Seb can read my mind.

"You're in critical condition. Everyone knows that. But because of that damned blog... everyone expects you to be dead."

"Well, I ain't dead."

"Not for lack of trying," Seb utters bitterly, the sharp edge returning to his voice.

"I need to get out of here," I grumble, because suddenly the feeling hits me like a sack of bricks and I need a bump so bad I would rip Seb Jefferson's nose off his fucking face to see if he has any leftover from his last big bender.

"You ain't getting out of here, Mick. I need you to listen to me. You're in some deep shit. I have Meg Nigel on the case paying triple her fucking fee, because this isn't her typical case. There are people after you claiming to have secrets that could sink you, Mickey. Whatever you've done, I need to know the truth and I need to know the truth right now."

I never thought at my height I'd encounter a man who towers over me, but Seb Jefferson's a big scary redneck who only looks punk because of his bleach blond hair and tattoos. Beneath it all, there's a beefy country boy who could rip my jaw off with one of his meaty coal miner's hands. He's like a big brother to me, but I know he could probably whoop me with a meaner back hand than my daddy.

"I have done nothing. It's all lies, Seb. All of it."

"It was five years ago, wasn't it?" he says. "You tried to tell me at your lake house. You were so damn drunk. I thought you were confused. What did you want to tell me? Let me help you."

"I *can't* tell you, Seb. I know you. If I tell you about five years ago. If I tell you why I started living this… It could screw over a lot of people.."

"Try me. I gave you that first bump of coke. This is my fault."

He believes it. That bastard actually believes that any part of my ruin is his fault. No. It's all me. It started with the pills to help me sleep. So I could stop thinking about what happened. Now, I just do it because I need it. I can't sleep without pills, can't wake up without coke. At least I thought I couldn't. I haven't had coke in a while…

I must have slept pretty well after the accident. And as for the attack…

Well, that was five years ago. I don't think about that anymore. Just Brent. And the fact that he could screw us over in an instant.

Seb continues, feeling guilty, as most addicts do. "I just wanted to get you high, and I wanted to shut you up. We were both young and stupid. Let's live to be wise old men. We can do this Mick."

I don't think I'll live to be old if I keep living like this. My mama warned me about music. Drugs. Sex fiends. My family's religious and she wanted nothing to do with my devil's music or my devil's lettuce or my devil's ripped denim.

She'll take the money, but she makes me cover my tattoos before I enter the house. Mama. I don't want her coming here, but she wouldn't. Not if there was a chance of encountering any part of my "life of sin".

"Yeah." I mutter. "My family. Does my family know?"

"Your ma and siblings are fine. They know you're alive, but… it's too dangerous for them to be near you right now. I know how you get, Mickey. If I don't give you drugs, you'll have J.T. or someone else it."

"Can you at least get me a cigarette?" I grumble. My arms are looking red and they're feeling itchy. That damn needle in my arm isn't doing enough. What the hell is in that clear bag, anyway?

Seb sighs.

"No. I can't. And you're in for a rough ride, Mick. The doctors here want to keep you here for two weeks to detox. After that, you'll be dealing with the court."

"This is bullshit."

It's my kind of bullshit. You know, the bullshit I caused by being a damned idiot.

"I don't trust your lawyer, Mick. I don't trust any of our fucking people. They care about the *Rebel Blood* brand. They don't give a shit about us. Meg Nigel's Angie's cousin. I trust her. She's… family. At least to my daughter."

"You think a black lawyer wants to represent the *Rebel Blood* bassist?" I groan, thinking about the unfortunate tattoo I have on my thigh. I ain't proud of the shit I did when our first album went platinum. I'd been high as a kite that night and I paid an artist $2,500 to open her shop and tattoo the rebel flag right on my body.

It seemed really smart, but now it seems stupid. Had someone dared me? I can't remember. I thought it looked pretty good too.

Brent nearly hit the damn roof.

"SHOW THAT TO THE PRESS AND I'LL CHOP YOUR BALLS OFF, FORD."

Seb knows about the tattoo, but few people do 'cause it's on my thigh. I keep those covered up and anyway, I ain't like that anymore. One thing traveling the country on our tour bus has done for me was exposing me to many people. I ain't the ignorant motherfucker I grew up as, and I don't want anyone to find out I was.

My stomach lurches as I wait for Seb to answer me. Triple her fee? How the fuck am I paying for that? Or any of this? My money goes to coke and the wind.

Seb sighs and tries to be comforting when he says, "Angie knows you might be an idiot, but deep down you have a good heart."

"Thanks."

"It's the line that's worked for you so far," Seb mutters. "Her friend knows that you're good people. She'll get you a good deal."

"Don't tell her about the tattoo."

"As long as you keep your pants on, she won't have to know. Get it covered up already."

I groan. Yeah. I should have covered it up three years ago. You just get used to it, you know? I grew up with the stars and bars outside my house. It just felt... normal. Now I feel like the fucking redneck idiot I am.

"I'm a fucking idiot," I groan.

"Yes, you are a fucking idiot. But you're our fucking idiot. We want you to get out of this, but you have to get clean, Mickey. This is it. I'm putting my foot down. No more bail outs, no more loans, no more getting your car out of ditches."

He raises a serious, bushy eyebrow. Seb looks like if the playground bully grew up and turned into Godzilla. I nod before I know I'm nodding.

The lead singer of *Rebel Blood*, Sebastian Jefferson, a man I consider closer than a brother, is finally putting his foot down. I told myself I wouldn't wait for rock bottom, because Seb Jefferson would catch me before I hit the ground. Now I know hitting rock bottom is worrying my best friend, who practically held my hand through hell when he ought to take care of his fiancée and kid.

We came up together. Young kids put in this fucking band and lured by the promise of living our dream. Making music, attracting beautiful women, getting money and the drugs... well, the drugs just became something we needed to cope.

I know I shouldn't put him through hell, but I'm still a selfish fucking addict and it's probably been what, five or seven days since I've had a hit? The more conscious I get, the more I crave it.

"You gotta bring me something more than what they're giving me," I tell him desperately. "I can get sober. I just need help to get through the hospital. It ain't right for me to be locked up here. I hurt people. I need to contact my accountant and give them money. I need to get a little money and then I can make sure that kid…. You know. Doesn't die."

Yes. If I get a little money, I can call Hyacinth. New pills cut with a little powder. *Oh, fuck. That would be great.* Seb snaps his fingers in front of my eyes, breaking my trance.

"Mick, calm down. I can't bring you any drugs. I can't bring you any liquor. Getting clean starts now. It starts right here."

"I want to get sober," I tell him, but I don't know if I mean it.

What I *want* is to hit up Hyacinth and ask her what pills she has and if she has any of the good stuff. I want to go to a nightclub and find a girl willing to go home with a motherfucker who can barely stand.

It's like Seb can see through me.

"I ain't giving you a choice this time. I know addicts. Sneaky fucking liars, all of us. If you get out of this without going to prison, you'll be doing things my way."

I grunt, and Seb grins.

"You are stubborn as hell."

"I am *not*."

"One day, you'll find a woman who lies through her teeth the way you do, Mickey Ford. She'll give you a run for your money."

I'm still thinking about my coke. Or maybe I ought to beg for the damned cigarette.

"You're a selfish piece of shit, Jefferson."

"Right back at you, buddy."

Angie comes back into the room with Calypso and a worried look on her face.

"Meg's here. She has a way to get Mickey out of trouble. *I think*. Although I don't know why that's your biggest concern…"

My throat tightens. Angie doesn't understand. We're a band. Nothing can happen to any of us or dozens of people can lose their jobs. Dozens. Not to mention the families most of us support.

I want to avoid jail if possible.

"I can avoid going to jail?"

"What she has planned is worse than jail," Angie says. "Meg thinks she can get a judge known for sentences where the punishment fits the crime. Careful what you wish for Mickey."

The next words come out with terror hanging on every word. I'm not a killer. I'm not a psychopath. I'm a man who's made mistakes. I don't *want* to hurt people.

"What about the people I hurt?"

"No updates."

"I need to do something for them."

"Already taken care of," Seb says. "I'm covering the hospital bills. We need these people to pull through. I can't have insurance delays fucking things up."

"And the dogs?"

Angie's face contorts in disgust.

"These beasts are enjoying themselves a little too much, if you ask me. Ever heard of obedience school?"

I groan.

"What happened?"

"Sam took a shit in the shower," Seb says, offering Angie an apologetic look. The look on Angie's face could blow a hole through the side of the wall.

"Thanks for looking after them, Angie. I owe you big time…"

Angie mutters, "I'll be happy when your untrained mutts are out of my house."

"Uncle Mickey, I drew you a mermaid!" Callie says, showing me her little tablet with a mermaid drawn on it with a blue tail, blue eyes, and brown spiky hair just like mine.

"That looks *exactly* like me." Sort of.

"Uh huh. And this is a sexy mermaid friend for you."

"Callie!" Angie gasps. "Where did you learn the word sexy? No, no, no. We don't say that at 5 years old!"

"She's *pretty*," Callie says, rolling her eyes, a little sass that her mama thankfully doesn't catch.

The mermaid in her drawing has brown skin like her mama. I guess Calypso V. Jefferson thinks all relationships are like her parents — one black woman and one white man.

I've never been with a black girl before. Getting the rebel flag tattooed on my thigh made me scared to approach a girl like that later on. I mean… I *am* ashamed of it. A bit.

And why bother get it removed when it helps me get with the *Rebel Blood* groupies? At least that's the way Mickey, the drunk idiot, used to think. I can already feel the sobriety coursing through me. Whatever that means.

Maybe Seb's right. I've done so much stupid shit when I wasn't sober. And now I've put people in the hospital and all I can think about it how to get another bump from Seb. I've lost my humanity and I don't know if I'll ever get it back.

5

A LAMB SENT TO SLAUGHTER

RAIN WILSON

I'm sitting in my cousin's Tesla wearing my stupid bar clothes and sipping on a chocolate milkshake from McDonald's. Meg's looking at me like I'm a disappointing mess, which I am.

"I know you couldn't have been in Ithaca. That means they involved other people in *Celebz Leaked*," Meg says. "Do you confirm or deny?"

She says the last sentence in the scariest lawyer voice I've ever heard.

"Confirm."

"Fucking A, Rain!"

"Meg, I'm sorry!" I mean that. Meg has done so much for me and I'm *so* intimidated by her.

"Rain, I don't know what's going on with you. Aunty Kirsten and Uncle Herbert are worried about you."

"I'm fine."

"You ran off at sixteen with Keith. That's not fine."

"They like Keith," I point out to her.

Meg grimaces and then reluctantly asks, "Did you take him back yet?"

"No."

"What is *wrong* with Aunty Kirsten? How can she support this?"

"I don't know. Keith has a job. He has a car."

"He lost his job six months ago, and he steals from you, Rain. He is in his thirties and steals from his teenage girlfriend."

"Only $500," I told her. "He's my man. I'm just lucky he isn't taking half my paycheck."

I know I'm trying Meg Nigel's patience.

She asks, "Name one good thing Keith does."

"He pulls out."

Meg glares at me with her perfectly microbladed eyebrows, then gags dramatically and says, "Don't take him back. Ever. Please. Promise me. Does he know about this *Celebz Leaked* stuff?"

"No. Girl, I told you Keith can't read."

"I thought that was a joke," Meg says, not bothering to conceal her shock.

"He can't. He doesn't read *Celebz Leaked*."

"Okay. And what about the other people? Who are they, Rain? I want names. I will track them down and I will screw them so hard they'll—"

"I don't want to talk about it. I'm done with that part of my life."

It's a lie considering **The Tyrant** made it clear I'm still on the hook for information, but once I get this done, I'll be out for real. I know Meg's plan for me has something to do with Rebel Blood.

She'll probably make me apologize and polish Mickey's kitchen floor with a toothbrush or some other ancient torture method. I can get information — just one last time — and get *free*.

"Done? Are you out of your mind? Mickey Ford's in the hospital. You are far from done. Have you ever heard of prison, Rain? Do you think you can fight well enough to survive prison?"

Meg's urgency scares me, like I might really go to prison. I hope she's bluffing, but I'm not sure. I'm terrified. Telling Meg anything could put her in danger and even if she doesn't approve of me and even if I betrayed her… I love Meg Nigel. She's the only semblance of a loving family that I have, even if she mostly expresses it by yelling at me.

I shake my head. I wish I could check my phone and see if **The Tyrant** messaged me back. Avoiding certain doom is way more important than letting Meg try to inspire me. Again.

"I mean… don't you feel guilty?"

"Yeah. A little."

"A little? Rain, you nearly *killed* him and that accident nearly killed several other people. Don't just blink at me like I'm one of your screens."

I blink twice, and I can see a vein popping out of Meg's head. Okay, I need to say something that's not dumb before she strangles me to death.

"I feel bad, Meg. But not about Mickey Ford. I have bigger problems than Mickey Ford… More people could get hurt."

"Like what? What could be a bigger problem than nearly murdering one of the most popular rock stars in America?"

"My life being ruined."

"Your life being ruined? You don't get it, Rain. It's already ruined. I'm in deep shit with Seb Jefferson because of the story you leaked and whoever else you know that's involved with that stupid blog will be in deep shit too. I don't understand. I bought you your first tampons. Since when do we keep shit from each other?"

"I told you. It's about my life."

"Is someone threatening you?"

I can't answer. I just can't make myself betray **The Tyrant**. I'm too scared. Believe it or not, some people are scarier than Meg Nigel on her worst days. I don't want to die. I haven't even had a life yet — at least not a life that Keith didn't choose for me. I wanted to go on a road trip. I wanted to see somewhere amazing and exotic… like *Canada*.

Meg interrupts my daydreaming sharply. "Rain. Nod or shake your head if you're too afraid to talk."

I nod. Meg sighs and then she nods. She's used to thinking quick on her feet in the courtroom and it seriously feels like she *always* knows the right thing to do. It doesn't hurt that she's a decade older than me.

"Okay. My idea might get us both out of this. They can't blackmail you if you're locked in a ten acre fortress that barely has any internet with a madman."

"A madman?!"

I don't mean to sound so dumb and desperate.

"Seb Jefferson asked me to be Mickey Ford's lawyer. Mickey was drunk as a skunk when they caught him on the highway. He might be in deep shit and for some reason a freaking celebrity thinks I can get him out of it."

It's crazy seeing someone like Meg doubt herself.

"Didn't you negotiate an NBA divorce last year?"

"Yes. But this is a huge viral story and I have a *rat* in my car."

My cheeks warm with shame. Meg has tried her best not to lecture me about all this, but I can tell she wants to lecture me and probably kick my stupid ass.

"I won't spill information anymore. Seriously."

My heart flutters. I don't want to keep lying to her, but I don't want to drag Meg even deeper into my problems. I made a mistake betraying her. I want to leave her out of this.

"What are you going to do about the person threatening you? Where's your damn phone?"

I purposefully ignore the question about my phone in case Meg thinks she's going to confiscate it.

I try to at least offer her a genuine answer. "Lie my ass off. Try to hide. I don't know."

"If you couldn't hide from me, you can't hide from someone blackmailing you," Meg says. "At least not without my help."

Little does she know that I've already been discovered.

"I know."

"Okay. Do you trust me, cuz?"

"Um... sometimes?"

"Good enough for me," Meg says and then she steps on the gas and peals off. I don't know what exactly her plan is, and she doesn't want to tell me. She plays *Sandcastles* by Beyoncé on repeat until we get to this weird enormous house about ten miles outside of Nashville. I've never been to this part of town, but there are enormous plantation houses spread out across large acres of land.

"Is this The Hermitage?"

"No. Didn't you go on the school trip to The Hermitage?"

Unlike Meg's parents, mine could never afford the school trips. I make up some excuse about how I forgot.

"You don't need to know where we are anyway," Meg says, pulling her car into a lot next to a fancy-looking Ford F-150. She gets out of the car and stares me up and down.

"I'm worried about you, Rain. And Logan's worried too. He thinks you're rabid."

Right. I bit Meg's "boyfriend" on the hand when he was supposed to be monitoring me. Oops.

"I freaked out. Sorry."

"Yeah. You freaked out because you sat in my office like a sneak listening in on my conversations."

"I'll do anything to make it up to you, Meg. Even live in this creepy dungeon. I'm sorry."

"That's what I want to hear."

We walk in through one of the basement entrances and Meg takes her shoes off as we walk through the door and I follow her lead.

"Angie, I have her."

I glance at the door, preparing to run in case I need to, but Meg can apparently read my mind and she clamps her hand down around mine... *hard*. Angie comes around the corner and stares at me with worry on her face rather than loathing.

"She's okay," Angie says, relieved.

"Yeah, she's okay," Meg says, giving me a skeptical once over. "She's a pain in my ass, but she's okay."

"Are you sure this is going to work?"

"I know this Judge. As long as none of those people die, we can get out of this. Rain will be safe. Mickey will be safe. And we can keep searching for the people who run that stupid blog without a troublemaker on the loose."

Meg gives me a vicious glare and Angie catches it quick.

"She knows, doesn't she?" Angie asks.

"She won't talk. But that's okay. I don't need her to talk. We'll need her here looking after him and making sure he doesn't fall off the wagon."

"Do you think that's a good idea? I mean… what if he finds out?"

"I think Rain needs a little practice keeping her mouth shut," Meg says calmly. "And when she's not keeping her mouth shut, she can try honesty. Maybe Mickey will respond to honesty."

Angie gives us both an obviously skeptical look. I glance down at my phone, pretending the words don't sting. Angie sighs and then shrugs. "Fine. Are you going to tell her exactly what bizarre plan you've cooked up?"

"No. I want her to agree to it first," Meg says. "Then I'll tell her. But it'll work. She'll be safe and it'll be easier to monitor them under the same roof."

"Agree to what?" I ask stupidly and Meg puts her hand on my head. I don't know why, but I get the sense that I suddenly understand what it feels like to be a lamb sent to slaughter.

6

GETTING ME OFF EASY

MICKEY FORD

"Mickey Ford, you are sentenced to 400 days of house arrest, one year of a rehabilitation program of the court's choosing, and 400 days of community service via an intensive daily mentorship program for a young artist chaperoned and managed by your legal representative, Meg Nigel. Court is dismissed."

Four hundred days of house arrest. This is what Meg Nigel calls getting me off easy.

Meg doesn't appreciate the scowl on my face. She calls this a deal.

"What's the problem? Take the deal. You own 10 acres of land in Nashville. Seb and Angie bought the house down the street and they can come over whenever you want. You practically own a small city, Ford. It's a good deal."

Good deal, my ass.

"I need a goddamn drink."

"No. You don't need a drink. You're already 10 weeks sober. Lean into it. You need to get your act together. My cousin is already waiting there and I need you to keep her out of trouble. You have to help her," Meg insists.

"Is she pretty?"

"She's 18, so she's 11 years younger than you. She's a baby, Ford. You're not going to be attracted to a baby."

I grin, giving Meg the full weight of my sapphire eyes. Instead of having their usual effect on her, she scrunches up her face with pure loathing.

"You are such an asshole," Meg hisses. "My *cousin* is only 18, and she has a boyfriend. Unfortunately. They got back together three days ago, so I'm pretty sure they're all hot and spicy for each other."

"How old is the boyfriend? Think I could take him?"

I kick my feet up on the dashboard of Meg Nigel's Tesla. My accountant can't release money for another car until I pay my restitution and Seb's sick of taking me back and forth for the hearings and sentencing.

"Her boyfriend is a very successful entrepreneur," Meg says, a strange note in her voice. I squint and search for signs of dishonesty, but if they're there... I don't see 'em.

"Oh yeah? Is he in tech?"

"Mickey? Can you focus? You aren't going to be hitting on her. She'll be staying in your house and staying out of trouble. During the day, you'll teach her the ropes in the entertainment business and give her some purpose in life. She has like… no direction. She needs help."

"And you think I have direction?"

"Somehow you make $15 million a year, so you have to know something. Teach her that."

"What the hell does that mean?"

"Figure it out, Ford. It's this or getting your ass handed to you in jail," Meg snaps impatiently. "I heard they liked pretty blue-eyed drug addicts in the state pen."

Damn. Seb was right that Meg doesn't hesitate before the claws come out. I don't want my ass handed to me in jail. At least she's right. They probably have wonderful drugs in jail, though.

"How can I get things delivered? I need… medication."

Meg glowers and I realize I'm way too dumb to get anything past her.

"You're under house arrest. You're getting nothing delivered that Seb Jefferson doesn't approve of. He doesn't want you smuggling drugs in."

"Fuck Seb Jefferson."

"Seb Jefferson is the reason you're not getting probed in the state pen," Meg says. "Be grateful."

"He's also the reason I'm sober as the day I was born in a car with a *beautiful* woman who won't pull over and let me have one last drink before jail."

"Ford? I've cracked tougher nuts. Flirting won't get you anywhere with me."

"Worth a try."

"No. It really isn't," Meg says.

"Your cousin look anything like you?"

"Yes," Meg says. "If you must know. But she's shorter, has darker skin and much longer hair."

"Sounds pretty. That boyfriend making you happy?"

Meg narrows her gaze and snarls, "I'm beyond happy with Logan, who can break you in half, by the way. Not worth it."

She doesn't know how pretty she is. Definitely worth a try. I wonder what she'd say if she knew about my tattoo.

Makes me hard thinking of trying to convince her to sleep with me, anyway. I guess I'm a sick motherfucker. It's the fame. It gets to your damn head. You want people just to see if they'll bend. It's like being a god from those Greek stories they read us in elementary school. Nymphs, nymphos… they're all ripe to be taken.

Plus, sick shit has happened to me. Shit, I don't want to talk about. I'd rather drown it out with liquor and if I can't have liquor, I'll need something else to make me forget. Sex.

Meg's cousin is out of the question. I don't want Nigel castrating me with her bare hands.

At least out here, the nightmares might stop.

Nothing bad happens in the countryside. At least that's what I believed after too many years of having shit hurled at me in LA — figuratively at first and then literally.

My new place is gorgeous and I can't wait to play football with my boys on the rolling fields. The land is beautiful and... mine. 400 days stuck on my property might not be so bad.

"Did Seb get the dogs in the kennel?" I ask her.

"Yes. They have officially moved your brutes in."

"They ain't brutes. They're Dobermans. Proud, muscular dogs."

"One of them ate my Jimmy Choo."

"I can replace your cigarettes."

"Get your ass out of here, Mickey. We're going to have this little meeting in a hurry so I can get back downtown for my date."

"Rain?"

First time hearing it, I think it's the prettiest name I ever heard.

"I explained everything to you clearly. Rain Wilson's my cousin. She's totally wayward and totally awkward and her life is a mess right now. I think you two will be good for each other. But no funny business, Ford."

"Funny business?"

"You're a musician. Don't try to sleep with her. Trust me, you don't want those kinds of problems."

"Why? Is she like a crazy nymphomaniac? I might like that..."

"She's eighteen!" Meg yells. "And anyway, she's not one of your little groupies. Your bicep tattoos won't impress her or whatever it is."

I stare at her stupidly until her expression calms. Those dumb blue eyes work wonders on women, even if they're spitting mad and allegedly unimpressed like Meg.

"You're going to give her a career. A real career that isn't slinging drinks in Angie's bar. No offense," Meg says once she's satisfied I'm listening to her properly.

"Why the hell would I want to do something like that? What's in it for me?"

"Staying out of prison since you nearly killed several cars full of people."

"Hm. Is she pretty?"

"You already asked that," Meg says, pinching my arm so hard that I let out a loud and involuntary yelp. "Now get out of the car. Rain is impossible to manage and so are you."

"What exactly do you have in mind with this *mentorship* program?"

"I don't know, Mickey. Impress me. You'll have an entire year locked up in your enormous mansion on your tracts of land. I'll show up to check in and once a week, I expect progress reports."

"How is this even legal?"

"Because you're famous and I'm a great fucking lawyer. Now get out of my goddamn Tesla. You smell gross."

"I smell like I need a drink."

"Out."

"I look pretty good, though, right? I want to make a good first —

"OUT!"

Meg Nigel might be easy on the eyes, but her sharp tongue probably scares the sane men away. She glares at me as if she knows what I'm thinking, and I salute her.

"Thanks."

My lawyer gets out of her car and gives me an uninspired once over. I haven't shaved in days and I haven't showered either. I'm wearing a shitty pair of Chucks, ripped blue jeans and an oversized navy and red striped sweater. I like hiding beneath big sweaters. When I was younger, I liked everyone looking at my body. My abs.

Five years ago, my life changed. Five years ago, I stopped liking anything at all except cocaine, amphetamines and booze. I still want to fuck my life up. It's just that they won't let me. Seb won't let me implode this fucking train even if I want to more than anything.

If the news about me gets out, I'll be America's most hated Rebel. That's why I wanted to kill myself on Route-81. I had enough whiskey in me to do it. I told myself I'd die that night and then I wake up to Seb's ugly mug, talking to me about restitution and sobriety.

This isn't what I want. I want an end to all of it. I want to disappear and have people start a rumor that I'm still alive in South America. I'm deep in the thought of ending it — a dangerous habit, I know — when I see the girl. She emerges behind Seb Jefferson's frame and flinches when he thumps his giant hand on her shoulder.

"Rain Wilson, meet your new mentor. Mickey Ford."

She's short — about five feet tall — and curvy. She doesn't look like she's eighteen. She looks a little younger except for the curves and the grown up expression on her face that shows Rain has likely been through too much. It's a common look in West Virginia, not so much in Hollywood where every line is pinched and smoothed flat with injected plastic. This girl has a proper face. A pleasant face.

Rain Wilson gives Meg a suspicious look. Then she glances at me and says two words that feel like a gut punch from a girl that young and pretty.

"He's filthy."

"Yes. He's been through hell," Meg steps in, defending me for once. "Rain, Mr. Ford is *kindly* letting you spend the next year here. No more running around the bar. No more getting into trouble. No more posting on the internet. You're going to hang out in the boonies and get your life together. Got it?"

Rain flinches and nods at her cousin. She looks terrified. This strange protective urge comes over me, but Rain doesn't appear to notice me.

Trouble. That's the first thing on my mind when I look at Rain. First, I forget about my rules. No girls with her skin color because I can't have her seeing my tattoo and committing some crime of passion. Second, I look at her waist and how it juts out into these *very* wide hips. She's more of a pear than an hourglass, but her butt is…

Wow. I can't stop staring at her, even if she's way too young for me to look at. And she got back together with her boyfriend. An entrepreneur? I could totally get her, anyway. I could seduce her. Girls can't resist me. They throw themselves at me. Why would Rain be any different?

Damn. She is insanely pretty. Those eyes…

Rain's finally looking me with enormous wide brown eyes that dwarf her other features. Except her lips. They're plump. Really plump. I'd be scared to have lips like that against mine. They're so full. Would she let me bite them? Would she think I only wanted to do it to hurt her?

Maybe that *is* why I want to bite down on her lips. And her ass. Damn. I'd like to take a bite of that. And what is she wearing? I feel like I was a teenager just the other day, but the kids today dress really weird. She has this little top that shows her belly button, almost like it's the 90s and then these weird big jeans. But the belly button part's nice.

Finally, I look at her eyes and she glances away from me bashfully.

"This is torture, Meg," she whispers.

"It'll be torture for him, too. Trust me. By the time you two are finished with each other, you'll wish I'd sent you both to prison."

Rain glances away from her again. Prison? What the hell could this mousy thing with her enormous ass have done to end up in prison? She's too pretty for crime. I stick my tongue into my cheek and try to listen to whatever her cousin's saying, but I can't even believe Rain and Meg are from the same family.

Meg's a pretty girl and all, but Rain is… stunning. I know exactly what I'd do with a stunning girl like her. She's a little on the petite side in terms of height, but I think I could make it work.

"So, Rain Wilson. Happy to finally meet the legendary Mickey Ford? You must be a huge fan for your cousin to set you up with this gig."

Rain glances nervously at Meg, who smiles and says, "Go on. Tell him whatever you need to tell him."

"No. I'm not a huge fan," Rain says.

Then she pulls out her cell phone and stares at it. Meg shrugs.

"Good luck whipping her into shape, Mickey."

"What exactly do you mean by whip her into shape?"

"Seb?" Meg says, turning to her best friend's new fiancé. "Did you come up with ideas like we asked?"

"An album. Mickey writes it. She sings. At the end of the year, I want these two sorry motherfuckers to bring me an album. 'Cause we'll need gold to clean up this mess, Mickey Ford. And you're going to play a part in mining it."

7

A NIGHT ALONE WITH MICKEY FORD

RAIN WILSON

I'm alone with Mickey Ford, the lead singer of *Rebel Blood*, for the first time and the only thing to jump into my head is "I have a boyfriend".

He looks up from the fireplace at me for the first time in forty minutes.

Yes, it's been forty minutes since Meg, Seb and everyone else left, including Mickey's staff. He has an ankle bracelet around his leg that covers up one of his tattoos. I know about *that* tattoo because I wrote about it in Celebz Leaked. Meg tells me Mickey doesn't know about what I did, but somehow, she wants this to be my stupid chance to make it up to him.

I say the stupid words out loud, "I have a boyfriend."

For someone who's been in an accident, he doesn't look hurt at all. I feel relieved and then I notice that I've been staring at him for too long after saying something super awkward.

"I know," he says, his tongue running over the cut on his lip as he looks away from me again and gazes into the fire.

"Nice house," I say, struggling desperately to make conversation.

"Got any liquor?" He asks without moving his eyes away from the flame. He's a little scary up close. The media makes him seem soft and sensitive, but he's nearly as big as Seb Jefferson and with his dark hair and brows, he looks more menacing.

His eyes are just as blue as Seb's. No, now that I've met them both, I can say that Mickey's are definitely bluer.

"No," I say. "I don't drink."

"I thought you worked at a bar."

"Yup."

"And you have a dream of being a singer?" He asks.

Dream? I don't have a dream. Life is for the lottery winners and the rest of us just get to work at Moe's.

"Nope."

"Going to marry your boyfriend?"

I ignore the question and take out my phone. My thumb aches. Plus, I don't know if the big bad wolf is texting me more threats. I wonder if my cell phone terrorist knows that half of *Rebel Blood* is on the case looking for her and I'm here in safety… allegedly.

I wish I could at least text Meg in case of an emergency.

"You don't have any signal out here," I say, pointing to my phone.

Mickey glances over at me again.

"Isn't it great?"

"Not if you have a life," I grumble.

But I don't have a life. Keith has probably just sent me the same dumb texts about how we're 'meant to be' — and by that, he means he's 'meant to be' on my lease while I pay the whole thing. We're back together again. He came over, we had sex for three minutes and then he unpacked his *Jansport* backpack in my studio. A roach scurried out of it. *Ah, home.*

It's nothing like this place. Keith doesn't even know I'm here because Meg told me not to tell him. I'm in no position to argue with Meg after what I did. I really am trying, despite what she thinks.

I think Keith invited his ex to our place anyway when he heard I'd be gone a few days.

"A man has his needs, Rain," he says — all the time.

I squirm uncomfortably in my seat. I guess my squirming bothers Mickey because his eyes dart from mine to my thighs and then back to mine again.

"Christ…" He snarls. "I really wish I had a drink."

"Isn't the point of this you getting sober?"

"Yeah, and they stuck me with some fuckin' teenager."

"Hey," I snapped, getting a little defensive, and also sick of the silence and Mickey's sour attitude. "I'm not a *fuckin' teenager*. I'm 18. I'm grown. How old are you, anyway? Not so grown up to not throw your car underneath an eighteen-wheeler."

Mickey raises one eyebrow slowly, barely reacting. Then he grins.

"You got a mouth on you, huh?"

"Yeah. Maybe I do."

He nods and strokes his chin, speaking in a slow West Virginian drawl.

"That's nice. I'm slow as fuck. I never know the right things to say. That's why I drink. Drank."

"That's stupid," I blurt out. "Drinking makes you dumber."

"I know. I told you, I'm slow as fuck."

Then he smiles and something really weird happens to me. The thought crosses my mind that I *get it*. I finally get why all the girls go crazy for Rebel Blood. There's something cheeky about the way he exposes his teeth and the way his cheek sinks into a dimple. Mickey's *hot*.

He's like basically an old man of 29, but that's still hot to me!

"Do you listen to the band?" He asks, leaning forward for the first time.

"No."

"Oh. You like rap or something?"

"Not everyone black likes rap," I say.

"Right."

"But I do."

"Oh. Cool. I probably don't know any of the rappers you kids listen to."

"Pap Smear? Lil Tay? Bald Baby? Lil Lizard Mix? Polka Digger?" I say.

Mickey shrugs and his sweater draws up, revealing a little hair beneath his abs.

He says in his soft West Virginia drawl, "I have no idea. You've seen the house and everything, right?"

"Yup."

"Great. Do you like the bass guitar?"

"I don't know."

He smiles, and this really weird thing happens. My chest feels like someone gave it a little squeeze. I felt nothing like that near Keith and the sensation makes me uncomfortable.

I shift in my chair again, but Mickey won't stop looking. He probably thinks I'm intriguing. Like a bug. But then his tongue darts over his lip and I wonder if I have it wrong.

"That's okay. I can play anything. I can even sing, believe it or not," he says.

"Don't sing," I murmur. That would be so embarrassing. I'd just have to sit there watching him, and I'm way too awkward for that. I always thought if some guy serenaded me, I'd kill myself. Not to be dramatic or anything. If Mickey Ford serenaded me, I'd die on the spot. This entire situation is too many crazy coincidences in a row. I wish I had someone to tell about tonight, but I don't. I lost my best friend because of The Tyrant and now I'm out here with a rock star who I nearly indirectly killed.

It wasn't entirely my fault, but that still feels like a copout.

Mickey chuckles and rubs his hands on his jeans.

"I won't sing, little lady. Don't worry. I don't know if I can sit here staring at you, though. You're *way* too pretty."

He sounds almost shy, which he can't be. I've written tens of articles about Mickey Ford and they all say he's a rude and obnoxious asshole. They don't mention how sensual his jawline is up close or how soft his voice is when he speaks naturally. It's not like he sounds weak, it's like he has a silent stoic power that draws you in.

"Thanks," I mumble to his compliment.

He's obviously just saying it to be nice.

"I mean it. Like… that boyfriend of yours… what's he like then?"

I can't talk to Mickey Ford, one of the hottest guys in America, about stupid Keith.

"He's great," I lie.

"Great money, big dick, all that stuff?" Mickey says.

I bristle awkwardly again. I can't believe half the words that come out of Mickey's mouth and then I have to remember that no one says no to him. Ever. He's what happens when no one says no to a man in like… several years.

Unfortunately, Keith has neither great money nor a big dick.

"A man doesn't need to have money or a big dick to please me," I say, like I know what the hell I'm talking about. I've only been with one guy. Keith. I don't want Mickey to know that because it suddenly feels shameful.

"He just needs to treat you right," Mickey says and for a moment, I think he really understands.

"Yeah. Exactly."

"Guess what, princess? A guy without great money or a big dick ain't treating you right. He'll be too tired from his shitty job to do all the tongue tricks you probably like."

His words shock me, but all I can think of is what Meg might say in her cool, collected voice.

"Do you really think this is appropriate?"

"My apologies. I don't get out much."

He doesn't seem sorry.

"What tongue tricks *do* you like?" Mickey follows up. "Sorry. Never mind. Forget I said that. It's late. I should leave you alone, Rain."

A horrifying thought occurs to me.

"Were you just trying to *flirt* with me?"

"I'm 11 years older than you and you have a boyfriend. You tell me?"

"If that's flirting, you're terrible at it."

Mickey's cheeks turn red. I don't know if that means he was flirting with me or not, but it's pretty funny.

"Don't worry," I say, before he can get too freaked out. "I suck at flirting, too. Keith did all the work asking me out."

"Keith," Mickey says, a hint of loathing in his voice. "I'd like to know more about this Keith."

8
I DON'T DO AGE GAPS

MICKEY FORD

Maybe if I keep her talking about Keith, I'll think about anything other than having sex with the gorgeous 18-year-old girl in my living room. First, she's 18. She's way too young for me. Like by about 7 years. I don't *do* age gaps — especially not after 5 years ago. D-day.

Meg Nigel didn't tell me that her cousin *is* extremely sexy. Her proportions are insane. I could get hard just calling her image to memory.

Her skin is dark and gorgeous with this giant features. Her voice is low and sultry, but she's so quiet and soft-spoken, I have to lean in to hear every word she says. Her eyes dart around like a deer searching for the screen in her hand, even now.

"How did you lovebirds meet?" I ask, already imagining ways to kill this Keith *character*. It's not jealous, but loathing. I have a sister as young as Rain, which I try not to think about when I look at her lips, but the thought of some guy touching her infuriates me, anyway.

I walk over to the other side of the room and pluck my acoustic guitar off the wall, sitting on the L-shaped end of the L-shaped couch. Rain curls up in the corner across from me, tucking her feet beneath her body and stressing her curves. I strum the guitar to stop myself from doing something crazy.

"The way everyone meets," Rain says. "He used to hang out by my high school in his car and holler at all the girls walking past. One day, I turned around, and he told me I had a fat ass for a tenth grader. He got me a job at Moe's. Next thing you know, he had me in his car and one thing led to another. He was my manager, and he always gave me the leftover guacamole."

"One thing led to another?" I ask, grimacing. If my little sister was caught up like that, I'd beat the motherfucker that touched her. Then again, I ought to have my ass kicked for looking at Rain like this.

"Sex."

Then we stare at each other for what feels like ages. It *is* ages because we sit a full minute in silence before I repeat…

"Sex…"

"Uh huh."

"How old were you?" I ask her, my stomach tightening.

"Sixteen. Or about to turn sixteen. Something like that."

"And you had sex?"

"Uh huh."

She's giving me a funny look, like she wants me to be taken with her whirlwind romance. All I can think about is how young she must have been. I was young when we started this job. Music. I had my fair share of industry friends who *changed*. Older men, younger women, these whirlwind relationships that seemed to be so loud and all-consuming and then the silent fizzle.

They lost their jobs, their albums, everything if they said no. Older men have power that they ought not to abuse. And I can see clear as day that this Keith character holds significant power over Rain.

I can't save everyone, but maybe I can save her the way Angie wants. I strum a little more and she bobs her head despite herself. She can't help but stay perfectly on beat. A bassist controls the beat, the rhythm of the music, and now I want to control the rhythm of the room and the rhythm of Rain's heart in her chest.

She's young, right?

I stop playing for a second and ask her plainly, "How *old* was this guy?"

Rain shrugs and reaches for her cell phone before anxiously setting it down again. No signal. She's all mine. I try not to act like the thought doesn't drive me wild. No liquor. No powder. But I've got... her.

She's a *woman*.

"He's not that old. He's 36 now," she says in her regular speaking voice, which really is as soft as a whisper.

Funny, I always thought all black girls were loud. I think better than to tell her that. Instead, I work out the math.

She's eighteen. 2 years ago...

"So two years ago he was... 34."

"Yup."

"That's sick," I blurt out before I can think better of myself. I'm always slow when I ought to speed up.

She flinches and then scowls.

"Don't talk to me like that."

"He was a grown ass man preying on a little girl. He's your boyfriend still? Meg Nigel okay with that?"

"Meg hates Keith. Angie hates Keith. They just don't understand what we have."

"And what is that exactly?"

"We have that real ride-or-die love. No matter how much he cheats on me or how hard it is for me to lose weight, we love each other. Forever."

"He cheats on you?" I ask, ready to rise out of my chair and break this Keith's neck.

"He used to. Ever since the circumcision, he's cut back."

Okay, Mickey. Try to do anything except ask her about her ex-boyfriend's foreskin.

"Why?"

"Oh, girls don't like the look of his uncircumcised dick."

Not the question I was asking, but somehow, a worse answer than I expected.

"I meant why do you stay with him?"

Rain shrugs. "He's my man."

"And what about this... losing weight. You don't need to lose weight."

"Keith doesn't like a big ass."

"What?"

"He says a big ass is for his side chick and he needs his main skinny. I just like cooking and eating too much."

She is clueless. Totally clueless. I suddenly feel guilty that Meg left this girl with me. Damn it. I can't screw this up. I can't screw *her* up.

"Ever think maybe it's time to dump this guy?"

"I'm not dumping my boyfriend because some celebrity tells me to."

"Some celebrity?" I scoff. I am not *some* celebrity. I am *Mickey Ford*. I've watched moms trample their daughters just to get my signature on their bra.

"Whatever," she snaps. "I just want my phone back, and if you want to keep me locked up in your creepy dungeon, I need entertainment. *Real* entertainment. This sucks."

Rain sticks her headphones in and she walks off. I play for a minute, because I don't have a clue where she's going. I haven't given up on her tonight.

She *will* dump her boyfriend. No signal. Out in this mansion in the middle of nowhere. 7 days until Meg Nigel shows up with the big bad dog Seb Jefferson to check on our progress. I can have a lot of fun with Rain in 7 days.

Not the dirty kind. I'll help her fix her life up. I'll get *her* life back on track. She'll be the perfect little distraction from booze and pills. Seb was right. I need to mentor someone. Meg was right too. I need to mentor the naïve beauty walking away from me.

Rain. Ain't that a pretty name? I like the sound of rain. I pluck the strings in the rhythm of rain on a tin roof top. Rain. Rain. Rain. Don't you ever go away.

"Rain!" I call her name.

"What?" I hear from the end of the hall.

"Come back."

"Why? So some dickhead alcoholic can judge me for my boyfriend?"

Ouch. Dickhead alcoholic?

"Sounds like you've been reading *Celebz Leaked*…" I mutter.

No reply from the end of the hall. Damn. I have to go after her. The house is nice — a large mansion with an old-fashioned exterior, but everything painfully clean and modern. I barely have anything personal here since this country home is my prison, so it's just… bare.

"Rain!"

Where the hell did she dart off?

9

5 YEARS AGO

RAIN WILSON

A roll of thunder across the Tennessee plantation sends a chill down my spine. We'll have a storm tonight and I'll be stuck here with Mickey Ford giving me weird looks, asking me sex questions and talking about Keith.

I don't want to talk about my relationship. I know... it sucks. I try to act like we're all happy, but when I tell my story out loud, I just feel lame. But everything about my life sucks. Mickey has a fabulous life. He doesn't get it.

I have to try to act okay with everything, but I'm not okay. The way he looked at me when I said I was sixteen...

I can't sit there and feel like a loser next to him. I *hate* Meg wants me to confess what I did to him. Now that I've met him I feel so much... *worse*.

But I also have obligations. **The Tyrant** expects me to find something juicy amongst Mickey's things but this house is bare, I don't have phone signal and I'm running out of time to make something happen.

I sit on the foot of a bed — I assume I'm in another guest room — and I hope if I stay quiet he'll just walk away or maybe find some alcohol and get drunk. Meg wants me to keep him sober, but I don't care about Mickey Ford... at all.

Unfortunately, I'm not quiet enough. Mickey finds me, appearing in the doorway all tall and lean, staring at me. He's lost weight since the court hearings, and he's all lanky, lean muscle and deep-set sapphire eyes.

He leans against the door, his biceps tightening and exposing his defined muscles. His body is flawless, and he smells *so* good. I hate that I notice it. I really thought he was filthy the first time I met him. Tonight he looks different. Less mean.

His shaggy brown hair falls to his shoulders, and he looks pensive and almost... sweet. Just thinking that about the man I spent so much time slandering makes me feel guilty. Meg worries I don't feel guilty enough, but it's all I feel. I just do what I think I have to so I can survive.

"Sorry if I offended you. I know... I'm a little old to be doing all the boyfriend talk with you," Mickey says.

"Yeah. You're like old enough to be my dad," I tell him, obviously joking. I don't know if he gets it or if I'm just not really funny.

"Hm. Not quite. But still. I can help you. Tell me why you want to be with Keith. This time, I won't be an asshole about it."

"I don't believe you."

"Pinky swear," he says.

Mickey Ford sticks out his pinky finger and there's a silver skull ring with two-diamonds for eyes on it. I reach my finger out and his pinky curls around mine. He's strong. He pulls me up off of the bed with just his pinky and whispers, "I promise."

"Okay. Fine. I don't want to be with Keith. I keep trying to dump him and he keeps coming back. I just… I have bigger problems than Keith right now. If I dump him, it'll just make my shitty life even worse."

He looks at me like he really cares. It's so weird to experience up close. It's like watching the poster on the wall of your teenage bedroom lean forward, just like the good sitcom boyfriend you wish he was. Mickey's not my boyfriend, obviously, but he's sitting in such a relaxed way and slouching so much that I can't help but feel comfortable around him.

"What's shitty about your life?" he asks, meaning it so much.

"Everything. You're rich. You wouldn't get it."

"Just because I'm rich doesn't mean shitty things haven't happened to me."

I still feel defensive. "Shitty things like what?"

He hesitates for a moment, then shakes his hair out of his face. He has a tattoo on his neck. *Young Love.*

"I never told anyone," he says. "What made me drink. What made me do this to myself."

"Let me guess, you didn't get a discount at Louis Vuitton?" I snap and immediately hate myself because the saddest expression crosses Mickey's face and he shakes his head.

"I saw something I shouldn't have," he whispers. "But no one can ever know."

My heart races as I lean forward and wait for Mickey Ford to tell me his deepest, darkest secret. The better part of me knows I shouldn't let him tell me. I should stop him and tell the truth, make restitution the way Meg wants me to do. *But girl, the tea…*

Mickey's fingers tremble as he plucks a few odd notes on his guitar. I don't know why he's telling me this. I'm the last person he should trust. He probably thinks I'm young, dumb and naïve. He's not entirely wrong, but he's still underestimating me.

I should tell him.

"This stays here, Rain. Between you and me. Student teacher privilege and all that."

"You don't have to tell me your deep dark secret if it's such a big deal," I say stupidly, as if giving Mickey one last chance to back out justifies the fact that I might have to give this information to **The Tyrant**.

I still care about saving my skin 10x more than I care about Mickey Ford. Yes, he's way hotter than I expected, but I don't know him. Plus, hot people always bounce back. I need to secure my freedom.

"5 years ago when Seb Jefferson was knocking up your cousin's best friend, I stumbled upon two of the producers at the label screwing a passed out 14-year-old girl and using my manager's office to do it."

He pauses and waits for me to react. I don't have much of an external reaction. People always complain that I keep my responses to myself. But I shift a little as I consider the weight of what Mickey has just told me. Rape. Five years ago, he stumbled upon a rape.

"I was in the wrong place at the wrong time, I guess. I still partied before... Not like this, but... Pretty hard. I couldn't stop myself from saying something."

He stops strumming definitively and his fingers curl around the head of the guitar like a lobster claw as he glares fiercely. He gives me an accusatory look and then snaps, "I'm not an asshole. I might be a drunk, I might be a flirt, but I'm not what they say I am."

I shrug because I didn't say anything. Mickey's reacting to whatever headline he thinks I've read or whatever he assumes I believe. Mickey sets the guitar aside and leans forward, shaking his shaggy brown hair out of his face. Holy shit, his jawline is insane.

That part looks way better in person. In the paparazzi pictures, you don't even notice his jawline, but it's hard not to notice only a few feet away from him. Why the hell did Meg send me here again? Is she hoping I'll "relate" to Mickey and then feel bad about the part I played in what happened to him?

He looks fine. Except for his injuries and except for the way he's still shaking. He runs his tongue on his lips, forcing me to notice them and then he mutters, "I shouldn't have been there."

"But you were," I say, even though I immediately regret saying something so stupid.

"I got her free," Mickey says, plodding on with the story like he doesn't have a choice. "I screamed at them until I could work her free and asked her name and age and everything. I told her to get out of there and get the police. I don't think she went. I think she just.... *ran.*"

He pats his pocket for an imaginary flask or box of cigarettes and then he swore under his breath.

"Fourteen," Mickey snarls. "The girl was only fourteen."

Now my stomach feels sick. Mickey gives me a concerned glance, but he clearly doesn't plan on stopping the story until he's finished.

"She wanted to be a singer. I was young and dumb, but not so dumb I didn't know wrong what I saw it. I threatened to go to the police myself and… well… shit got out of control."

Mickey pauses and then stares at me with a scarily blank expression. That's it? It's bad, don't get me wrong, but it's an abrupt end to the story. My heart throbs. I don't know what the hell Mickey wants me to do with this information, but I can't help sitting in rapt attention, waiting for him to tell me what happened next.

"What do you mean shit got out of control?" I ask him after the silence goes on too long for me to handle.

"They got me too," he said. "Beat my ass nearly to death. Took my phone. Rape. Gunpoint. That whole thing. And they have pictures of me they got off my phone. Not pictures of the… attack. But let's just say, I ain't had the cleanest life."

"Was it something illegal?"

Mickey shakes his head. "237 naked pictures, to be exact. Not to mention information about my family, people I've dated, personal shit worth millions. Brent, my manager, has all the back-up copies. If I don't keep my mouth shut, I'm fucked."

"Holy shit."

"That's not the worst part. Someone knows. Someone's blackmailing me."

My eyes dart nervously to his. Mickey tries to calm me down, which only makes me feel worse.

He puts his firm hand on my shoulder. "Don't worry. I'm safe now. We're safe out here. So I don't want you to worry about anything, Rain."

How can I stop myself from worrying? I'm in the middle of something way bigger than me. Something I don't understand.

"Do you have the pictures?"

"If Brent has them, I don't know why I should destroy them. I need reminders of my screw-ups. Maybe that'll be enough to help me change."

Mickey doesn't sound hopeful.

10

I DON'T DATE WHITE GUYS

MICKEY FORD

"That's it then," she says. "Shitty things have happened to you."

"Yup."

She looks down and her expression is... guilty? That doesn't make sense. I've only just met Rain, and she has nothing to feel guilty about. I'm the one who ought to feel guilty. I want her... I want her more than I've ever wanted another woman.

It's the sobriety, I tell myself. It's screwing with my head. If I were high, I'd be passed out somewhere far away from the innocent eighteen-year-old that I have no business looking at or touching.

"So," I say to her quietly. "We're in a bed."

She shifts a little and my eyes can't help but look at her thighs. Her butt looks nice, too. And soft.

"This is the weirdest mentorship I've ever had," she says. "Maybe we should… talk about the fact that I can't sing."

"The album?"

"I'm *not* a singer. This is a ridiculous idea."

"Could you at least try it?"

"No."

"Oh, say can you see," I sing, waving my hands in hope Rain will follow along.

The sound that comes out of her mouth defies the fact that her speaking voice is the most beautiful thing I've ever heard. Her *singing* sounds like a cat mated with Kim Kardashian and recorded the sound on a Fisher Price cassette recorder.

"Okay!" I yell. "That's enough. The acoustics in this bedroom are way off."

"No. I just suck at singing. Keith says the only thing I'm good at is killing roaches."

"Keith…" I snap. "That's right. If you can't hit middle C, at the very least, we can get rid of that bastard Keith."

"*We* aren't doing anything," Rain pouts. "I don't have any signal and I never agreed to dump him."

"*You* don't have any signal. *I* have a way to get whatever I want. And we're walking to the edge of this property where we can get exactly two bars and then… *we're* breaking up with Keith."

My ankle monitor covers the expanse of all ten acres — for exercise, naturally.

"You can't force me to break up with Keith."

"Yes, I can."

I lunge for her phone and I'm surprised the thing comes away from her hand so easily since she's practically glued to it.

"MICKEY!" Rain yells and she lunges after me. Oh, hell no. I act like an idiot with Earl 7 days a week, so running away from an 18-year-old waitress is light work.

"Where the hell are you going?"

"My ankle bracelet allows me to access all ten acres of this property freely!"

"Mickey, stop! I love Keith!" She shrieks.

"No, you don't!"

"He's the love of my life!" she yells.

"The love of your life cheats on you?"

She's already out of breath, but doing her best to chase me down.

"He has depression!" She yells back.

I glance over my shoulder and pick up the pace.

"You can't seriously love that asshole."

"I do!" she answers, but honestly, it's not even remotely believable. I finally see a beloved bar and I struggle to unlock Rain's phone and she jogs the distance between us, panting miserably with each labored step.

"I can't unlock this."

The stupid thing only requires her fingerprint. Just when Rain's in reach, I pull her forward, dragging her close to me and I press her finger forcefully to her cellphone, opening it up.

"Mickey stop!" She shrieks frantically. "You're close to the edge! You'll activate your ankle bracelet."

"Ha!" I yell triumphantly. I don't care about going to jail because I finally have Keith's phone number. At least I assume he's the guy in her phone called "Baby Boo Keith". Rain tries to reach for the phone, but she's much too short to have any hope despite her desperate flailing around. After two rings, Keith picks up, and I put it on speaker.

"Hello?" Keith says. "Kadisha? Is that you? I don't have this number saved."

I clamp one hand over Rain's mouth and I tell him plainly. "Keith, that you? Rain's boyfriend?"

"Who is this? Is that stank hoe cheating on me?"

"No. She isn't," I snarl. I want to kill this motherfucker.

My rage mounts instantly. Stank hoe? He can't possibly be talking about the vision in front of me. I ought to beat his ass. Or shoot him.

"Good," Keith continues. "Tell her sorry ass to get home. I need her to clean the shower before Lucinda comes over. I done told Rain not to leave her toothbrush and shit out when I'm having company. That nasty hoe leaves for two goddamn days and —

Rain bubbles up beneath me, but I just clamp my hand down harder over her mouth and pull her against me in case I need to shove her face in my chest to stifle her screams.

"Rain is not cheating on you at the moment, but she is ending your relationship. At least, I'm ending it on her behalf. You are not to contact her and you will vacate the premises of Rain Wilson's home or there will be a security team to escort you. I'm sorry, Keith, but your time is up. Rain's done."

I don't wait for a response before I hang up and then I fling Rain's phone as far across the property as I can into a giant pond. She gives out an ungodly shriek.

"WHAT DID YOU JUST DO?!"

"I dumped Keith."

"You DROWNED MY PHONE!" Rain shrieks, her face contorting with fury. Her nostrils flare out with rage and her face gets rounder like a bulging airbag of rage.

"You're welcome," I snap, my cheeks already turning red with frustration. "I saved you a lot of trouble getting rid of that Keith character."

I brush my shoulders off because Rain ought to be grateful. Given it's my first day as her mentor, cutting off the dead weight in her life is a colossal success. Rain doesn't seem to care or appreciate my hard work. Her voice gets low and she looks at me like I'm stupid.

"I need that phone you don't understand what kind of trouble I'll be in!"

"Explain it then."

"I can't! You wouldn't understand. You're too *dumb* to understand."

She gives me a furious push.

Too dumb. Damn. Rain can tell she's struck a nerve because she emits an involuntary gasp and then looks up at me. She glances at me and then at the house.

"Why you little…" I mutter before I give chase. Rain takes off like a hound after a fox, except she doesn't realize that in this scenario, I'm the hound. She's the fox. She shrieks an apology as she runs toward the house.

"Why are you chasing me! Mickey, I'm sorry! Fine, I shouldn't have said that!"

She's lucky the dogs are sleeping away in the kennel or they'd love chasing after her, too. I learned from Angie that they enjoy chasing perhaps a little too much.

"I'm tired of your foul mouth. I'm chasing you so I can whoop your ass," I scream as I tear back toward the house as fast as my legs can take me.

"Whoop me?!"

"I'm your damn mentor," I say. "It's allowed."

"That doesn't mean you can whoop me! That's *abuse*."

She's slowing down and I grin once I realize I'll catch her. I probably won't whoop her, but I want to scare her into acting right. That's what Meg wants, right?

"It's only abuse if you tell anyone," I yell as I close the distance between us.

"That's not how that works!" She shrieks, darting just out of my grasp and zig-zagging back. Damn. That little move took me by surprise. I ought to be faster than her, but now that she's switched directions, I might have to use another tactic.

"Stop running!" I call after her. "Fine! I give up. I promise I won't whoop you. And I'll get your phone back. I'm just a fuck up. I'm just a fuck up and I'm really fucking attracted to you. Okay."

She stops in her tracks, but she doesn't turn around. My heart turns into a small, hard lump in my throat. It's cancer, I tell myself. I love her so much that I've made myself all lumpy and sick. Rain slowly turns around, all the best parts of her jiggling. She's still several yards away.

"Attracted to me?" She repeats disdainfully.

"I know. I'm fucked up. You're ten years younger than me. You're getting over your ex and... I can't ever sleep with you. Meg would kill me."

"She'd do worse than kill you," Rain says.

Great. She probably thinks I'm a gross old creep.

"We should go back to the house," Rain says. "It's going to rain again. I don't want to get caught."

I take a few steps closer to her and she allows me to approach, giving me wide doe eyes.

"I *really* want a drink," I tell her.

"I know. But tonight we should probably just... keep our distance and focus on the whole mentorship thing."

"Right. Yeah. Keep our distance."

"Trust me, Mickey... I get it... You'll be stuck here for a year. But you and I can't ever be anything. Or whatever. I'm not into *Rebel Blood*. Like at all. And I don't date white guys."

"I don't date black girls," I snap back.

She steps back and I feel guilty for hurting her. She doesn't get it.

"That's racist," Rain grumbles.

"You just said the same thing."

"Well, my way isn't racist," she says. "I just want to protect myself from bullshit. *You* wouldn't get it."

Her eyes flicker with rage but soften once they meet mine.

"I know a lot about wanting to protect myself," I whisper. "Thanks for being here. Thanks for letting me come clean to you."

"Yeah. Whatever," she says, but she doesn't pull away. What I feel for her is so... complicated. I know she's young but Rain is strangely... magnetic.

"Sorry for pissing you off. But you are way too good for that guy. He cheats on you, Rain. You deserve a man who wants you. Only you."

Our eyes lock for a moment and I think we're getting somewhere. Then Rain rolls her eyes. We're right at the door to the house when Rain looks away shyly.

I want to say something else, but then her eyes flutter toward mine again and I see that she's scared, worried, or something. She's about to bolt.

"Good night, Mickey," she whispers and then slips into the guest room. Damn, I missed my chance. But tomorrow, I'll have another. And the next day, another. I have one year and by the end, I'll have Rain... forever.

11
I'M DONE PLAYING GAMES LITTLE LADY

RAIN WILSON

Without my phone, I'm screwed. If I can't contact the brains behind Celebz Leaked, I won't know what **The Tyrant** plans next. **The Tyrant** could be back at my place right now, negotiating the public release of my sex tape with Keith as an ally.

I should have told Meg, but I still can't bring myself to confess my stupid actions to her. I still feel so *dirty*.

There's one bright side. Keith is gone. I feel like I just woke up from a long nap. Now that the breakup is done, I can't believe how seamless it was.

I don't even feel sad. It's like I tossed a backpack full of bricks off my back. Could it have been that easy? I mean, he's still in my house for now, but I doubt Meg will even let me go back there. I wouldn't even know how. I have no more money left in my account, so I couldn't leave this place if I wanted to.

Keith took my debit card two days before I got to Mickey's place to buy some black and milds, and he over-drafted my account for $50 to buy Plan B. He said I was controlling when I asked who it was for.

I smile as I lie in Mickey's bed. That will never happen again… Ha. I'm free. And I had a freaking celebrity break up with him. It doesn't matter that it's Mickey Ford from *Rebel Blood*.

Mickey might not be so bad after all. Unfortunately, that's not enough to save him. I'm going to hack into his phone while he sleeps and send whatever I can to *Celebz Leaked*. I used to do this all the time to my older brother so I could tell his girlfriends that he was two-timing them.

Plus, I became a night owl after my night shifts at Moe's — those times when Keith would ignore his girlfriend's phone calls to help me with my high school homework. I almost failed out because of his goofy ass. Maybe Mickey's right about Keith. He's a scumbag and I'm grown now. It's time for me to act grown.

I know I can do better with my life.

It's not like my singing career has promise. I saw the look on Mickey's face. I have no talent. I am seriously the most boring, basic person on the planet. I don't know why Mickey would say something so stupid, like he's "attracted" to me. I guess he's just a scumbag guy trying to sleep with me because we're in Meg's little morality experiment.

I know I have options. In one of those options, I have a shot at freedom.

We won't have to work together when I leak all his information and get one step closer to securing the bag and booking a flight to freedom. Sorry, Meg. There's a better way out of here than singing for Mickey Ford.

Swing low sweet *Spirit Airlines* and carry me to somewhere upscale like… Kansas.

Mickey thinks I'm asleep when he stumbles through his kitchen muttering about needing a drink and complaining about the food his staff left warming in the oven. He barely eats.

When he *finally* falls asleep, I sneak out of my room and walk around the house. My eyes adjust to the dark quickly.

I know what I'm doing is messed up but at the end of the day, Mickey has tons of money and probably eighty-thousand women who would sell their own kids just to go on a date with him. He's attractive, but he's almost too attractive.

Now I need to find some way to contact **The Tyrant** and share my new discoveries about Mickey.

The Tyrant must already know about the pictures and when **The Tyrant** finds out, I can get the actual pictures and information from Mickey, I'll be *free*.

It's horrible what happened to him. I know from experience how horrible it is to worry about your nudes getting leaked, but what the hell does Mickey have to fear? He's a millionaire. He'll bounce back.

The rape stuff was sad. I won't tell The Tyrant about that. She'd only have fuel for her homophobic fires. I might be shady, but I'm not a total piece of shit. Okay, leaking his nudes is pretty bad, but I draw the line at gossiping about rape. That part makes my blood run cold.

He didn't go into details or anything, but it makes what **The Tyrant** said about him so much worse. No one deserves that.

Padding through his house in the dark, I feel like a creep, but it's the only way I can truly appreciate how amazing his countryside home is. I don't want Mickey getting a bigger head than he already has by gushing to his stupid face. His house is so big that you can go days without seeing people on the other side of it.

I guess it's sweet that he got Keith off my back, but that doesn't justify the fact that Mickey is privileged and he doesn't *deserve* the privilege.

I push his bedroom door open. I don't bother opening it carefully because if he's going to wake up, I want him to do it now before he catches me digging through his things. *Damn, his bedroom is huge.*

They painted the walls this deep brick red, and he has a giant four-poster black bed in the middle with literal notches made on one poster. I hope to God the notches aren't counting hookups because there are well over a hundred of them.

"Mickey," I whisper again to test if he's really asleep. So far, so good. Now I need to find his phone. I'm sure he has one somewhere. I check his side table and bingo... Mickey Ford's cellphone. His bedroom is dark except for a small night light plugged in near the entrance. I run my finger over the smooth back of the phone and then I hear an unfortunate sound... a low, threatening growl.

I gasp and then glance over my shoulders. There's a dog here. Not one dog... two. They're both growling at me as I stand there holding Mickey's cell phone and stuck in a situation that will quickly become compromising if I don't get away. I thought Meg told me the dogs slept outside in one of those luxury kennels. She knows I don't mess with dogs...

I try to hold my breath and think of a way out. I know I should put Mickey's phone down, but I can't stop myself. If I just hold my position and grab his finger, I can unlock the phone, do what I need to do, and then I'll pretend I only came in here because I was running away from the dogs. The plan makes sense. It's probably one of the best plans I've ever had.

"Shhh," I whisper. "It's okay, puppy..."

The dog's growling continues, but it doesn't move. I lean over, pushing my braids out of the way so they don't tickle Mickey's sleeping face, and I grab his hand. My heart feels like a little frog bouncing off the walls of my stomach. Mickey doesn't budge, and I am eternally grateful that he sleeps like the dead. Normal people use their thumb to unlock their phone, right?

I try the thumb, and it doesn't work. Crap. I try his index finger and it works. It freaking works. I feel like I just discovered the holy grail. Mickey's background is a picture that says "sobriety is worth it". All he's done so far is complain incessantly about sobriety. Whatever.

Everyone knows the good stuff is in the "Photos" app. I'm practically licking my chops with glee and grateful that, as dumb as I may be, I'm fantastic at remembering phone numbers. No one my age remembers phone numbers —

except me. It'll be nothing to get this info out of here and sail to freedom. Money, escape from Keith… maybe I'll even get myself a Nissan Altima. I'm giddy with excitement, so I don't notice that the growling's stopped, and it's stopped for a good reason.

The dogs are calm because their master's awake. I jump out of my skin when Mickey's deep West Virginia voice drawls, "What the ever living fuck are you doing in my bedroom?"

The light emanating from the screen highlights the genuine terror on my face. I want to leap back and make a run for it with Mickey's phone in tow. He has an ankle bracelet. I don't have to outrun him forever. I just need to get to the edge of his property and leave that sucker in the dust.

I take my first step away from him, but the dogs bark and Mickey's forceful hand clamps around mine. I scream and drop his cellphone. The 237 pictures of him I'd selected are now plainly visible, even in the dark room. Mickey flicks his bedside lamp on and his grasp on me tightens. This is the wrong time to notice it, but Mickey sleeps shirtless and when he sits up in bed, the blanket falls away from him and holy shit… he's not just shirtless. Mickey Ford sleeps naked. He drags me onto his bed and I shriek as he forces me to sit next to him.

"Move and I swear, Rain Wilson. You'll be sorry."

It is so hard to hear a word he's saying when a CREATURE falls out of the sheets from between his legs and just hangs there with Mickey, blissfully unaware.

The dogs keep growling and Mickey sighs.

"Quiet, Sam."

"Your dog's name is Sam?"

Mickey shoots me a glare.

"No," he says. "You won't do this. You won't distract me."

His grasp on me tightens and I get the feeling I'm in *way* over my head.

Mickey grumbles through his sleep, "I can tell I've already underestimated you. Pippin, sit."

Sam and Pippin both respond to the command and their ears perk up. The dogs are enormous. They could both tear me limb from limb and now the bedroom's illuminated. I realize how close a call I just had. It feels dangerous to take my eyes off Mickey's giant beasts, but I can't ignore him for long.

"What were you doing with my cell phone, Rain? I've been thinking something ain't right about you. I've been thinking something ain't right about all of this. I'm done playing games, little lady. You're going to tell me the truth."

12

ONE PROBLEM SOLVED BY SEX

MICKEY FORD

"I just wanted to see," I say. The lie is horrible, but Mickey's no Meg Nigel, right?

"You just wanted to see? That's why you sneak in here in the middle of the night, getting me out of my damn bed…"

She glances over at me. Then down. What the hell is she looking at? *Shit.* I'm naked. I'm sitting right next to Meg's eighteen-year-old cousin and because this midnight scamp went crawling through my things, I didn't cover myself properly. At first I think she's looking at my cock, but as I draw the pillow over my bare crotch, her face contorts in horror.

"Is that… a…"

"Yes. It's a confederate flag. I was stupid. I was young, famous and country as fuck. $2,500 down the drain."

"I need to go."

She gets up, but I can't let her go. I stand up and drag her back down so she's sitting on the bed.

"Not so fast."

"Can you at least cover up?!" she snaps. "You really are a racist! You're a conservative murderous racist!"

"Murderous!!?"

"That's what the confederacy is about, you idiot! Slavery. Which is about murder."

I ought to cover up. I'm already half stiff just sitting near her and now that she's on the bed next to me, I can smell her too.

What is it about black women that they always smell so good? Angie's like that, not that I'd be stupid enough to tell Seb Jefferson I think his lady smells nice. Rain smells even better to me.

"I'll cover up when you tell me the truth."

"I won't tell the truth until you cover up."

"Rain. I haven't had a drink in over two weeks and right now all I want is to get higher than a motherfucker and spend the night with a beautiful woman who moans loud and lets me eat her from the back. I'm stuck here with a kid who I just caught stealing from me. I don't want to talk about my damned tattoos or anything else. What would your cousin *Meg* think about this shit?"

Rain's eyes grow wide, like she never considered the notion that I might tattle. I won't, but she doesn't know that and man, her eyes are sexy when they get all wide and scared-like.

"You can't tell Meg! And this is your fault for throwing my phone away. I *need* my phone," Rain snaps, her voice filled with shocking vitriol for such a quiet woman. I'd pegged her as demure, but I can see that she burns with a blue fire, barely noticeable but hotter than most engorged flames.

"This ain't about your phone. You're over here going through mine looking at pictures of…"

I glance down for the first time and look at the pictures she's selected. My cheeks turn red. I don't know why I'm bothering to cover up now since Rain's seen it. 237 pictures of me in compromising positions. Half the pictures she selected are on my phone because I receive messages once every 90 days, reminding me that powerful people hold the keys to my destruction. The night of my attack. Now I really need a drink. A big fat drink.

Rain gives me a nervous glance and then she says, "Please, don't tell Meg. I'll make it up to you."

"You're a liar."

Rain stares at me, and for the first time, I see what I missed. She ain't quiet because she's shy. She's quiet because she's listening and this little lady is a lot more clever than she lets on. That's the good part about being dumb as rocks. I can see when a woman's turned on like a light and Miss Rain Wilson is on…

"Yes," she whispers. "I am."

"Give me the phone."

She hands it over.

"I'll get you a new phone soon, Rain. I'll talk to Seb and it'll have games or whatever. But still no internet. And this... we still need to talk about this."

"I'm sorry."

"I confided in you. The first thing you do is go look for evidence. What the hell were you going to do with that? Betray me?"

I can hear how angry I sound and I pull back. I can't bring myself to scare her, even if I just caught her going through my things. She has one of those faces that's impossible to be mad at.

"I just... I don't know..."

My voice deepens and I can feel myself turning into the monster I try to suppress with booze and pills. Mickey Ford... I was a bastard back in high school and I got into more fights than my parents could handle. I'd always been a rough and tumble country boy, which made it ten times worse what they did to me. I place a hand on her thigh, a firm but controlling hand.

"Is this about money?"

God knew what he was doing when he made it so that pretty girls usually need money.

"Yeah," she says. "I needed money."

"I have money."

"I know."

I touch her thigh a little more and look at her. "I could give you money."

"Okay... why do I feel like there's a catch?" she says, catching on quickly to my intentions for a woman who appears so naive.

"You're pretty.... We're here together. If we became... *friends*. I could help you out."

"Friends?"

"Friends who have sex."

Rain nervously glances up at me then grows immediately indignant. "I'm not having sex with you for money!"

"But you'd sell pictures of my bare ass to God kn—

"Okay, fine!" She interrupts. "I'm sorry. I know it was wrong. But I'm *black*. You can't expect me to have sex with you when you look like..."

I move the blankets.

"When I look like what?"

I lean back, propping my arms behind my head and giving Rain Wilson a full view of what she's been eyeing in her peripheral vision in a desperate attempt to project subtlety rather than desire.

"Stop that," she says, getting off the bed, but keeping her gaze fixed on me.

"Stop what?"

"Your dick is out! That's harassment."

Yeah. My dick is out, and it's probably harassment. There's only one problem. I don't care. If this little brat thinks she can steal from me and scamper around my house in the middle of the night while I lie around bored, she has another thing coming.

I grin and tease her a little "How much money you want?"

"I'm not a hooker."

"I never said you were. Consider it a gift to a really *hot* friend."

She gets outraged then and I think it's the hooker thing.

"I'm not your friend!" she yells. "And I'm not really hot. I'm nothing! I'm just a stupid girl with a stupid boyfriend who worked at stupid Moe's and then got a stupid job at a stupid bar. Now Mickey Ford is showing me his stupid dick, and this is just dumb!"

She's getting hysterical and I sit up again, adjusting my cock so it hangs properly on the top of my thighs. It sort of moves on its own, though, rolling over my thighs as Rain stares.

"You ain't *nothing*," I tell her, meaning it despite myself. "You're way way more than that."

"You said it yourself that I'm a thief. You called me a liar. You're right. I'm all of those things. Meg wants me to be here and learn from you, but I can't even last one night."

"What you're saying is you feel like a failure?"

"Yes!" she screams at me. "I'm a huge fat fucking failure and I'm totally screwed and not just because of Keith or the fact that your *giant* dick is out."

Then there's silence. *Dead* silence. She's just brought up my dick, and it's like hearing his name is waking him up. I know I ought to cover up again, but I can't help myself. I'm a man.

For some stupid reason, there ain't anything we're more proud of than getting it hard and ready for entry between a pair of soft thighs.

Right now, Rain's thighs are more than doing it for me.

"Welcome to the club," I tell her calmly. "If there's anyone screwed up here, it's me."

Her eyes dart from my cock to my face again.

"Yeah," she says, as if the realization that I'm a bastard just hit her. "Good point. What kind of guy just shows his big hard dick to a strange eighteen-year-old girl."

"You barged in here, rifling through my things. You stumbled upon me naked. If you're so dang curious, have a look."

Rain folds her arms, and despite herself, she peeks. Yes. It feels good knowing I have her here.

"You think I care about tattoos and six-packs?"

"Count the pack. I'm pretty sure you'll find there are more than six…"

"Shut up," she says, but I can feel her eyes roaming over my chest. Counting.

"My biceps are pretty nice, too. And my hands."

I flex my hands, stretching my long, dextrous fingers. Tattoos cover nearly every inch of me. I like tattoos.

"They're guitarist's hands," I continue. "Never had any complaints from women."

"Maybe you were too drunk to remember the complaints," she snaps. "And come on, notches on your bed?"

"The dogs did those."

I chuckle. There's something about Rain's attitude that gets me… excited. It's like the whole woman is a challenge.

"Come to bed with me and all your problems will go away," I say before she can think of something sassy to say.

Rain scoffs.

"Name one problem solved by having sex."

"Horniness?"

I might be stupid, but even I can figure that one out. Rain fidgets and then huffs.

"I'm not horny," she says. "I've *never* been horny. Sex isn't even that great. I'd basically just have to lie there while you talked about how good you were. I'll pass."

"Great. Then we'll spend the rest of the night here and you can watch me."

My hands grasp my shaft and she flinches. I grin.

"Um… I'm going back to my room."

Maybe I am bad at flirting.

"I don't think so, Rain. I can't have a thief wandering around my valuables. It's up to me and I think you'll be sleeping right here tonight."

And always, I muse to myself. Because I can guarantee once I let this woman into my bed, I won't want to let her out.

13

COOPED UP LIKE A SLAVE

RAIN WILSON

"You can't keep me cooped up here like a sex slave."

Mickey finally stops gripping his dick like a goose he's trying to strangle. He gets out of bed and struts toward the door. Naked. I want to move but I'm stunned by his physique and where would I run anyway?

He's so much taller than me. I'm only five feet tall, so he's more than a foot taller than me and his body is... insane. Mickey's cut everywhere and he's covered in tattoos. A lot of guys look gross with that many tattoos, but most of Mickey's tattoos are hot.

My stomach tightens with raw anger at the confederate flag tattooed on his thigh, but then he walks past me and I'm staring at his ass.

Holy shit. His ass looks like it was carved out of marble and there's a tiny heart tattoo on one cheek. Maybe he's not as racist as I think, and he's just dumb enough to let people tattoo anything anywhere. See? I'm getting hypnotized by his ass. *Basic.*

I'm so busy staring at his ass that I hardly notice Mickey locking his bedroom door.

He slides the key onto the gold chain around his neck before replacing it and facing me. I try not to look at exactly where it hangs on his broad chest. His dick is still out. But he's only halfway hard as he looks at me.

"Why the fuck did Meg send you here?" he snaps, getting serious and slightly scary. At least he's trying to scare me.

"Nothing. No reason."

"Lying. Again."

How can he see through me?

"What do you care?"

"I've known you 24 hours and you want to sell me out already. I don't like the idea of a beautiful woman doing such a thing."

"Women can do whatever they want."

He grins and leans forward.

"Yeah. They can."

He presses his thumb against my lips. The slight contact from the nude superstar sends a strange thrill through me.

"What do you know about sex?" He whispers.

"I'm not a virgin."

"Good," he whispers, all too pleased with himself. "I like that. Do you like sex?"

"Um... no women like sex, Mickey."

"I like sex because it requires honesty," he whispers. "You can't lie to someone you're sleeping with."

"I'm pretty sure you can."

"Not really," Mickey says. "And I know once I sleep with you, you won't lie to me anymore. Do you understand?"

"Not at all."

Mickey leans forward and kisses me on the lips. I try not to freak out about the fact that a celebrity rock star is kissing me on the same day that I broke up with Keith. What makes me freak out even more is Mickey leaning in deeper and his kisses feeling so much better than any kiss I'd ever had. The only guy I kissed before was... well... Keith.

I pull away and Mickey grins.

"Wow," he whispers. "You're a lot sweeter when you kiss."

I'm too shocked by his kiss to play it cool.

"How did you do that? How did it feel so good?"

"I thought you kissed before."

"I have. It's just... normally there's more... teeth? Keith's a biter."

Mickey chuckles, and then he touches my face and brings me in close again. I can't help myself. I don't care that he's naked or anything. I press my hands against his chest and let him kiss me. I can feel the monster between his legs stiffening as I lean against him, but I can't stop myself from kissing him. I feel like I just tasted the best ice-cream in existence and now I can't break away. Instinctively, my fingers grab onto his shaggy brown hair and he groans as tangle my fingers in it.

"Fuck yes," he whispers. "You are wild."

"What does that mean?"

"Nothing," he whispers. "Come here."

He touches my hips then and brings me close, kissing me more and leading me slowly toward his bed. My heart races as the thought suddenly crosses my mind that seducing women is child's play for Mickey. The notches. He wants me as one notch. All the notches on his bedpost probably mean I'm one of thousands of women. He guides me gently back onto the bed, but before Mickey slides between my legs, I press my hand to his chest.

He stops kissing me and gives me a curious look. He suddenly looks as awkward as the teenage boyfriend I never had, but always dreamed of. He looks like the weirdly hot music guy in school with his hair and his bare skin drawing against mine.

"What's wrong? Too fast?"

Yes. Yes, it's way too fast.

"I just broke up with Keith," I whisper.

"Yeah," he whispers. "I know. I ain't a cheater."

"Neither am I," I whisper back to him.

"Listen," he says, pushing hair out of my face and kissing my forehead. "You have nothing to worry about. I'll take care of you. I'll make you cum."

He says it with such confidence that I can't help feel wounded defiance. How the hell can he be so sure that he can make me cum? Orgasms are events that happen without Keith.

But Mickey's blue eyes gleam with confidence. I hate to say it, but up close, I don't even find his eyes so terrifying. The sapphire holds me fixed on his bed, wondering how the hell I got myself in this position.

"I don't want to be your prostitute."

"Fine. I won't give you money. Fuck the money. But still… I want you."

"Isn't the point of sobriety not getting everything you want?"

He chuckles and kisses me gently on the lips like we're long lost lovers and not enemies.

"I'll get everything I want," he whispers. "The first thing I want from you is… to see you."

He touches my waist and I inhale a sharp gust of air as he slides my shirt up and whistles when he removes my shirt.

"They're soft," he whispers, rubbing my breasts through my bra. "Really soft…"

I can feel his hardness pressing against my thigh as he massages my boobs. I don't want him to stop, but then he does.

"I've never seen a black girl's tits," he whispers.

I struggle against his grasp. I shouldn't be enjoying myself in Mickey Ford's arms. He oozes gross fetishization. Or something. I don't know what to call it, but the way he's looking at me and staring at me makes me feel… wanted.

"Couldn't you just look them up?"

His grasp on my breast grows more firm. I gasp and again try to wriggle away from him. The sensation of his fingers running over my nipples becomes impossible to ignore. Sex. I want us to have sex when he touches me like that.

His warm breath against my neck as he speaks breaks down my resolve.

Mickey's face turns red and he shrugs. "Never thought about it."

Right. I have to remember myself here. Mickey is a bored addict, and he thinks he can have anything he wants. This is exactly what **The Tyrant** talked about.

I shove my hands against his chest and find a firm pillar of musculature. Mickey might look lean, but he's strong.

"Okay, well… I'm not your little sex experiment," I say, my mouth drying up as I ignore the instinct to squeeze his chest muscles. My hands on him don't seem to bother him. I could probably get away with doing what every girl in America wants to do.

Okay, not every girl. There are Seb girls and Earl Wayne Jr. girls… then there are Mickey girls. They'd always swarm Celebz Leaked after a new story threatening to show up at **The Tyrant's** house and burn it to the ground.

You can just tell he'd be a great boyfriend. He might not get the shine Seb Jefferson does, but he's so hot! — Anonymous Comment

Honestly, I would kill my boyfriend and fuck Mickey Ford that night if he gave me the chance. — Anonymous comment

Mickey's hand on my face draws me out of my memory.

"Why not? I'd like to experiment with you. I heard you were... you know... wilder."

My stomach tightens. He's so attractive, but every time he opens his mouth... he says something so dumb. I squeeze my eyes shut and try to ignore my stupid teenaged heart, which doesn't realize that it's supposed to stop pounding like crazy when a white guy says something problematic.

"That's so racist," I whisper, sounding so much gentler than I feel. Mickey pushes a braid out of my face and kisses my cheek.

"Racist?" He whispers. "Little lady, we're all racist. Okay. So tell me about white guys. What do you think about white guys in bed?"

He draws his finger over my shoulder and I shudder against him. The way I feel when he touches me is nothing like what I felt with Keith. I bite down on my lower lip to stop myself from saying something stupid to Mickey.

I want to tell him the one stereotype I heard, which is that white guys have smaller dicks. Except I've already seen Mickey's dick and that 100% does not apply to him.

His dick is actually so big that I almost doubt it's human. I keep trying to ignore it pressing against me but it's so warm and present that it's hard to ignore. It's getting harder too.

The dick. Mickey's touching my boobs and it's making him insanely stiff.

I think it's going to happen. I think I'm going to have sex with Mickey Ford.

"I don't think anything about white guys," I say to him, and then our eyes meet.

He chuckles and flashes me a cocky smile that makes me feel small and inexperienced.

"I think you want me," he whispers. "And I think… if you're going to steal from me, I'm going to keep you very close…"

His fingers wrap around my waist and then Mickey's hand slides down to the front of my pants. His cobalt eyes are crazed with desire as he slides his hand down my pants and I meet his fingers with a loud and urgent gasp of pleasure.

Mickey grins, his fingers moving between my lower lips forcefully.

"Cooped up like a sex slave, you say?" he whispers… "I like the sound of that."

14

RAIN COMES

MICKEY FORD

"Why am I not surprised?" She snaps. "Of course you'd like the sound of slavery."

"Careful," I whisper. "I've got my fingers in your pussy. I know I'm getting you real wet."

She squirms and can't help herself. She's soaked and I bet she tastes good. I want to get every drop of pussy juice onto my tongue.

I press my finger to Rain's chin and pull her gaze to mine as my fingers slide between her legs. She's soft... really soft. And she's soaking wet. Fuck. I don't think I've ever had a girl that wet near me. I usually do whatever groupie is up for it just to get off, but with Rain... I want more. The first step is to get her to stop hating me. The next step is to make sure she can't escape and rummage through my things.

I slide my finger into her deeper and she moans. Loud.

"What are you doing?" she gasps, pressing her lips against my shoulder with desperate affection spilling out of her. The juicy wet pussy between her thighs gushes against my hand as I get close to making my black girl cum. She's really pretty as she gets close. She gasps and she kisses me again with those crazy soft lips.

Kissing her is even better than I thought, and I want her again. My grasp on her waist tightens and I kiss her on the lips as I push her close to the edge. Her moans get louder and sharper and I lift her off the ground to make her cum with one last thrust of my fingers as I rub her to orgasm. I spread her lust-wracked body on my bed and climb on top of her, kissing her as she gasps for breath.

Mine. She's mine. The urgency I feel for her defies any desire for any drug. I never wanted a groupie that smelled like vodka and her own vomit the way I want Rain. She smells like an angel. I bet she tastes like one too. I spread her thighs apart, and she yelps, shutting her thighs quickly. No. I want that...

"Open up," I demand.

"What are you doing?"

"Eating your pussy. Now open up."

Her hands cover her mound, and a flash of anger surges through me. She can't stop me. Not yet.

"Rain..."

"You can't put your mouth down there, it's nasty!"

"What the fuck is so nasty about it?"

Rain rolls her eyes like I'm the clueless one.

"First of all, my period."

I push my finger into my mouth.

"You're all clean right now."

She gives me a truly horrified look.

"What?" I ask her, continuing to lick her sticky sweet pussy juice off my fingers. Fuck. She tastes better than booze. A lot better.

"Second, the pussy is just the female butt in the front," she says.

"Huh?"

Rain groans and buries her head in her hands.

"I don't know. It's just gross. Keith always said it was gross and whatever. It's gross."

I pull her hands away from her face and lie next to her, trailing my fingers down her bare stomach until I get to her pussy. She glances away bashfully as I gaze at her.

There's nothing I want more than to kiss her, make love to her, and taste her. I need to taste her.

"You talk a lot of bullshit. Even more than I do. Women are meant to be tasted. That's why you taste so damn good."

She wrinkles her nose with utter disgust.

"I don't taste good."

"Yes. You do."

She tastes way better than good. Her pussy tastes like some type of elixir. She's ridiculously wet and soft and those lips…

it's like they come with built in flavor already. She's soft. Sensuous. Mine.

I run my tongue over my fingers again, and I've already licked her all up. I need more. More... I slide my fingers inside her panties again and Rain moans as I get all the juices I can on my finger and pull my hand out of her tight black panties.

"Taste yourself," I command her.

Rain tries to scramble back, but I roll on top of her, pinning her to the bed with my hips. I'm so hard I think I'm going to burst, but I'm not letting this troublemaker out of my bed without giving her a taste of the juiciest cunt I've ever had in my life.

"Do it."

"You're a freak," she whispers, but she doesn't try to run away. She looks... intrigued. I grin.

"Yup."

"And you're racist. I'm not licking a racist hand."

That part nearly makes me laugh.

"Why not? I just made your black pussy cum. That wasn't racist now, was it?"

"I hate you."

Rain squirms again, and I hold my finger to her face.

"Taste."

"No!"

As she opens her mouth to say no, my finger goes in. Instinctively, her mouth clamps down and she squeals, but has no choice. She sucks her juices off my finger and when I pull my hand away from her, she gasps and pushes against my chest.

"Asshole!"

"See? It wasn't so bad," I tell her, laughing as she makes a face and then realizes that she doesn't taste bad. At all.

"That's not the point!"

She pushes me again, but this time I grab her arms and pin them over her head. She's here in my bed, wet enough to take my cock and squirming desperately against me. I don't know if quiet Rain's wilder than any other woman, but the way her hips squirm against mine gets me harder than any other woman has. It's been a long time since I've really wanted a woman. Since I wanted a woman like this.

My forearm pins Rain's arms to the bed and her eyes can't help wander to the rest of my tattoos.

"You need to get it removed," she whispers.

The last thing I want to think about is my stupid tattoo, but she can't get her mind off it.

"I know."

"Do you really feel that way?" she says, her vulnerability beneath me striking me. "Is this like... a race thing."

A race thing? I mean. It *isn't* a race thing. Maybe. I don't know. But there's something pretty about her nipples. There's something intriguing about her soft outer folds and the pink flesh covered between them. I like the way her hair smells and the way it's wrapped in this soft long braids. I want to touch the braids and wrap them around my fingers.

"I don't know," I whisper, running my tongue along her neck. It doesn't matter if it's a race thing as long as I get her in the end. She's positioned firmly between me and my mattress. We have plenty of time before Meg or Seb Jefferson shows up and I plan to make good use of Rain Wilson before then. She excites me.

"It's not right," she whispers.

"Okay. Sorry. I can't help it. Back where I grew up… you'd get… I dunno… Let's just say you couldn't bring a black girl home."

She flinches and then tries to squirm away again. No. I don't want her going anywhere. I like her right where she is, exactly where I have her.

"Mickey Ford," she whispers, using my full name, which sounds weird spilling out of her mouth. "I… I don't know if I can do this."

I press her more firmly into the bed. Her eyes are both wide and terrified beneath me.

"Why not? I scare you?"

"No."

I caress her hips and want to spill inside her. I bet she would feel good. Tight. She's really tiny, except those hips and that butt.

"Then what?"

"You're an asshole," she says confidently.

Most people think I'm an asshole.

"Maybe."

"You dumped my boyfriend," she says, but I doubt she should complain about that.

"Yes."

"You're racist."

"Not anymore."

"Charming."

"I was never America's sweetheart," I murmur, kissing her cheek. "I left that to Jefferson."

I was the sweet one at first, and then I became the bad boy. Drugs made me cruel. They made me careless. Drugs nearly made me kill someone.

"Stop," Rain breathes.

No. I don't want to stop with her. I want to have her tonight.

"Why should I? You want this. I know you want this."

She glares because I'm saying the entirely wrong thing — the line that works on groupies but gets you canceled everywhere else.

"You don't understand, Mickey," she says. "I'm here because Meg wants to punish me."

"Great," I say, grinning widely. I can work with guilt.

"You can get revenge on her," I tell Rain. "Prove to her you're a grown woman who does what she wants… follows her own urges…"

I kiss her neck and find her nipples again. They're mesmerizing. And large. I enjoy touching them, but I want to see more of Rain naked. Rain struggles against my forearm with a scowl.

"You're pinning me down."

"Yup."

"I… It's not about Meg," she says, her chest rising nervously.

"You brought her up."

"I'm explaining," Rain snaps with all the huffy rage that only a teenager can muster. "Meg sent me here to punish me and she sent me to be with you because she thinks it'll make you seem… human to me."

"I see. So you're a secret fan, idealizing me from the sidelines. I understand."

I bend my lips but stop right before kissing her.

Rain looks at me like I'm stupid. Then she says words I never expected to hear from a woman who just spread her pussy all over my fingers.

"No, Mickey. I leaked information to *Celebz Leaked*. I'm the reason you got in the accident."

15

A RICH HIPPIE

RAIN WILSON

Mickey's next words surprise me. I think he'll let me go or maybe move off me so he can take a swing at me. I think he'll do anything except what he does next. His forearm presses into me harder. I cry out involuntarily as his hips press into me harder and Mickey's face turns so dangerously red that it almost looks like he's choking.

"What?"

"It was me," I croak out. "I'm sorry. I'm really sorry…"

I want to hide my face but my hands are currently pinned beneath Mickey Ford, the crazed former drug addict and the celebrity who I targeted online for years with other members of my online group chat mini-cult. Now I'm here, pinned beneath Mickey Ford and not only do I have to answer for what I've done, but now, I'm utterly at a crazed white man's mercy and he has a symbol of hate tattooed on his thigh.

"Stop your whining," Mickey says, his voice deep and sharper than I've ever heard him speak before.

"I'm sorry," I whisper again, hoping it sounds like anything other than whining to him.

"Is that why you were going through my shit?" he snarls, his eyes roving over me. Demon redneck eyes. They're scary in person, just like I thought.

I move my hands, hoping I can get away from him, but there's no way in hell that's happening. Mickey can overpower me easily, which I should have considered before this stupid bid at honesty.

"Y-yes..."

"Fuck," he hissed. "Meg Nigel's trying to fuck me over."

"No, please! It's not her fault. It's mine. She wanted me to come here and apologize and make it up to you..."

"You can make it up to me," he whispers, sliding my panties off. This isn't what I expected to happen next. My hips instinctively part as Mickey slides my underwear off. He groans as he presses his fingers between my lower lips again. His fingers are rough and masculine, powerful in a way that I've never felt before, and the way he touches between my legs is so... raw. He's still pinning me to the bed as his lips touch my neck firmly.

"The way I see it, Rain," he snarls. "I own you for the next year. That's how you can make it up to me. You'll warm my bed. You'll do every word I say... and maybe if you're lucky, I'll let you leave my house at the end. But I have so many things I need to do to you... and I ain't going to stop myself."

Without another warning, I feel it. The head of Mickey's insanely large cock presses fiercely against my bare entrance. No condom. Nothing.

"Mickey," I gasp. "I could get pregnant."

"You won't get pregnant," he says confidently before sliding the tip of his dick inside me. I can't argue because holy shit… pain. Mickey's big. He's bigger than big. He's enormous.

"Mickey!"

"Quiet…"

I gasp as he slides the rest of the head inside me. I can feel the stretching between my legs and its painful.

"It's too big… It's way too big…"

"Is Keith smaller than this?"

I don't know how to break it to Mickey. 99.986% of human males are smaller than this. I can't break it to him because he withdraws and replaces my pain with a moment of relief. My chest heaves and I gasp, wriggling my hands beneath Mickey's firm grasp again.

He pulls out of me. Not tonight. We're not going to have sex tonight.

"If you'd let me eat you more, this would go faster," he grumbles, his tongue darting over his lips as his eyes fall between my legs again. He's so determined to put his tongue between my legs.

"It's dirty down there," I protest again. I secretly want him to taste me again. It felt good. But I still barely know him. The right thing to do is resist.

"You are not dirty down there," he growls. "Now spread your legs, woman. If I'm going to get my cock in you, I'll need you wet."

Mickey spreads my legs apart lewdly and I feel like I'm about to dip my toe into the most taboo sex act imaginable. I know everyone now is like a super-freak, but Keith definitely never put his tongue down there. Keith's all I know... And now, I know Mickey Ford.

Mickey's thumbs part my lower lips as his tongue slides dangerously between my legs, running along my clit as his fingers slide along my lower lips. He groans as he presses his tongue between my legs and tastes me. I imagine he'll wince as he juts his tongue out awkwardly, but he pushes in without a moment of hesitation, licking me at first and then sucking hard on my lower lips. I gasp and rake my fingers through his hair, meaning to push him off, but sinking my hands into his shaggy, dark brown hair.

I've written over a hundred posts guessing that Mickey Ford smells like a potato salad left out on a sunny day, but that couldn't be further from the truth. He smells like leather and sandalwood, more like a rich hippie than a dirty hippie. And his tattoos... I obviously hate that stupid confederate flag tattoo, but I can't stop to think about it when Mickey's doing that with his tongue.

I gasp and unravel completely in Mickey Ford's arms. I don't want to feel so vulnerable to him, but I can't help it. His touch is light when it needs to be and then firm. That first painfully delicious orgasm isn't the first.

Why? Why the hell did Mickey Ford find out that I'm a horrible person and then stick his tongue in my pussy?

I don't have longer than a moment to contemplate before he removes his tongue and slides it along my outer thighs. He chuckles as I moan loudly. He kisses the tops of my thighs and then my stomach before whispering, "What did you write about me? Which parts?"

His West Virginia 'r' terrifies me yet gets me instantly wet. His voice speaks every word with masculine determination. His fingers run over my belly button and he clamps his hands down around my waist.

"Which parts, little lady?" he whispers. "I need you to tell me exactly what you're responsible for…"

He teases me with his finger, spreading my lower lips apart as he gazes into my eyes.

"I'll know if you're lying," he whispers as he touches me between my legs. "So tell the truth, Rain."

I tell him. I sat in the Meg Nigel's office, picking up information and working as the world's most low-key celebrity spy. I started off making guesses about what *Rebel Blood* was up to and then I got information. Good information. Mickey doesn't move his hand away from my stomach until I finish telling him the truth about me.

"Good girl," he whispers, kissing my cheek tenderly. "I'm glad you were honest."

He pushes hair out of my face and then I think Mickey will let me leave his bed. I think he'll change his mind about me now that he has what he really wants. I've seen what he's carrying between his legs and there's no way he can fit it inside me. He just… can't.

"That's it," I whisper back. "I can leave?"

"Fuck no," he snarls. "I think I'm going to keep you and you're going to make it up to me," he whispers. "Now come on. We're going to sleep. I'll get the damn tattoo removed. And I'll have plenty of time to get my cock in you."

My stomach lurches anxiously for several reasons.

We? I find out what Mickey means when his giant bicep clamps around me and he pulls me close to him.

"I ain't going to have you sneaking around my house. You're staying right here, little lady."

Before I know it, he's snoring and I'm trapped. And Mickey's warm. It can't hurt to close my eyes for a few moments. I'll worry about **The Tyrant** tomorrow.

16

GETTING MY MOJO BACK

MICKEY FORD

I can smell her in the morning. Her pussy tempts me to spread her thighs apart and wake her with my tongue around her clit, but I can't because I'm going to wake her up like this. I blow my trumpet. Loudly. Yes, a literal trumpet. It's time I whip this tiny sex pot into shape.

Rain shrieks and awakens, yanking her arms forward and quickly realizing what I've done to her. She screeches and jerks her arms forward again, yowling like a coyote when she realizes I've tied her to the bed with my neck ties.

I'm always swimming in fucking neck ties for award shows and meetings, but I hate the feeling of 'em around my neck. I quite like the sight of them wrapped around Rain Wilson's arms She screeches and tries to reach for one knot with her teeth.

I was a Cub Scout. She ain't getting that knot out unless I cut it out.

"Good morning, Rain."

"Mickey! What are you doing? Let me go!"

"I don't think so."

"Meg could get here any minute. You can't just keep me tied to your bed. She'll kill both of us!"

"I don't care."

"What?! Do you want to go to jail? Prison! Imagine what the damn gossip headlines will say then."

She trails that comment with a loud and frustrated shriek, followed by more yanking on the ties. I fold my arms. I cover up my thighs with my jeans so as not to offend her more than I have already, but I ain't covering up my chest.

"What do you want?" She snaps.

There's always something someone wants, isn't there?

"I want you to cure my addiction. One year, all about you and me, and then I'll let you go about your life and I'll go about mine."

"I'm not qualified to cure your stupid addiction," she snaps. "HELP!"

"You know we're alone for 10 acres, right? The only chance you have is the dogs."

"No! Not your stupid dogs."

I think I'll have an easier time of getting her to agree with backup. I whistle so both Sam and Pippin appear in the doorway, tails wagging eagerly and ears pricking as they notice Rain on the bed.

"MICKEY!" she screams. "Don't let these beasts come near me! I know white people stay letting dogs up in their bed, but it's not for me!"

"Agree to my terms."

"I don't even know your stupid terms!" She shrieks.

Sam gives me a confused look. I point to the bed and he takes a few steps toward Rain, who lets out a horrified shriek. She kicks out her legs like a madwoman and screeching.

"TELL ME THE TERMS!"

I whistle for Sam to come back, and Rain visibly relaxes. She won't like my terms, but she will agree with them.

"I want your services."

"What?!"

"Sex. Whenever I want it. However, I want it. For a year."

"I thought that was just dirty talk."

"Nope. And I need you to agree in sound mind."

"What's in it for me?!"

I gesture toward my body.

"I can make you cum without getting my dick near you. Imagine what'll happen when I finally fuck you."

She squirms and wriggles back defensively against the headboard she previously tried so hard to escape.

"I can't do that," she says, her thighs closing and my access to Rain's perfect cunt slowly disappearing.

"We'll get you that album. We'll do everything Seb Jefferson and Meg Nigel want from us. We'll have to keep this a secret. Obviously. But I think we ought to have a little fun and to tell you the truth… I ain't ever had sex sober."

"That's sad."

"Thanks."

"Sorry," she says.

"Don't be sorry. I just… I need practice, that's all."

"So I'm not your experiment but… I'm your practice."

"Right. Yeah."

"Don't expect me to stay catching feelings for you."

"Of course not. You once wrote that I was the ugliest redneck motherfucker to walk this Earth."

"You read that?"

"I read everything you wrote, Rain Wilson. But don't worry… now that you've agreed to my terms, I'm going to make sure you're thoroughly and entirely punished for what you've done."

I can't help but chuckle at the next terrified look to cross her face.

"What do you mean, punish me?"

"I don't know what I mean yet. But you'll find out."

"Great. Are you going to let me go now before your dogs rip me apart limb from limb?"

"Sam? Pippin? They're named after hobbits, for Christ's sake. They're friendly."

"Said every white person ever before their damn dog attacks an innocent person."

I smirk, enjoying the view of her fruitless struggling and her terror. They're only Dobermans. She keeps struggling even when it's pointless and the look on her face is both terrified and... adorable.

"We both know you're far from innocent."

She snaps back. "You got a fucking confederate flag tattooed on your thigh. How stupid are you?"

I scowl and Rain glances at her binds as if she's just remembered that she can't escape from me when she gets all smart-mouthed.

"Pretty fucking stupid, Rain. I only learned how to read 'cause of Rebel Blood. I could always understand music but... I didn't learn how to read until I was seventeen."

"Oh."

"Yeah."

"So you are stupid..."

My cheeks flush.

"I'm *dyslexic*. So yeah, I learned nothing in school in the slow classes and I knew nothing except West Virginia racism until I came out to L.A. Yes, I'm fucking stupid and I fucking regret what I've done, but what I'm more ashamed of is the fact that I never learned. When I have a kid, I'll be different."

"Get it removed," Rain snaps. "I'll die tied to this bed before I sleep with you while you've got that thing on."

"I got my dick in halfway. That counts." Doesn't it count?

"It doesn't count. And you barely got the head in. I don't want your racist dick inside me. Period."

"But you'll let me eat your pussy?"

"I'm a complicated woman, Mickey Ford."

"Since when does the prisoner get to make demands?"

"Prisoners have rights now, Mickey. Welcome to social justice America. Now get it removed, untie me, and we can figure out how to keep this arrangement a secret from Meg until you get your mojo back or whatever."

"My mojo?"

"The sex moves you need to impress your hordes of stupid groupies."

"Right."

"And you can teach me sex moves for when I take Keith back… or whatever."

The thought of her going back to that stupid son of a bitch makes me want to keep her tied there until she comes to her senses. But I'm about to get what I want… I'm so close to having exactly what I want.

"Fine. I'll call Seb. I'm sure he'll be happy to do it. How fast can you learn a song?"

"We both know I can't sing!"

Rain's lit a fire under me. Whether she can sing or not, if I can get her to scratch out the lyrics to one of my latest, Seb will think we're making progress and I can get closer to a night with this troublemaker warming my bed. No offense to Sam and Pippin, but unlike my dogs, Rain doesn't fart in my face when she sleeps next to me.

I get her free from the bed and explain my plan.

"I don't need you to sing. I just need you to prove you've made progress. Go into my studio, try not to steal anything, and get my black journal. Pick any song you want and learn it. Okay?"

"Whatever."

She rubs her wrists and examines them for marks before throwing a fierce stare in my direction.

"I don't even want to know how you did that without waking me up."

"I guess I found some of my mojo," I tell her, grinning stupidly from ear to ear.

Score.

17

RELAPSE

RAIN WILSON

Mickey doesn't let me get out of his bedroom without putting his hand on my waist and running it over my ass.

"You're fucking hot," he whispers. "Really fucking hot. I can't wait to finally have you."

Mickey's delusional. If I was 'fucking hot' I'd be dating the hottest guys on the planet, not Keith's ex-girlfriend or a celebrity's sex project. I'd have half a million Instagram followers and those Balenciaga shoes that look like socks. I'd have everything. Instead, I have… a sex dungeon with crazy Mickey Ford and we only have a few hours until Meg and Seb arrive to check on our progress. I tiptoe out of the room once he lets me find my way to his studio.

It's huge. Seriously, you could have a party with, like, fifty people right down here. There's a little desk there with pens and crumples pieces of paper. Mickey writes the fewest songs for Rebel Blood. Everyone says that it's because he's too drunk to write anything good. Considering the bags of empty wine bottles still down here, I imagine that's true.

I reach into his desk for the black journal and then... I find something. Inside his desk, behind a stack of papers that he never asked me to look through, is a cellphone. It's ancient. It's a freaking Blackberry. I told you it was ancient. My mom had one of these. My heart races as I press the button on the side. It works. It freaking works and by some miracle, this indestructible ancient phone connects and finds a bar. I can message her. I don't have to wait for her to find me and blackmail me to oblivion.

I probably only have a few minutes down here before Mickey Ford gets suspicious. He told me not to steal anything. I don't have any plans for stealing. I just need to send some juicy details to **The Tyrant**. Something to stave off the inevitable rage storm from my conspicuous absence. I know Meg thinks I'm safe out here with Mickey, but she doesn't get it. I'm not truly safe as long as The Tyrant walks the streets and has access to a cellphone. I send a text message.

+1-(607)-555-5660: It's me, Rain. Here's something you can use…

I send as much as I can, my stomach lurching with guilt as I shut the phone off and slide it back in the desk, grabbing Mickey's journal and bounding upstairs before he can get suspicious.

"I don't have to check your cavities, do I?"

He chuckles and mutters that he was joking when he sees the dismay on my face. I hand him the journal. He sighs and cracks it open.

"My handwriting's still garbage," he grumbles. "And I mix the letters up but... you get the point."

He opens the journal to a page written in red ink.

"Try singing this one. It's a love song."

I glance quickly at his bare chest before glancing back at the page. The red ink on the page matches the ink on one of his tattoos. I want to reach out and touch both of them, but Mickey's finger draws my focus back to the page.

"Here. Sweet Southern Woman."

"Is that about an ex-girlfriend?"

He gives me a suspicious look, but I can't help it. It's my instinct to search for information like that and now I have access to a secret phone... it's like I've fallen off the wagon again.

"No," he says. "It's about a woman I ain't met yet. My dream girl."

Then his hand falls away from the page and the uncertainty tightening into my stomach turns into outright fear. I've made a mistake, haven't I?

I know I'll regret what I'm about to say, but I can't stop myself.

"You're not as much of an asshole as they say you are."

He chuckles softly.

"Not at all, Rain."

When Meg and Seb arrive, putting on a show is easier than I expect it to be. They suspect nothing. Mickey doesn't even look at me once Seb and Meg are in the room. All he cares about is pressing Seb into bringing him some mystery drug or booze.

Seb Jefferson's the 'mainstream' boy band crush, not like they're a boy band anymore... They're still just as popular as they were in their early twenties. It's like America gets crazier the older and more 'mature' they are. After twenty minutes of entertaining Seb and Meg in Mickey's living room, Meg turns to me, clearly suspicious that I've been quiet for so long.

"You've managed to keep her here for over *five* days without her cellphone? What does she do all day?"

Seb denied Mickey's request for a phone until we have at least one song recorded...

I glance at Mickey, and he suddenly turns red. Great. So much for subtlety. Luckily, Meg doesn't seem to notice.

"I'm working on learning from the best," I muster with as much enthusiasm as possible. It's not entirely a lie. Technically, Mickey is the best guy I've ever slept with. I'm not as proud of that as you might think. Meg shrugs.

"As long as you're improving your job prospects, this is good. I can't believe this is working. And it's so *quiet* out here. When I need to get away from Logan, can I crash in your guest room?"

Mickey turns ten times redder then mutters something about Meg, always welcome as long as he's under house arrest. I take several minutes to notice that the only person quieter than I am is Seb Jefferson. The 6'7" tall giant glances over at me and I feel frozen in his gaze. He and Mickey both have blue eyes but his are icy, while Mickey's are a deep cobalt shade. Either way, Seb's terrifying gaze lands on me.

"Miss Wilson, I need help to get something out of my truck. Will you come along and allow the attorney a moment with her client?" Seb says.

I feel a surge of fear as his eyes fix on me. I wonder if he smiles more around Angie because to me, he looks cranky and fifty times more terrifying than Mickey Ford.

Meg cheers up at the chance to get into lawyer mode. Seb gestures toward the door and I follow him, a sudden nervousness creeping up on me. I glance back over my shoulder to look at either Mickey or my cousin for reassurance, but both are already immersed in conversation. Seb parks his truck in the driveway across several spots every time he visits. I glance over and stop at the top of the 4 steps down to his truck.

"You don't have anything in the truck, do you?"

Seb turns to face me and thrusts his hands into his pockets.

"You caught me."

"So what do you want?"

"Your cousin covered for you."

Now my heart's racing. Fast.

"W-what?"

"Don't deny it," Seb says calmly. I feel puny in his shadow. He's neither smiling nor scowling, and the neutrality in his face terrifies me ten times more.

"I don't know what you're talking about."

He raises a dark brown brow that matches the color of his grown-in roots.

"I saw the *Celebz Leaked* article this morning. I bought that house for Mickey Ford and I know every inch of it. Someone took a picture in that studio and there's only one person it could be."

I freeze and goosebumps prickle over my flesh. I stare at Seb, not because I'm brave or standing my ground, but because I don't know what he'll do to me. Mickey obviously doesn't know that I've already betrayed him, but now that Seb's looking at me like this, I know he'll find out, eventually.

"I…"

"Meg's a good cousin. But I'm not a good anything, Rain Wilson, not without Mickey," Seb says urgently.

His eyes narrow and I sense what he's saying is a threat, even if he has said nothing objectively threatening.

"I understand."

"Have you slept with him?" Seb asks bluntly.

That question hits me like a sack of bricks. I follow my instincts.

"No."

"Good. Don't. Mickey Ford can't stand to get his heartbroken… and you'll break his heart, Rain Wilson."

"I'm here to learn my lesson. I swear. I had a relapse but… I'm done. Meg wants me to stop and I will."

Seb grins.

"*Relapse,*" he says knowingly. Seb's a former drug addict, even if he doesn't look like it anymore. "Keep that up and you'll hit rock bottom. I don't think you want that, Rain. And Mickey can't handle it. So keep your legs closed and don't overcomplicate things."

I feel suddenly ashamed. Dirty. And terrified. I shouldn't have sent the message. And Seb's right. If I keep this up, I'll hit rock bottom. After singing Mickey's song, after listening to him, after staying up all night with him… I don't know if I want that.

18

MY DESSERT

MICKEY FORD

It worked. We kept our secret and now I'm alone with her again. The staff left dinner and now, Rain is mine for the night. My thigh winces from the work I had done earlier. While Rain and Meg caught up, I had Seb bring his people in to set up in my massage room so they could remove my tattoo.

Now, I really wish I had a drink. The tattoo's gone, but there's a red blotch on my leg that looks like a bruise with some remnants of the blue ink. It ain't exactly graceful, but for Rain, I'll do anything.

She's pretty. She's pretty in the way I never saw in West Virginia. As I was growing up, they'd always say I was a pretty boy, and I'd leave the state just 'cause I was too pretty to stay.

That's how I feel about Rain — she's too pretty to stay with me for long. And too young. I remember what it was like to be eighteen. Though few eighteen-year-olds have a net worth of $15 million like I did.

With her cousin gone, she glances wistfully at the front door as it closes. Now that I'm seeing her in daylight — and I'm properly and completely sober — I notice how threadbare her clothes are. Her socks have holes and her underwear doesn't quite fit. We're standing awkwardly in the foyer and I don't want to gawk at her, or make her feel uncomfortable by offering her my oversized sweater.

I'm only wearing it because of the smell of marijuana permanently etched in the wool. I might never smoke again, I might as well enjoy the smell while it lasts in my clothes. Rain sighs impatiently. She's waiting for my next command, or perhaps there's something on the tip of her tongue. I can't tell.

We have to be somewhere next, but I haven't thought of where. The house has everything I need for complete entertainment for the next years — everything except the drugs and booze I requested.

Whenever Rain's around, drugs are the last thing on my mind. It's not just that I'm alert worrying

"Mickey, I'm sorry," she blurts out. Her lips are so perfect that I can hardly listen to her words as she talks. I just think about sucking on them. Or biting them. I've already pushed her far enough now and I have to be careful. One wrong move and she could tear off down that driveway with Meg Nigel and send my ass to prison. Properly.

But sorry? That's a new word from Rain that grabs my attention.

"For what?"

She gets all sad and mumbling when she's guilty about something. I pick up on that quickly because she seems to spend so much time guilty.

"I messed up. Again."

"How?"

She explains what she did. The studio. The text message. I try not to show her how it hurts me that she'd betray me so soon after I already forgave her. I stuff my fierce anger and remember that she's a decade younger than me. Ten whole years. I don't want to know how stupid I was ten years ago.

Still, I can't let her get away with this. Not like I will, anyway. I'll get her into bed tonight and fix her right up. But for now, I want to understand the little minx. How can I know that she's bad for me and want her so badly? I guess it's the same with pills, isn't it? At least if Rain fucks up my life, I can take her to bed and make her pay for it. With heroin, I just wake up without my wallet buck naked in West Hollywood, a significantly less glamorous situation.

"What's your problem, Rain?" I ask her calmly. "Why would you do something like that so soon after entering our... arrangement."

Her eyes dart nervously toward mine and then she looks away, rubbing her lip nervously with her thumb and then mumbling a response.

"I don't know."

She gives those infuriatingly soft responses that make it hard to want to punish her. But damn it, do I hate her teasing. She turns me into a tyrant, who then only wants to punish her and screw her... and make her beg for the man she allegedly hates so damn much.

"You betray me every chance you get and you don't know why? We have an *arrangement*, Rain. Don't you have a sense of honor?"

She thankfully doesn't point out that nowhere in our arrangement did we promise to tell each other the truth. But I don't want her to keep lying to me. I want her to trust me.

"Why do you keep lying?" I say, taking another step closer to her and wanting so desperately to move her from this verbal waltz into the foyer back to my bedroom. I resist the urge to touch her until she answers.

"I don't trust people," she says softly, lowering her gaze and sending this surge of protective angst through me. That's partly my fault too. I even said out loud that I didn't do age gaps, but when I found myself close to her, there was something so painfully irresistible about her. It wasn't the fact that she was eighteen.

I touch her cheek and lift her gaze to mine because I can't stand another moment without holding her eyes in mine. When she denies me contact with those large brown eyes, I get angry. Furious, even.

"And I don't trust men."

I push hair out of her face, but I can't bring myself to punish her or kiss her. I'm frozen, staring at her and hating myself for wanting to sleep with a teenager who hates my guts.

"Okay."

She sighs and says, "Are you saying our arrangement can't work? Did I screw up already?"

I hate that there's a hint of hopefulness in her voice. It makes me bitter. And cruel.

"No. Our arrangement will continue. Thank you for your honesty, Rain."

Her shoulders relax, but she shouldn't let her guard down.

"Our arrangement will continue *now*," I whisper, running my hand down to her neck and wrapping around it. I don't squeeze, but her gaze meets mine and her terrified expression dares me to do it.

"What are you doing?" she whispers.

"Teasing you," I whisper back. "You're quite the little brat. Rifling through my things. Texting information. Causing me problems. Clearly, I'm not punishing you enough."

I squeeze gently, not enough to hurt her, but enough to make her feel the control pulsing through my hand.

"Trust is powerful," I whisper, running my thumb over one muscle in her neck, noticing how weak it is in my firm grasp. I could break her. Her chest shudders nervously.

"I've been hurt a lot," she whispers. I relax my grip slightly, but keep my hand around her neck. I feel she'll be a lot more honest if I keep her like this. I move her against the front door, pressing her back against it, keeping her pinned there with a gentle palm wrapped around her neck.

"People have hurt me too, kid."

"But you're rich," she hisses. "That's the difference."

"It didn't stop me from getting raped. That didn't stop me from doing drugs. Life is about a lot more than being rich."

"Easy for you to say."

I take my other hand and run my thumb over her lips. They're soft. She shivers as I touch her. She's scared. Terrified. I lean over and touch my tongue to her earlobes. She melts, her neck filling the space between my fingers as she arches forward to meet my tongue.

"Stop lying," I whisper.

When she doesn't answer, I run my tongue along her neck, making a space between my firm palm so she can feel the soft wetness. She moans. Loudly. I can't stop myself from going further. I take my hands and slide it under her barely there dress. It's so thin, I don't know how she's warm in this mansion.

"I can't," she whispers, gazing at me voluntarily this time as my hand finds its way between her legs.

"Fine. Then stop lying to me. I don't give a shit what you do to everyone else."

"Why should I stop lying to you?"

"Because I can help you, Rain. I can protect you. But I can't do that if you don't tell me the truth."

"No one can protect me," she whispers, just as my fingers find her clit. She moans as I rub her slowly, one hand around her neck and the other in her panties, finding her soft clit. The sparse hair around her lower lips moistens as I spread her lips open. She gasps as my thumb massages her clit and I press my hips against hers.

"If I fail you, that's it," I whisper. "I'll let you go and I'll spend the year alone."

She moans again, not exactly a response to what I'm saying, but a response to my finger hitting her most sensitive spot. She moans a vague "yes". My hands trail lower and then I work her entrance open and slide a finger inside her. Shit. She's so tight and having my fingers inside her with one hand wrapped around her neck is getting me really hard.

Her hands fall to her side and then she surprises me by reaching forward and cupping her hand around my cock outside my jeans.

"I'll tell the truth," she whispers. "From now on... I promise."

I think she's earned her orgasm now. I move my fingers inside her and press my lips to her chest and neck until she climaxes. Once she's finished, I drop to my knees and hike that little dress up. Her tummy undulates nervously as I kiss her navel and move my tongue to her panties. They smell delicious. My teeth easily tear away the cheap fabric, revealing my dessert.

19

MICKEY IN MY PANTS

RAIN WILSON

My panties slip over my thighs and Mickey makes a low, groaning sound in his throat as he exposes the space between my thighs. He holds my panties between his fingers for a moment and then he crumples them. He has a funny way of punishing me, teasing my underwear off slowly and then pressing his finger just between my soaked bare thighs.

He's both cautious and loving, sensations I'm unaccustomed to. I can't deny how much I enjoy his gentleness. I wish I didn't. I wish I could still hate him the way I did when **The Tyrant** had me under her firm control.

Mickey's tongue laps juices up off my inner thighs, his slow tongue darting out and teasing me.

"Damn. You're wet," he whispers.

Yeah. Soaking wet. Having Mickey Ford, the bassist from *Rebel Blood* between my legs with his tongue sliding between my legs, slowly tasting my pussy with his eager tongue drives me wild.

I cry out as Mickey pushes his tongue between my legs without giving me a moment to respond. I want to push him away, but his tongue feels so damn good as he spreads my thighs apart with his long tongue.

He's still holding onto my underwear as his tongue slides past my lower lips and then wraps around my clit.

I moan, loud. Mickey squeezes my thighs in response, grabbing my thighs and then moving his tongue faster around my clit. I cry out again and Mickey licks at my clit and running his tongue down my lower lips and then pushing deep inside me the louder I moan. A few minutes of his lips around my clit and something tightens inside me.

Mickey pulls his lips away and I gasp. I'm close… so close… But he's stopping.

"I want the truth from you," he whispers. "Before I make you cum, I need to know the truth."

His voice is gruff and demanding. I find myself in no position to argue with him. Mickey has all the power here. He's larger than me.

I am a soaked, whimpering mess and Mickey knows it. That's exactly why he's teasing me like this. Weakening me. I want to resist Mickey's questions, but now that I know what an orgasm with Mickey Ford feels like… it's exactly what I want.

He grins mischievously as he observes my reticence, holding me with deep consideration in his cobalt gaze. He pushes my arms over my head and strokes my hips slowly. Does he just want information, or is this something more?

I run my feet over the ridiculously soft sheets on Mickey's bed. I'm here. I'm in Mickey Ford's bed and maybe if I just tell him the truth, something will change.

Maybe it's time for me to make something happen in my life. Maybe instead of sneaking around, lying and cheating, it's time for me to do something different. To trust someone. But can I trust Mickey Ford?

I know every dirty, gossipy detail about his life. I know he had a freaking confederate flag tattooed on his thigh like some type of racist. My throat catches as I observe the red stain, which looks more like a birth mark than a hate symbol.

"Afraid?" He whispers. But it comes out so thick and West Virginian. *Fraid?* I don't want to be. I want to trust that he isn't... evil.

At least right now, with his eyes boring into me and my thighs soaked with his spit, he feels different than I expected.

"I can't tell the truth."

"So you are afraid."

I nod and he kisses me, taking my lower lips between his and then sucking on them until my hips buck upward instinctively.

When he pulls away, I feel breathless. He doesn't kiss like a racist. And he doesn't touch me like a racist either.

"I'm so scared," I whisper. "I want to tell the truth, but I'm afraid..."

I've never admitted that to anyone. I don't even know why I feel safe enough to tell Mickey the truth that I won't even tell my cousin Meg.

His hands are back on my hips and he runs his thumbs over my hip bones, clearing his throat as I adjust my position so my butt feels more comfortable and my hips nestle gently against his.

"What could scare you?" Mickey murmurs, running his hands over my body again, making me feel like I'm ridiculously sensual and ridiculously vulnerable at the same time. Mickey slides his body over mine. He kisses me on the lips. Why does his shaggy brown hair smell so good?

"You ain't scared of anything," he whispers again. "You'll come right into the house of the man you nearly killed and get him into bed. So if something scares you, it must be pretty big."

I don't know why Mickey doesn't realize that I'm a loser. I don't know why he thinks I'm so fearless. I'm only eighteen. I haven't been through *that* much. And I'm definitely not fearless.

My legs wrap around Mickey, and his hard torso stiffens in my grasp. He's like every boy crush I had, but… better. His body is lean and tight. His tattoos are badass and… I don't want to hate him. I want to feel him.

His kisses are even more overwhelming than touching him and he can't seem to get enough kissing. He grasps my cheek and draws my face to his, kissing me until he's ready to put his tongue in my mouth.

His tongue feels soft, warm, and eager for me. I grab his cheeks again and try not to think — period. I can't think about the fact that I'm kissing and making out with a genuine celebrity because if I do, I'll faint, and if I faint, I can't be sure Mickey won't tie me up again until he gets his way.

"It is big," I whisper.

"How big?"

My throat catches. For the first time since I've entered his giant country home outside of Nashville, I begin to think that Mickey might just differ from what I assumed. He presses his fingers between my legs, sliding between my wetness and groaning as he comes into contact with me. Even the slight contact calls all my senses to attention.

"How big, little lady?"

"I could go to jail," I whisper, the catching in my throat suddenly tearing. I don't cry often, but now I feel the tears coming into my eyes as it all suddenly hits me. The truth. Years of terror. Years of fear. My mistakes haunt me daily and now, Mickey Ford's lying on me and he's offering me... protection?

I don't know what he's offering. For all I know, when I tell Mickey the truth finally, he'll hate me even more. He'll hate me for throwing him under the bus just to keep myself safe.

"Jail? You're 18," he says. "You won't go to jail."

I know he's trying to help.

The disbelief nearly makes me want to clam up and avoid telling him, but then Mickey presses his lips to mine, ever so softly.

"Listen, kid. I know what I said...about taking you... punishing you... making me pay... but if there's more going on, I'll help you. I think I've punished you enough."

His hand brushes the space between my lower thighs again. Punishment… You'd think sleeping with my worst enemy would be a punishment, but it's only made me see how human he is. This can't be what Meg had in mind when she sent me here.

He's warm. Mickey Ford is so warm. I put my hand on his back and his weight presses into mine.

"Hey," he whispers. "Come on. Tell me."

"I did something horrible when I was sixteen. The dumbest thing I've ever done…"

Tears prick my eyes again and as one falls, Mickey presses his thumb to my face, rubbing my tear away. His lips find my cheeks again.

"What? Tell me, kid."

"I filmed myself masturbating," I whisper. "I was underage and… someone else has the video. Maybe lots of someones."

My chest tightens and then releases. Now I'm sobbing and I feel like such an idiot. The hot models that Mickey Ford hooks up with probably don't cry while his big dick presses eagerly against their thighs. The models who Mickey Ford hooks up with probably look nothing like me and they definitely aren't self-conscious.

Mickey's eyes considering me only makes me nervous. I feel dirty for my confession and I can't tell if he has pity or judgment in his cobalt gaze.

He's already said that I'm the only black girl he's ever been with. And we haven't even been together properly. I'm not even waiting for Mickey's response. I'm just crying and feeling the weight of everything crashing down around me like a wave. Telling Mickey feels good, but I know I'll have to pay for it.

"Have you told Meg?" he whispers, still soft, still touching me. His voice sounds so smooth and calming. I forget that **The Tyrant** is worth fearing.

"No."

"And whoever's blackmailing you wants you to get information on *Rebel Blood*?"

I nod. Mickey grins.

"See? I ain't as stupid as they say, am I?"

He wipes another one of my tears away with his thumb again and then follows up by grabbing my cheeks and kissing me — passionately. I can't stop myself from kissing him back because Mickey's not just kissing me like a horny dude (like Keith, basically). It's romantic. It's the most romantic kiss I've ever had and it makes me feel like I'm really in a movie — and for just a minute, I get to get the guy.

I grab Mickey's face back and we hold onto each other as our lips spread apart and our tongues jostle with each other until Mickey rolls onto his back and I follow his lead, rolling on top of him. My hands fly to his chest and I can't help but notice how firm and strong his chest feels beneath my palm. His hands clutch my hips and I feel nestled in my seat atop him. His shaggy brown hair falls away from his face, exposing his sharp jawline again.

"I'll help you, Rain. It's illegal for anyone to have that. Anyone. But this is the last time you lie to me. Promise."

His grasp becomes more firm with his serious tone.

My heart races and for the first time, I mean what I'm going to say to him and suddenly everything about Mickey feels like it means something.

"I promise."

"Good," he whispers. "We can handle this, then. Whatever happens, we can handle it together. We have… three hundred and something days left together, right? That's enough time to solve all our problems."

"Create an album, stop a vicious blackmailer… help you quit booze… pills and all that other stuff."

When I list it all out loud, it sounds impossible, but Mickey Ford's eyes gleam with desire and excitement. His fingers lock tighter around my face and I feel a jerking movement as the third leg between his thighs pumps against me, wanting me desperately.

"And sex," Mickey says with a grin. "Lots and lots of sex."

20

WHERE THE TROUBLE STARTS

MICKEY FORD

Soft spread thighs straddling me turns me into a beast, only in need of rutting and fucking. But Rain's thighs... they do something different. My hands travel over them as I appreciate the sharp contrast of her skin. It's so much darker than mine and when I pinch her flesh or spank her, she doesn't turn red.

Her skin tone is rich and her large lips and features mean that every beautiful part of her is ten times more accessible to me. Her bare cunt, covered in tightly coiled pubic hair, shaved neatly around her folds, drives me wild. I kiss her again and then roll her onto her back, so I can stare into her eyes as I make love to her.

Making love to a woman without looking at her eyes means you might as well not make love to her at all. I stroke hair away from her face and send my fingers between her legs to feel her wetness again. She's still soaked, and her cunt is even hotter than before. My cock's so stiff, I'll burst if I don't get inside her soon. Hell, I'll erupt anyway.

"Wait," she whispers. "Keith stole my last birth control pills."

"So… you're pregnant?" I whisper, touching her soft stomach and getting harder at the thought of her body becoming pregnant. It's instinct, isn't it?

I don't even think about the consequences, just the image of her stomach growing large and smooth with a baby Ford. Lord knows the world needs more baby Fords.

"No," she whispers, touching my shoulder gently, like she's too scared to touch me back. "It's not that."

"Okay. Protection?"

My chest pounds. I don't have protection and I don't want it. I want her bare. I've had lots of women and I always used a rubber but I have this burning desire to feel Rain that defies all reason.

"Yeah," she whispers, her small tongue darting nervously over her youthful lower lip.

I stroke her hair and kiss her round forehead.

"We're 10 acres away from the main road and several miles away from civilization. We got nothing."

"Great," she whispers, running her hands through my hair. *Fuck*, that feels good. I want her to want me almost as badly as I want her.

"I'll pull out."

"Every guy says that," she whispers.

"Listen. I don't have to… if you don't want to. And… I think I had a vasectomy."

"You think?"

"I've done a lot of drugs."

Then, she surprises me. Her hands reach for it, and I gasp as Rain boldly wraps her fingers around my dick.

"I'm touching Mickey Ford's cock," she whispers, a little triumphant smile crossing her face that I don't even think she's aware of. Her fingers feel fantastic.

Damn. Now I *really* want to cum. There's something so powerfully sexy about the way she says 'cock'. It makes me want her more than anything.

I ease the rest of my clothing off and before Rain can protest, I press the head of my dick against her entrance. This time, she gasps in anticipation. Big. Rigid. Hard to fit between her gorgeous thighs. But worth it.

I press my cock into her an inch. Rain cries out. Her back arches and my desire for her only mounts.

"Easy, girl," I whisper.

"It's big."

Yeah, it's pretty fucking big. The worst part is that I don't know if I can fit inside her, if it will hurt her too much or if she'll put me off. I don't even know if I can pull out in time. I'll try… but Rain is… beautiful.

She smells good, too. It's natural for a man to want to cum inside a woman that smells good. Trust me.

My hips press an inch forward against my will and Rain's panting grows louder. I only have the head of my cock buried between her lips and feeling her heat wrapped tightly around that small, sensitive part of me only pushes my instincts to drive into her up to a fever pitch.

My weight presses into my forearm as my hips drive forward. *Fuck*. Rain's tight. She's so tight that she feels almost wrong. My cheeks flush and my mouth hangs open from the surge of pleasure as I drive into her. Tight. I've never been inside anyone so tight.

"More…" she whispers. Her voice is so soft…

"You ain't hurt?"

"It feels… so big… really good…"

She whimpers again as I slide the rest of my cock inside her, unable to resist my drive for her another minute longer. Rain cries out as I fill her with my entire length.

Our bodies press together like they're meant to be, and the euphoria is immediate and potent. Like a drug. My drug. My hips ease forward another inch, burying my cock deeper between those perfect legs.

Rain groans now, and I can feel the head of my cock almost like a knot that's so deep in her that it's nearly at the base of her stomach. My fingers find her clit and I press down with a slow rubbing motion, tightening the sensation of my cock buried inside her while I find her womanly pleasure center and tease it to arousal.

Rain's so wet and unaccustomed to pure pleasure that her response is immediate and intense. My hands move faster against her clit, massaging along her outer lips and stimulating her with my fingers so she can feel the way my big white cock stretches her.

I gaze at her pink fleshy center and then lean back over to stare at the most important part of Rain… her soft brown eyes. My forehead presses to hers and then our lips meet. She moans as my fingers keep working her.

"C'mon babe," I whisper. "Cum for me…"

I move my hips slowly and Rain moans. She won't last long like this. She *can't*.

I take her lower lip between my teeth, my hardness urging me to pound her harder and faster.

I murmur into her ear, "Cum for me…"

She cries out… *loud*. I withdraw my hips and thrust into her again. This time, she moans and then arches her hips up against my fingers as she cums ridiculously hard. Rain cries out twice as loudly and I grab her hips as I move my cock into her, driving into the tight wet pussy climaxing hard around my dick.

A slow start yields to more passionate lovemaking. I grab Rain's arms and pin them over her head. I take this opportunity to observe her pure, unmarked body. I'm covered in tattoos. Some I regret, some I hate, some I love. But Rain's eighteen and her skin is smooth and untouched. The perfect shade of brown.

I lace my fingers with hers and press her hands into the bed as I make love to her, hips moving slowly against hers as her little whimpers and moans show she's slowly sliding toward another climax.

I grab her cheeks again and kiss her. I love cradling her face between my hands as my hips drive her into the bed and I plunge my cock into her tight black pussy. And damn... she's tight. It's both the width and the angle, a tight squeeze on my cock but the perfect vice grip as I drive into her textured walls slowly.

"Cum for me," I murmur, running my tongue along her bare neck. "I want to see you cum again..."

She can't control it, but her body responds to mine as my fingers find her clit again and I push her to another eager finish where orgasms and thrusting blend to become one pleasurable rocking movement of our bodies in my bed.

Minutes turn to hours and Rain's pleasurable orgasms turn into bursts of pleasure until we soak my bed and I still haven't cum. Hours. It's been hours of enjoying her and now that her pink center has turned red with pleasure, I need to finish.

"I can't..." I groan, edging my hips into her deep and slow. "I can't stop myself..."

Rain grabs my butt cheeks and pulls me into her deeper.

"I don't care," she whispers. "Cum inside me."

Her chest arches up and her nipples standing on end make me eager to obey her command. Cum inside me... Those three little words.

That's where the trouble starts.

21

MAYBE IT WAS A BAD IDEA

RAIN WILSON

O*kay.*
Maybe it was a bad idea for me to let Mickey Ford cum inside me. He's supposed to be my mentor, for one thing. That makes this totally fucked up on principle. Second, we aren't supposed to be having sex at all. We're supposed to be sitting around making an album and learning how to be wholesome instead of total screwups.

But *sex*...

I've had sex before Mickey, but it was mostly lying there. Once, Keith called me "Ariana" during it and I cried for three days. Until Mickey, that had been the best sex of my life because at least Keith said sorry after and took me to Moe's for chips.

But Mickey's giving me wide blue eyes like a puppy and I don't feel like a screw-up for once.

First… orgasms. Mickey gives me orgasms, and he doesn't seem to find it difficult. He knows exactly what to do to make me cum. At first, I think it's magic, but it's obviously skill.

I feel wanted. And not in the same way I do with Keith. I feel like Mickey Ford… *sees me.*

"My Lord…" Mickey whispers. "You are… divine…"

I can almost forget he's a monster according to the tabloids, a dangerously stupid, self-obsessed playboy with eyes too blue and gorgeous for his own good.

I can almost forget that he had a freaking confederate flag tattooed on his leg… which is just gross.

"Do you hear me?" He whispers. "Divine…"

He says the word with the fervor of a true believer and damn, I want to believe him.

Mickey kisses my neck again, a low growl emanating from his throat as he pulls me close to him. He smells so good… but didn't we just have sex?! How the hell is he still hard.

Mickey grins once he notices my anticipatory freeze.

"Scared?" He whispers. Like hell. But Mickey slowly raises my hands over my head again and I feel less scared than… eager. He pins me to the bed and sighs appreciatively.

"More sex," he whispers. "Then more honesty. If we're both going to fuck things up, we might as well do it together…"

I smile despite myself, and Mickey touches my cheek.

"Finally," he whispers. "You never smile… But damn, Rain… your smile is gorgeous."

Gorgeous? Keith always laughed at me for my goofy smile, which now falls away as I give Mickey this foolish doe-eyed expression. He says this stuff like it's no big deal, but he's the first guy to say stuff like this to me.

He chuckles at the change in my expression and runs his thumb over my lips.

"I mean it. I could write songs about that smile."

Maybe it's just some stupid line. He probably says that about every girl he sleeps with. That's what musicians are like. They're song whores. They write songs about everyone.

Mickey bends his head to kiss me and I hope that it isn't a stupid line because he tastes and smells… amazing. He's a great kisser, so good that he makes me feel all awkward and fumbling. Where do people even learn to kiss?

Whatever. It doesn't matter, as long as the kissing doesn't stop…

He presses his hardness against me again, his eyes closing against his will as this expression of pure bliss crosses his face and he moves just an inch inside me. Mickey's body becomes a pillar of taut muscle as he eases into me slowly again and then presses his hand against my pussy.

His fingers know exactly what to do between my legs and it isn't long before one orgasm after another surges through me. Mickey's giant dick feels like a tight knot in the base of my stomach and just when I think I'm way too small to be sleeping with a guy that big, pleasure surges and I want more… more.

I thought I'd never been horny before, but I didn't know good sex. I didn't know what sex was like when a man wants you and needs you. Not just me or other woman. Mickey pays close attention to *my* pleasure, pulling out of me and then entering me from behind with his finger on my clit.

When something makes me moan or buck my hips, he watches me and keeps doing it until he's ready for me to finish. The orgasms are... incredible.

When we cum together, he pulls out of me and then draws me close, wrapping his arms around me. It's almost like he's my proper boyfriend. It's almost like what's happening between us is... *real*.

He strokes my shoulder and then murmurs to me softly. I turn to face him, a concerned look on my face.

"What's wrong?"

"Seb warned me not to do this," I say, hating how horribly childish I sound. Rebel Blood doesn't control me and Seb Jefferson definitely doesn't.

Mickey grins, and I think he misunderstands. I'm not the one in danger. He is.

"Did he now?" Mickey murmurs, scowling and then touching my face.

"He doesn't want me to hurt you."

Mickey grins. "You put me in a coma for several days. Too late, little lady."

My cheeks feel all weird and warm, something that only seems to happen near Mickey.

"Sorry."

He reaches his hand between my damp thighs and grins.

"Don't worry, I think you made it up to me."

His fingers dance along my inner thighs and my stomach twists in knots. He enjoys my body. He doesn't complain about my pubic hair the way Keith did and he doesn't complain about... me.

"Yeah. Right. Sure," I whisper awkwardly.

Mickey touches beneath my chin and kisses me. It's exactly as comforting as he intends. I love kissing him. When he pulls away, there's a smile on my face. It crept up on me unconsciously, but now I don't want it to go away.

"Don't let that bastard get you down. Come on. Spread those legs again."

Mickey's insatiable. I make a plea for us to be better than this.

"Shouldn't we record like... one song?"

"One more time," he murmurs. "One more time and then... we can get some work done."

"Cool."

I hear Mickey's dog scratching at the door eagerly. Those dogs are relentless. Mickey doesn't seem to notice, and then he thrusts in me just as his giant dog pushes the door open... and *stares*.

"*Mickey!*" I shriek. He doesn't care. This crazy white boy doesn't care because he thrusts into me. Hard. I cry out and the dog lets out a goofy bark. I shriek and Mickey grabs my hands, pinning them over my head.

"Mickey, your dog's watching us!"

Mickey chuckles.

"He's a dog. What's the big deal... now, stay..."

The dog stiffens its back, and his other Doberman sniffs his way into the room curiously.

I cry out against my will as Mickey's hardness makes me scream. Then squirm. Then I climax again. Mickey doesn't care that his dog is staring at him. He pounds me hard, making me cum repeatedly until he finishes. I can't believe how good it feels to have him cum inside me. It feels crazy to let him do this and yet... it feels right.

He pulls out of me. Laughing. I can't help but giggle too because his smile is *really cute*.

"Best not go for doggy style right now."

"That's not funny," I snap, pulling the blankets over me and giving his feral Doberman a fierce glare. The dog's tongue hangs out suspiciously and it gives me a threatening bark. I yelp and pull the blankets up higher. Damn, Mickey's bed sheets are soft. You can't find soft ass sheets like this at Walmart. Or anywhere I shop.

He rolls over, still hard, and his stupid dog barks again and then walks toward the bed. I shriek and scurry behind Mickey, who still can't stop laughing.

"You don't like dogs?"

"No! They're gross. They smell like..."

I bite my lip. **The Tyrant** liked joking that dogs smell like white people, but I think better than to tell Mickey Ford something like that. It's pretty... unkind.

Now that I know him, it's difficult to be unkind to Mickey. He just stares dumbly and lets it roll right off him. It's like bullying… well, it's like bullying a puppy.

It doesn't feel right.

His dogs don't have a clue about what feels right and they don't care that I'm naked and wet.

Pippin climbs onto the bed and Mickey scratches behind his ears.

"Smell like what?"

"Nothing. Never mind."

Sam offers a bark that sounds like he's trying to snitch. I gasp and hide behind Mickey even more than before. I swear these dogs could eat a person alive.

"Come here. He's friendly. I promise… I won't let him hurt you."

I'm still skeptical, but my chest does something funny when Mickey says, "I promise."

Sam bounds forward and bends his head so I can scratch right between his ears. My throat tightens, but I scratch the dog's head. Relief floods through me when the beast doesn't even bite me.

"See? He's fine. Now come to bed."

He wraps his arm around me, and I run my fingers over his tattoos instinctively. Mickey presses his lips to my ear and murmurs, "I want you, babe. I fucking want you."

22

BIKINI MISHAPS

MICKEY FORD

I don't expect the first forty days of my imprisonment to pass as quickly as they do. Rain and I have three songs recorded with lots of help from auto-tune, my vocals and training Rain in my studio.

When she's done singing, I take her around the house and we just… hang. It makes me feel like I'm back in high school again, in West Virginia, just lounging with a girl after class.

She ain't high maintenance like a model, but she ain't easy, either. It's hard to get her to smile and when I can get the tiniest smirk on her face, it feels like a victory.

It feels better than coke. Better than drinking. Rain's better than all of it. If Meg wants her to heal me… it's working.

She brings the goodness out of me. She's soft and quiet, a welcome respite from the insanity of crowds and flashing lights and cameras. I imagine coming home to her after a show, finding her on the tour bus in those crazy sweatpants she wears that make her ass look like a perfect grey marshmallow.

She's the type of girl I always wanted… a *normal* girl. Sure, she makes mistakes, but I'm the band's screw up. Rain's fuck ups haven't hurt as many people as mine have. I don't think that girl ever went to the cops.

Once I joined the band, I lost my chance at normal. I lost my chance of approval from my religious West Virginia family — at least until the money began flooding in.

I traded in my crushes on short-haired tomboyish girls with freckles for supermodels that looked good on social media. Tight little waists, all the same standard size, with ribs sticking out and bones jutting everywhere into me. They got the same spray tans and the same stylists to dye their hair the same shade of blonde. They dressed in the same clothes and they were all… boring.

There's nothing that inspires me in the redundant flood of identical groupies throwing themselves at me. Boring groupies, boring models, boring ex-girlfriends. Sex becomes a game — what can I make them do. It gets boring, lonely and mechanical. They're beautiful but empty, just like Los Angeles.

I prefer Nashville. When this is all done, I'll move Rain downtown. If she'll have me.

None of those girls I knew were anything like Rain.

She's different. And today, I think I can keep her. I think I can make it work so that we're together… forever.

"Are you watching me sleep?" she grumbles, opening one lazy eye as we lay out by the pool.

Her comment snaps me out of the moment. Damn it, Mick. Stop being such a creep.

"Maybe."

"It's creepy."

What's unnerving is Rain's body in a bikini. Not unnerving. Just pretty. These new bikinis ride up and this one sits between her butt cheeks, which are all jiggly and exposed. That tiny bikini top covers her gorgeous B-cup boobs, now pressed into my lounge chair instead of into my chest. After forty days of Rain Wilson in my bed, I don't think I'll ever get bored.

"You're still staring," she accuses.

"So what if I am?"

I grin and wait for her to lash out at me for my boldness. She shrinks instead.

"There's nothing to see."

She flicks open her new phone and a rush of anxiety surges through me.

"Tell me you aren't blackmailing me again," I mutter, peering over her shoulder.

"Nope."

Rain flips over and I'm going to lose my mind. I'm too hard to sit at the end of the pool with her anymore. So I don't. I take my shirt off and dive into the water. It's refreshing. Real refreshing. When I rise above the surface, Rain sits at the edge. Glaring.

"You just splashed me."

"Sorry."

I grin, thrusting my hands through my hair and then reaching out to grasp Rain's eagerly extended hand.

"C'mon in."

"I don't enjoy swimming."

"You can hold on. Come on!"

Before I can encourage her again, I notice Pippin scampering behind her. I try to hide my smile as I know what's coming next. My Doberman puts his paw on Rain's back. She screams when she realizes what's happening, but it's not enough time to stop my dog from pressing his paw into Rain's back and shoving her into the pool.

"My phone!" Rain yells at the last minute, barely getting it on the beach chair as she falls in. I scoop her up, holding onto her bare waist as she thrashes desperately before realizing her feet can touch the bottom of the pool.

"Careful."

The water's up to her neck as she stands, so it looks like a furious head is floating in the blue water.

"Your dogs hate me."

"They do not."

"Pippin pushed me! Again!"

"He knew I wanted you close. That's all."

I grab her waist and pull her in for a kiss. We've been doing a lot of that lately and doing an even better job of hiding it from Seb and her cousin Meg. It's a lot easier than I expected it to be for Rain to keep a secret. And the sex... man, the sex is amazing. She's gorgeous, which helps. And she's so easy to tease and play with. She can go for hours and she is... hot. Really hot.

Rain lets me kiss her. Then she lets me pull her bikini string between my fingers until it comes off, sliding off her body and floating away in the pool. She gasps as I reach for her breasts beneath the water. I touch her dark nipples, rolling the hardened nubs between my fingers and then pressing her against the wall of the pool.

"You like that, don't you?"

"Shut up..." she gasps, as I slide my fingers into her underwear and touch her soft lower lips through her bikini bottom. Oh yeah. She is so soft. So smooth... I rub my fingers over her outer lips and Rain gasps when I finally reach my finger over to her clit. The sensitive hard nub stands out against her soft lips and my cock stiffens beneath the chlorinated water.

"You feel amazing," I growl, massaging her breasts more as my hands slide into her panties. Rain moans loudly, but I want more than her moaning. I want those crazy, large lips against mine. I push her against the wall of the pool and kiss her hard, my hands working her pussy like crazy as she moans. I'm ready to make her cum all over my hands.

"AHEM!"

I jump back from Rain instinctively. Fuck. Oh fuck. Her breasts are out. I throw my hands up to cover Rain's breasts and Meg Nigel shrills.

"GET YOUR HANDS OFF MY COUSIN'S BOOBS!"

I pull away and then turn red. Really red. Meg is still losing her goddamn mind.

"Rain Wilson, you get your ass out of that pool right now!"

Rain covers her own boobs, and she looks up at Meg with abject horror on her face.

"It's not what it looks like!" I call out. "She um... She lost her bikini top."

"She lost her bikini top?" Meg screams. "Do you have any goddamn respect for me, Mickey Ford? Do you have a single brain cell in that stupid head of yours?!"

"We were shooting a music video!" Rain calls out, her hand madly scrambling through the water for her bikini top, which keeps getting further and further away.

"A music video? With what camera?!" Meg shrieks, taking a pack of gum out of her Louis Vuitton purse and flinging it at my head. I dodge it and barely avoid getting hit with a pen from her law firm.

Meg has lost her patience. With both of us. She reaches for Rain and pulls her hands away from her boobs, yanking the screaming five-foot-tall girl out of the pool and wrapping a towel around her.

"I need an explanation right now!" Meg squawks.

Rain shrieks again as she nearly slips on the deck. My heart surges with a powerful, protective urge. My ankle bracelet blinks red under the water as I grab onto the deck.

I hop out of the pool, my instincts telling me to get between them. My instincts telling me to protect Rain. Unfortunately, my instincts are wrong. I step between them and Rain lurches forward… vomiting… everywhere.

Meg shrieks, leaping back dramatically. "My Jimmy Choo!"

Her screaming isn't enough to make a dent in Rain's aggressive projectile vomiting. Rain leans forward, her wet braids hanging over her face. I reach for Rain's hair.

I forget that Meg's there for a moment and put my hand on Rain's back. Her heart's racing like a butterfly on coke.

"Babe, you don't look so good."

"BABE?!" Meg shrieks. "You're her mentor! She's a freaking kid, Mickey! I swear to God, I'm going to slaughter that fucking redneck. Seb promised me you'd keep it in your pants."

Meg has officially lost her lawyer cool. I rub my hand against Rain's bare back as she crosses her arms over her chest, covering her breasts as she continues to empty the contents of her stomach on my pool deck.

Rain emits a final dramatic retching sound and Meg turns to her, disdain fading from her face as concern replaces it.

"Wait, why are you throwing up? Did he drug you? Are you doing drugs?! Are you trying to turn her into a crack whore!?"

I swear, my lawyer is looking for a reason to kill me.

"No!" Rain says weakly, wiping her mouth and then leaning her body into mine. "He's sober and I'm sober! Calm down."

"I wouldn't hurt her like that," I say stiffly. "I promise. She isn't well. That's all."

I wrap my arm around her tightly. This is all about to change, isn't it? We've been caught. If Rain walks out of here, there's nothing I can do. Not without alerting the police.

Meg glares at me.

"You wouldn't hurt her? She's eighteen and I caught you with your hand down her pants. This relationship is OVER! Do you hear me? It's totally inappropriate. You're nearly 29, Ford. Pick someone your own age!"

Rain bravely moves her hands away from her breasts, clenching them into fists to stand up for herself. I can't stop myself from staring at her tiny B-cups. Her breasts are cute and the nipples are even cuter.

"Meg, stop! I don't want to leave. We're still working on the album."

"I don't care. I'm not going to sit back and watch another grown ass man take advantage of you, Rain. I love you. I love you like a freaking sister. You deserve so much better than a rock star who only wants to use you for sex."

Use her for sex? That's not what this is. Meg doesn't get it. Yes, I started following my horny instincts but... Rain's more than some girl I'm sleeping with. She's... pretty. She's soft. She's mine.

My stomach tightens as Meg holds onto her.

She grabs Rain's arm. I wrap the towel around Rain, a lump in my throat. Maybe Meg's right. Maybe messing with Rain was going too far.

"Rain… I'll call you. Don't worry. Go with her and we'll talk."

I want to be strong. I want to act like I have some control here.

"Don't you dare," Meg hisses. "Don't you dare give her hope when you're only going to break her heart."

23

MICKEY'S VASECTOMY

RAIN WILSON

I'm back in my stupid studio apartment again. Keith's gone. He took my furniture, my laptop and the seat from my toilet. Weirdly enough, he took the roaches with him too. I haven't seen a single one since I got back to my place.

I cleaned from top to bottom the first night Meg brought me back. She tried to help, but I was so angry, I didn't want to say a word to her. She keeps trying to tell me she's doing this for my own good, but she's forbidden me from ever seeing Mickey again. He can't even contact me and I can't contact him. It's so dumb.

She doesn't get it. I'm not some stupid, love-struck teenager. I don't want to see Mickey Ford because he's manipulating me to fall in love with him.

I need to see Mickey because I'm pregnant. I told Meg I had food poisoning from too much caviar at Mickey's, but that was yet another Rain Wilson lie. When am I ever going to stop being so basic and messy?

Apparently never. I took four pregnancy tests before allowing myself to believe the truth. Mickey Ford knocked me up. So much for his stupid vasectomy. New rule, never trust a guy who says he had a vasectomy unless you snipped him yourself.

I'm going to have that big idiot's baby. In fact, our baby is probably going to be super dumb, because we're both stupid. *Sorry, kid. I ruined your life before it even started.*

There's a knock at my door and I assume it's Meg, because she stops by every day at noon to win back my affection and make sure that I'm not talking to Mickey or Keith. When she comes over, I think I'll finally come clean. I'll force myself to tell her I'm pregnant and I'll tell her about the stupid video Keith has. Maybe the police really could help. The Tyrant could still kill me... And yeah, that scares the shit out of me.

Whoever's at my door knocks again.

"I'm coming! Who is it?"

There's no answer at the door. Great. I roll my eyes, expecting Meg to have a boba tea in one hand and her purse in another, but when I open the door, it's Keith. And he isn't alone. My worst fears have come true.

"Hello, Rain," **The Tyrant** says. "I brought your boyfriend. Can we come in?"

The Tyrant grins, and a shiver runs down my spine. A little voice in the back of my head tells me *run*. But, I ignore it. Never ignore that little voice, okay? I wish I hadn't...

Keith won't make eye contact with me. He shoves his hands in his pockets as I glare at his loathsome face, wondering what drugs I must have been on to allow this imbecile into my life.

"I don't want you to come in," I snap.

Keith rolls his eyes and shoves his hands into his pocket.

"Too bad."

The Tyrant shoves the door open and Keith brazenly walks into my apartment. I kid you not, a little roach crawls out of his shoe and follows him in. I crush it beneath my foot.

Is Keith the source of the damned roaches?

Whatever happens, they can't find out I'm pregnant. I don't know what The Tyrant will do if word gets out that I'm carrying Mickey Ford's baby. I have to act tougher than I feel with my stupid sweaty palms.

"What do you want? My cousin's coming over in a few minutes."

The Tyrant glances at Mickey. I only hear two words before what happens next.

"Get her. Or I'll report you to the police for screwing a sixteen-year-old you fucking pervert."

The next thing I know, Keith's coming at me with a hand and a giant rag. It happens too quickly for me to react properly. Rain, you idiot. You shouldn't have let them in…

I scream. I squirm. But then everything around me fades to black. There's nothing I could have done short of not opening the door. But how could I expect that my ex-boyfriend and my blackmailer would kidnap me? This isn't how my life is supposed to go. I'm basic. I'm simple. I go to work, I come home, I use the internet, I sleep. Exciting things don't happen to me.

Everything changed when that stupid blue-eyed rock star came into my life. When I let my obsession with Mickey turn into blogging and then bleed its way into real life… I made my bed.

Now, I have to lie in it.

When I finally wake up, I know I'm in an apartment, but I don't know where it is or who it belongs to.

I sit up sharply and find it surprising that I'm not chained or handcuffed to a bed. Ha, there's a door too. I rush to the door and naturally, it's locked. The windows are locked too and there are burglar bars — and not the kind you can squeeze through if you're five-feet-tall and relatively small. These are heavy duty.

Shit. I've been kidnapped. And my mouth hurts. I touch my lips and wince from the tiny bubbling bruises around my lips. *This ain't shit motherfucker really used chloroform to get my ass.*

My heart pounds when I realize that (obviously) I don't have my phone. I have no way of communicating and no way to get out.

I touch my stomach and a surge of terror rushes me that's so unfamiliar yet instinctively maternal. The baby. Whatever they used on me could harm my baby. I can't be more than a few weeks along, unless Mickey got me good that first night. He probably did.

We shouldn't have had unprotected sex. But what's a girl to do when one of America's hottest celebrities presses her into his bed and promises her pleasure beyond her wildest imagination... then delivers?

I was stupid, powerless, and incredibly horny. Doomed from the start.

I approach the door and knock, hoping that yields some response. Maybe there are other people in this building who may want to help me.

"Help!" I say — not too loudly, but loudly enough that I hope the right person hears me.

I don't have to wait long before the handle twists and the door opens. This is the furthest thing from the right person.

"Calm down, Char. Of course I didn't hurt her," **The Tyrant** snaps bitterly. Okay, I'm seeing double.

This has to be one of those pregnancy symptoms, right? Because there's no way in hell what I'm seeing is real. There's no way in hell that **The Tyrant** has a... twin sister.

Two pairs of terrifying olive eyes stare at me. Honey blond, frizzy curls frame both their faces. *Char* stares at me and then wrinkles her nose in disgust, turning back to **The Tyrant.** Please, tell me her real name...

"This is too far. I helped you. I gave you everything so you could build a career, but you're taking it way too far," Char says. "This is more than a gossip blog."

"Since when did you become such a prude? She won't tell anyone. She's a little bitch. She's *my* little bitch."

The Tyrant steps into the room grinning, and I step back. She isn't that tall, but when you're five-feet, everyone towers over you. **The Tyrant's** probably around 5'7". I note what details I can in the vain hope that I'll make it to the police. I already knew what she looked like before, but this time,

Meg finally found out what they had on me and she doesn't want me to worry, but the FBI could get involved. If they find out, they could leak it, so I have to keep quiet until the feds build their case.

A little voice in my head tells me I won't make it that far. They won't let me get out of here alive.

Char finally does it. She uses the Tyrant's real name. Well, her nickname.

"You've gone way too far, Lottie. Way too far."

The Tyrant leans against the frame of the door, smirking at me and ignoring her sister. Sorry, *Lottie?!*. I see why she came up with the pseudonym. Lottie isn't a bad name, but it's not exactly what you'd expect for a hacker/gossip queen. Lottie, short for Charlotte, is a name that belongs to someone kind and classy who bakes banana bread.

"Hey, Rain. Enjoy your nap?" The Tyrant teases. Wait... *Lottie*.

I stay as far back as possible and search for weapons. There aren't any weapons. Obviously. But I have to try...

"Why did you bring me here? What's going on? Meg was coming to my house. She'll find out what you did."

"She's right," **The Tyrant's** twin says. Char. And now I know The Tyrant's name... *Lottie*. It must be short for Charlotte. Or something. I try to stay calm. I need to find a way out of here, but if I'm going to do that successfully, I need to be patient.

"Since when do you have a twin?"

I speak slowly. Quietly. Aware that anything I say could make *Lottie* lose her cool. It worries me that she doesn't seem bothered by me knowing her name. I'm no expert, but when that happens in movies, it's because the psycho killer doesn't plan on letting you leave alive. I don't even know where the hell I am.

"See, Char? She's just as stupid as I told you she was. No one will find out that she's here and we'll just use her for information until we can convince the buyer to take the stupid website off our hands."

"This isn't right."

Lottie snaps. "You're in too deep, Charlene. The moment you betrayed Seb Jefferson, you lost your moral high ground."

Charlene gazes at me sadly and then turns her attention back to her sister.

"Three days. You have three days to work it out."

"Don't worry. Three days is plenty of time for me to get information out of her."

"Stop talking about me like I'm not there."

Char and Lottie both glance at me. I step back into the room, suddenly scared. Char's ethics apparently stop short at saving me or helping me out of here. I'm stuck. Pregnant and stuck.

Okay, new rule: if I get out of here alive, never trust a rock star who tells you that he *thinks* he had a vasectomy.

"We'll come back when we need you, loser," Lottie sneers. "Just keep quiet and try nothing stupid."

24

I WISH I WAS DRUNK.

MICKEY FORD

"MICKEY FORD OPEN YOUR GODDAMNED DOOR!"

I wish I was drunk. I wish I was drunk more than anything. Or high. I haven't been sane since Rain left. My staff notices that I don't leave my room. I listen to the songs we made for the album repeatedly, but nothing works. She doesn't have her cellphone or if she does, she isn't answering my calls.

I love her.

I think it started the first day I saw her. I didn't want to look at an eighteen-year-old like that. I never thought I'd look at a woman Rain's color like that. I guess I'm 28 now. I'm less ignorant. Less stupid.

Less likely to survive the next ten minutes because my lawyer has taken off her lawyer shoes, and she's beating down my door like I owe her rent.

"MICKEY I CAN SEE YOUR DAMN SHOES UNDER THE DOOR. OPEN UP!"

Great. There's no getting out of this one. Meg Nigel wants to kick my ass and I might as well let her.

"Come on in."

I hold the door open and she doesn't even walk in.

"You look like shit."

I run my hands over my face. Fuck. How many days has it been since I shaved? This is too fucked up for words.

"Thanks."

"Where the hell is she?" Meg asks next, her neck craning so she can get a full view of my house.

"Where the hell is *who*?"

"Rain, you idiot. I showed up at her place 45 minutes ago like I do every day and she's run away or something."

"Well, she isn't here."

"Don't lie to me, Mickey. I have security cameras all over her place. I've gone to great lengths to keep my naïve cousin out of trouble and somehow getting you involved in this ended up being a *huge* mistake."

"Rain's a big girl. She probably just wanted to get some air."

"She disappeared from her security cameras, Mickey. Rain doesn't have those skills to hack a camera. No offense, but she uses that phone for like pictures and nonstop texting. She doesn't have the tech savvy to just... disappear."

"Maybe she didn't run away," I say, trying not to let Meg

know how angry I am. I ain't ever been the angry sort of guy, but if Meg got Rain into trouble, it's in my best interests to know exactly what sort of trouble that may be.

Meg folds her arms and then glances behind at her Tesla.

"I brought Logan to shake you down if necessary, so for the last time Mickey, I need you to tell me the truth. Do you have her here? Is there a sex dungeon in this place?"

"She ain't here. That's the truth. But if she's missing, I'll come help you find her."

Meg sticks her hand out, pressing it firmly against my chest.

"You're under house arrest. You aren't going anywhere."

"Rain's in danger, you said so yourself."

"That's not what I said. I said that she ran away. And you can't go breaking out of house arrest to find her. They'll send you to prison, Mickey. Do you understand what prison is?"

"Believe it or not, I'm not a complete idiot."

"It's not about that. I'm your *lawyer* and even if we're in this disastrously unprofessional entanglement, you can't leave this place. Logan and I will find her."

"Do you even know where to look?"

"No. But trust me, I'll find her. I always find her."

But there's something different about the way Meg says it and something different in her voice overall. She worries for Rain in a way she hasn't before and it's been so long since I've seen my girl that… I worry too.

The last memory I have includes the smell of her vomit. I want her again. I want Rain...

But I won't stand up here and argue with Meg Nigel. If Rain's in trouble, I know just how to find her. I watch Meg disappear with her Tesla, and I pick up the phone.

"What do you want?" Kara answers, with all the sweetness I expect from her.

"Bring Earl down to the house. I need you."

"I ain't bringing you drugs."

"I've been clean for over fifty days, Kara. I don't want drugs. I need my friends. Please... something's happened to—

Right. Rain's a secret. I haven't exactly told my friends about her.

"The mystery girl you've been pining over the last two months? I read your songwriting blog, Mickey. It's my job to turn your insane ramblings into music we can actually sell."

"Shut up."

"I'll come over with Earl, but I hope you ain't planning anything crazy because if Seb finds out—

"I don't care if Seb finds out."

"So you won't mind if I tell him then?" Kara asks, testing me. She dyed her hair magenta last week and cut most of it off, sparking questions about the Rebel Blood backup guitarist that she doesn't want to answer.

Kara understands secrets better than any of us. But she knows that starting beef between me and Seb can only lead to bullshit.

I call her bluff. "Tell him if you want. It doesn't matter. As long as I find her."

"Okay. Fine. I won't tell him. And what do you mean, find her? I thought she lived with you."

Kara usually has some dating drama going on that she doesn't have time to bother with us.

"Just get over here."

It takes a painfully long time for Earl and Kara to drive out of the city. Earl brings his horribly obnoxious sports car and a new girlfriend who looks like she wants to kill him.

Kara gets out of the car and glares at both of them, wrapping her long red flannel shirt around her bony shoulders as she storms ahead to the entrance of my mansion.

"Careful," Kara mutters. "Earl brought another one of his depraved sex fiends."

The girl following Earl bends her head demurely as she stands next to the hillbilly giant. He removes his Stetson to fix his hair and then grins as she stands submissively beside him.

"Olivia, why don't you get into the house? Make yourself comfortable."

"Yes, master," Olivia whispers. She winces as she walks past him.

The woman pushes past me and I give Earl a quizzical stare, which he meets with a beaming smile.

"What do you do to them?" Kara whispers.

Earl grabs his belt buckle and moves it around his crotch.

"That's between me and my *ladies*. Don't worry, this one's really well behaved."

Kara makes a disgusted face.

"Your last whore propositioned me. So perhaps you could keep your sex freaks under control."

"I've got money, they've got pussy. It's called a relationship, Kara. You should try it."

"No, thanks."

"If you joined us... I think that might be pretty hot..."

Earl shrugs, still grinning, and they're both about to get into an annoying argument that has nothing to do with finding Rain, who is definitely in trouble.

"My sexuality is not a damned fetish," Kara continues, punching Earl in the arm as he laughs and sticks his hands in his pockets.

"Listen, Kara. It ain't the sexuality that's the fetish... it's the pussy."

Kara gives him another well-deserved punch, but it's my time to cut in.

"Can both of you shut up? I lost... my *girlfriend*."

"Since when do you have a girlfriend?" Earl snickers. "I thought you just smashed and passed groupies along. How many girls have come out here to service your landlocked cock?"

Kara rolls her eyes. "Hold on. It's obviously that teenager Seb stuck here to teach a lesson."

Kara smirks and then cackles knowingly. "God, how naïve can you people be? I'm gay and even I couldn't survive 24 hours next to Mickey without thinking about —

Kara trails off as she realizes what she's just said.

"Hold on... you're gay?!" Earl says stupidly.

"You've met five of my girlfriends, you big moron."

"I thought you meant girl friend in the platonic way."

"Tell me this is a joke..." Kara snaps. Earl's grinning, so he's definitely just being an idiot to get under Kara's skin. We all know she's a lesbian.

"Can you two focus!?"

Kara sighs, rolling her eyes again.

"Yes, I just said you were really hot, Mick. Can we move on? America agrees that you're the hottest in *Rebel Blood* but... according to the internet, Earl has the biggest dick."

"That is *not* true," Mickey says.

"America agrees. I have nothing to do with it!"

"We might as well take them out and measure 'em," Earl says, beginning the act of unbuckling his pants while Kara dramatically shrieks at him to stop.

I interrupt again. "Can you both stop!? My girlfriend is in danger and I haven't seen her in a damned week. I need to break house arrest. I need to find her. But I need you to slow Seb down because when he finds out, we'll try to stop me."

"Uh oh," Kara mumbles.

"Uh oh, what?"

"I wasn't bluffing you meathead. Seb's on his way. If you're going to break the law... you'd better head out. He's madder than a wet hen and he thinks he knows who betrayed him. You know... *Celebz Leaked?* Meg's work and his work finally intersected. It's Charlene."

"His tech girl?"

"She's more than his tech girl," Kara says. "She has her hands so deep in Seb's business that she got him to think it was Daisy. Seb mentioned something about the FBI and Rain but... I don't know."

"Celebz Leaked," I whisper. "She's in trouble. If they're the ones who have her, I need to get her. Now."

If *Celebz Leaked* is involved in what's happened to Rain, I'm definitely breaking out. She's afraid. And that means she's vulnerable. I have to protect her. It doesn't matter how stupid it is.

25

RAPE HER

RAIN WILSON

I scream as Lottie flicks her long-handled Bic lighter on, a tiny flame flickering at the end. She grins and allows the fire to disappear. The threat still lingers.

"It's time to talk, Rain. You've spent three days eating my food and sitting in complete silence. I don't want to torture you. I don't want to release your sex tape to everyone you know, but… you're forcing my hand."

"If you do that, you'd be distributing child pornography. That's illegal."

And the Feds are already onto them.

"You don't get it. I don't want to be in this business anymore. It's tired," Lottie says, running her finger over the flame without so much as a grimace.

"Tired? Is that what you're calling consequences for being a piece of shit?"

Lottie slaps me across the face. Hard. But at least she doesn't use that stupid lighter on me. I've been slapped before. By my mom. By my dad. By Keith.

Shame knots in my chest. I can't betray Mickey anymore, not even if Lottie burns me alive. I can't betray him or our baby. I have to keep my secret.

I stare Lottie right in the face. *Show no fear, Rain.*

Lottie snickers. "Listen. I tried to reason with you, but… it's not working. Keith!"

I think she's joking at first, but the door to my bedroom prison opens and Keith walks through the door, dressed in his uniform from his new job at Food Lion. He grins when he sees me.

"Seriously? You tied her up."

He turns to Lottie, who wears jeans, a t-shirt and a messy bun. She couldn't even bother dressing like a bad ass to torture me and as for Keith…

Maybe he still has enough love for me in his heart to let me go…

"Keith! Keith, please… don't let her do this to me. This isn't right!"

Keith ignores me, sticking his hands in his pockets and shrugging.

"What do you want me to do?" He asks Lottie.

"Are you kidding me?!" I shriek. "After all I've done for your broke ass, you won't even acknowledge me?"

"Listen, Rain… you dumped me."

"You cheated on me! Several times!"

"Is it my fault you're so damned…"

"So damned what, Keith!?"

"Do you really expect a man to settle down with a girl like you? A man needs to have a woman who reflects him. I need a ten, Rain. And you… you're not a ten."

Lottie laughs. My cheeks flush with hurt. I don't want to let his words get to me. His hatred. His loathing.

God, I hate Keith. I hate Keith more than I've hated anyone and now that he's here, helping my worst enemy make my life a living hell, I'm willing to risk it all. I try to get out of the chair and scream that I'm going to beat his ass, and then I hear a sound that was all too familiar on my block growing up.

The pop of gunshots downstairs. Lottie turns sharply to Keith.

"Did you hear that?"

"Gun shots."

"Stay with her."

"And do what?"

Lottie grins.

"What we discussed, of course. She won't give me what I want, and I'm tired of looking at her stupid face. Rape her. That ought to loosen her up."

Rape her.

The words linger in the air and then the door shuts behind us as Lottie wanders off to check out the noise downstairs. Can't either of them tell that was a gun?!

"Keith, I don't know where we are or what's happening, but that woman is *crazy*! She's been threatening me for years. She has dirt on everyone she meets and there were just gunshots downstairs. We don't know how many damned enemies she has, so please just let me go."

Keith's staring at me. I meet his gaze for the first time since he entered the room. His hand's on his belt buckle. Wait, why is his hand on his belt buckle? He's not actually going to…

My stomach lurches. He's hard. *He's hard.* No.

"KEITH! KEITH WHAT ARE YOU DOING?!"

He approaches me, and then he pulls it out, and he puts his hand on my head. Oh, hell no. *If Keith thinks I'm not going to bite down on that small ass thing like the ridiculous baby carrot it is…*

I shut my mouth tight and kick my legs out as best as I can with hands tied behind my back. Keith doesn't care. He grabs my head and then shoves down toward his crotch. Before he can force my lips over his cock, the door opens and he jerks away from me in surprise.

"Damn, I need time to turn her out!"

"What the fuck did you say about my girlfriend?" A voice behind Keith snarls from the doorway,.

This isn't possible. If he's here, he'll go to jail…

"MICKEY!"

No. Mickey can't do this. He'll go to prison. I can't find my voice. I just nudge my chair forward and nearly fall over. No...

Mickey Ford pulls out a handgun with a pearl handle and points it at Keith.

"I'm going to jail, anyway. I might as well add murder to the charges. It'll be what, an extra year?"

"Mickey, NO! Don't kill him!"

"He was about to force his dick into your mouth."

This is *not* because I give a shit about Keith.

"I don't want you to go to jail!"

Mickey shoots. Keith and I both scream, although Keith's scream is significantly more high pitched than mine.

"Mickey!"

"I only shot his damn foot!"

Keith yelps and then collapses.

I get straight to the point. "Where are the others?"

"Which others? I fired a couple warning shots downstairs but... I have seen no one else."

"Untie me!"

"Rain..." he says my name urgently as he drops the gun into his holster and ushers over to me, stepping over a screaming Keith to get to me.

"This white man just shot me! This is a hate crime! Rain! Rain help!"

Keith cannot be serious... First, I'm tied up. Second, he was about to rape me. He's insane if he thinks I'm helping his sorry ass. Mickey doesn't untie me right away. The blue-eyed idiot kisses me. Hard. I lean forward to kiss him back and as we're kissing, since I'm still tied up, I totally lose my balance and my chair tips over.

I scream, and Mickey catches me before I hit the ground.

"Shit. We'd probably get out of here."

My heart beast as he holds me and I don't want him to let me go. I want to kiss him again. Mickey notices and he kisses me slow and deep. We don't have time for this, but neither of us can stop kissing each other.

"Did you just cheat on me?!" Keith gasps. I don't even dignify him with a response. My heart is racing like a horse on steroids and Mickey's fingers work the knots around my wrists open.

"We don't have a lot of time," he says. "Rain... when the cops come..."

"You're going to prison, aren't you?"

Mickey nods and I feel a sudden tightness in my chest. Is now the best or the worst time to tell him I'm pregnant? Keith lunges for Mickey's ankle and that crazy motherfucker points the gun at Keith's face.

"I've dreamed about this for a long time," Mickey snarls.

"How? You didn't even know what he looked like?!"

"Doesn't matter," Mickey says, cocking a gun. "I might be famous, but this is how we settle girl problems in West Virginia..."

"MICKEY STOP!" I screech. "I'm pregnant!"

He stops and then both Mickey and Keith look at me and say, "Is it mine!?"

I want to tell Keith that of course it isn't his baby since we haven't had sex in like… 100 days… but before I can say anything, the door bursts open again and there are police. Everywhere.

"Mickey Ford, put your hands up… you're under arrest."

"Rain…" he says, trying to get an answer out of me that just won't come out. It's like there's a lump in my throat and as much as I want to just blurt out that I'm pregnant with his baby, I freeze. Maybe it's the cops. Maybe it's Keith's bleeding foot leaking on the floor. Maybe because this is *not* how I pictured my pregnancy announcement going.

I can't bring myself to say a word. The cops fill the beat of silence.

"Shut the fuck up and do what we say, Ford. Your ass is under arrest!"

26

MICKEY'S WHAT-ECTOMY?

MICKEY FORD

Seb sits on the other side of the glass, phone pressed to his ear and a scowl permanently etched on his face.

"Of course it's your baby, you idiot. What the hell were you thinking? You *knocked her up*?"

He looks like he wants to reach through the glass and strangle me like Bart Simpson. Look, Seb knows everything about my life. At least he knows what happened all the years I spent doing drugs while he got clean.

"Didn't I get a vasectomy?"

"That was a tonsillectomy, you *irresponsible* motherfucker," Seb snarls, and I can tell he's doing everything in his power not to call me a fucking idiot. Don't worry, I've got this.

"What's the difference?"

"One is in your throat, you goddamned buffoon!"

I don't know where the hell Seb learned all this shit because I don't have a clue what he's talking about.

"Listen," I explain. "She's cute. Can you blame me?"

"You can't knock up a teenager because she's cute, Mickey. Damn it!"

"I love her."

Seb presses his head against the glass and I can tell he's hoping his head either breaks it or he falls unconscious and out of the misery of talking to me.

"Do you really? Because this ain't a game, Mick. Meg's cousin is special to Angie, and she's special to Meg. Do you understand what that means? If I want my woman to be happy, which I do, I can't allow you to go around knocking girls up that means something to her."

Seb ain't exactly the king of keeping it in pants. I shrug and mutter something stupid. Then I try saying something better.

"I love her, Sebastian. I'm serious. I'm in jail because I love her so much. And you shouldn't even be here giving me a hard time. Charlene betrayed you and worse... she has a twin sister who's been threatening my girl."

Seb clenches his jaw. He's on the traditional side. He values loyalty over everything and to find out that one of his own betrayed him and then through Daisy under the bus has sent him for a loop. They disappeared from the house that day — Charlene and Charlotte, the twins behind *Celebz Leaked*.

"It doesn't matter if we find them or not. They sold the website. Your arrest gave them the big story they needed, and they skipped town."

"You okay with that?"

"No. I am absolutely *not* okay with that. But we have a bigger problem, Mickey. You're bringing a kid into the world and you're in jail."

"At least I'm not the one pregnant."

Seb rubs his temples in frustration again.

"Mick, you're in *jail*. That means you have more access to drugs than you ever would on the outside. Despite your bullheaded stupidity, I'm trying to get you out of there. I need you to prove that you love Rain and you love that baby by staying clean. Do you think you can handle that?"

Maybe Seb was right, and it was worth a visit to come down here. I already turned down several offers of drugs.

"I love her. I'll stay clean. For both of them. I promise."

"Don't fuck this up, Mickey. I missed five years of my daughter's life because of drugs. I won't let that happen to you. Even if you're a fucking idiot."

"Is she here?"

"Meg didn't want her to come."

I lean back, disappointed. I deserve that. And she doesn't deserve to see me like this. They lie to you in the movies. The jumpsuits aren't always orange. Mine are this filthy grey color and they smell like sweat.

Seb continues. "I thought it was a horrible idea, but... she's pregnant with your kid. You two need to talk. I'll get her."

We have thirty minutes left in this visit and finally, I get to see Rain again. Two weeks in jail without her and I miss her like the desert misses a downpour. Seb leaves for a few minutes and my anxiously beating heart worries that the last thing I see for the day will be Seb's back. When he returns, she's with him, and even prettier than the first day I saw her.

She glances nervously at the glass and Seb points to the phone. Rain licks her sweet lower lip and approaches the chair, sitting and picking up the phone. We look at each other through the glass.

"I never slept with Keith," she says. "Not after... us."

"Yeah. I know. I knew that. I'm sorry."

We stare at each other through the glass and it hurts that we never had a proper conversation about... us.

"You saved me. Don't be sorry."

"I miss you like hell, little lady."

The tiniest smile crosses her face. "I miss you too."

She glances down and a surge of pain and hurt rushes through me. No. I need every minute of those eyes as I can stand. I need to etch every contour of her round face into my memory while I'm cooped up here because I don't know how long it will be. I don't know if I'll see her again.

"Rain," I say her name softly, the single syllable nearly catching in my throat. "I love you."

"Stop…" she whispers. "Please… stop. I don't deserve your love."

"What?"

"I told Seb I wanted to see you, but it's because… it's my fault you're in here and I'm sorry. I'm just a screwup. I don't deserve you, Mickey. I lied. I betrayed you. And now you're back in jail. I don't want to be a burden or a gold digger so… I'm going to tell Keith the baby is his and go back to my life."

"What?"

"You're rich. You're famous. When you get out of there, you have millions of fans waiting on an album and waiting for you. I'm just a messy teenager who couldn't keep her legs closed."

My cheeks flush like they've been touched by the summer sun, and Rain won't look at me again. Why the hell won't she look at me?

"Rain. I don't want that. I don't want you to do that. I love you. And that's *my* baby. You can't give my baby to Keith!"

"It's not your baby. Not after today. I'll lie to Keith and you'll be free. My mama always told me that the only way I'd get a guy to stay is if I trapped him with a baby… I never wanted to become that… and now I've blown it with the only guy I had feelings for. I put you through too much and it's not worth it. Not to be with a girl like me."

"What do you mean, a girl like you?"

"You had the confederate flag tattooed on your body, Mickey. You're white. You like white people and white things. Your fans are all... They wouldn't accept me. I've done enough to screw with your life. I'm sorry, Mickey, but I have to go."

"RAIN!"

She puts the phone down and rushes toward the door. Seb gives me a confused look and then hurries after her. *Goddamn it...*

27

EVEN PREGNANT

RAIN WILSON

Even pregnant, I'm a massive loser. I can't even be cool as I break up with a guy who *isn't* my boyfriend and I'm already ugly crying as I yank the giant backdoors open and climb into Sebastian Jefferson's truck.

I can't even celebrate the fact that I'm sitting in a celebrity's truck because I'm way too depressed. This sucks. I'm sitting in the backseat of Seb's truck, while Angie sits up front and Seb climbs into the driver's seat.

"What happened?" Angie whispers to him. "Why is she crying? I lied to Meg to bring her here, so you'd better come clean."

"I don't know what happened," Sebastian grumbles, glancing over his shoulder at me. "Rain? Did Mickey say something stupid to you about the baby? Because I swear to God, I'll box his stupid ears clean off. If it was a race thing, I'll kick his ass."

I shake my head and bury my face in my hands. Great. All these hormonal tears are making me feel like a big, stupid baby. I'm sitting outside the jail crying my eyes out in a celebrity's car and I'm too wrapped up in my tears to feel that bad about it.

Eventually, I choke out, "He didn't do anything wrong."

"Then what happened?" Angie snaps. My ex-boss doesn't know how scary she can be. Now I know them better, it's no wonder she turned Seb Jefferson into a good guy. She probably scared his ass straight.

"I dumped Mickey," I tell them. "I'm going back to Keith and I'm going to raise this baby on my own."

"Keith?" Angie asks, the pitch of her voice going up several octaves so she's practically hitting a whisper note.

"He's been hitting me up and said he's sorry for almost raping me and…"

"Do you even have feelings for Keith?"

"No."

"What does Keith provide for you, Rain?"

"I don't know. He's just there. But it's totally inappropriate to make Mickey take care of my baby. I'm not a gold digger."

Angie doesn't even say anything. She just glances over at Seb and purses her lips.

"I *told you* Meg got in her head. We should have gone in there with her and then we could force them to do what's right. I don't want them to repeat our mistakes…"

Seb strokes his jaw and then shrugs.

"Maybe Meg's right. That stupid motherf — OUCH! What was that for?"

"I pinched you," Angie says. "Because you are *not* being productive. Rain? We're going to take you home, okay. And then you and I are going to have a little talk. And don't text Keith."

Seb glances over at Angie and then mutters, "Meg's going to kill you."

"Meg has never been a single mom. She doesn't get it. And I know Mickey Ford. I've seen him with Calypso. I've seen his heart. He might be an idiot, but he's not half as evil as you are and you're a great dad."

"Thanks…" Seb grumbles. Angie has a way of weaving in her compliments and insults, so you aren't sure whether to be offended or flattered.

"Don't get offended," Angie teases, her tone lightening up considerably.

"Easy for you to say…" Seb grumbles back, but there's a hint of a smirk on his lips that tells me he secretly enjoys Angie's harsh teasing. She kisses him on the spot where she just pinched him. "I like you evil just the way you are, big guy."

"And I like you sassy," he murmurs, leaning over and kissing her. They kiss so hard, I think they're going to consummate their flirtation in the front seat. I clear my throat and Angie catches herself, pulling away and tucking hair behind her ear before clearing her throat.

Just watching them flirt makes me feel so weird and lonely. And there's this part of me that just wants to search Mickey's name online and binge read stories about him. He can go back to being America's heartthrob and I'll go back to being… I don't know… one roach in my apartment?

Ugh. This sucks.

Something's weird about the route Seb's taking. He just missed the turn to my place, and he definitely knows where it is considering he picked me up for this secret meeting that Angie helped arrange. The meeting I just used to break up with Mickey. Weird. Maybe he knows a shortcut.

I close my eyes and try to think of anything but Mickey's lips running over my nipples and then teasing their way down my belly. I try not to think about his stupidly thick West Virginia accent or all the dumb things he says about race. When I first met him, I wanted to yank his ears, but since we started sleeping together, his stupid little comments just made me laugh.

It's like… he does genuinely want to know things, but it's not exactly the right climate to look like an idiot over race issues. We talked about that stuff. We had something… real.

But I'm too much of a loser to end up with something real. It's my fault Mickey's in jail and if we're together, I'll only ruin his life even more than I already have.

I realize that Seb just pulled his ridiculously pimped out F-150 into a lot that *isn't* my apartment. It's one of these fancy downtown places that looks like it should be in New York. I don't really go to Downtown Nashville often and I'd definitely never end up at a place like this.

"Where are we?"

"Somewhere we can talk," Angie says. "That's all you need to know."

"The last thing I need is to get kidnapped again…" I mutter under my breath. Angie offers me a sympathetic look.

"Listen," she says. "I care about you, Rain. And I know that right now, you're scared. You're pregnant and you don't know what to do. I got pregnant when I was your age. Let me be here. Let me help."

"Do you know what my mom said when she heard I was pregnant?"

"You can tell me, honey," Angie says, turning on a sweet side I didn't know she had. "Please. I just really want to help."

I don't know if Angie Victor can help me. Some people were just born to be a lost cause. I'm one of those people. My life just can't seem to go right, and now I've dragged Mickey down with me. I can feel another crying session bubbling up in me. *Don't cry, Rain.*

"I don't know what to do."

Angie offers me a sympathetic look. Maybe she'll finally give up on me.

"At least you'll have the dogs for company."

"The dogs?"

"We caught Callie riding Pippin down the stairs like a horse. We need these beasts contained. Mickey said you loved the dogs."

Great. Like my predicament couldn't get worse.

28

KNOCKED UP A FEW BEAGLES

MICKEY FORD

I am *not* letting that woman out of my sight so she can give my fucking baby to a loser like Keith. Damn it, Rain. I know I'm a screwup, but I'm not so much of a screw up that I'll let another man raise my kid. Especially not when that man has the brains of a dead mouse.

Fuck. I need a way out of this. I know I did this to myself. If I'd been thinking, I might have sawed my foot off. I couldn't do something so sensible, though. I had to just run clean off the property with the biggest rifle I could find in my collection.

Drugs? I don't give a damn about drugs. I just want Rain. I want the mother of my child. I loved her before then. I think I realized it when Meg Nigel caught us. I didn't even care about getting into trouble. I just wanted Rain safe.

I care about her way more than drugs. More than anything. When you love someone, it rips you to pieces to hurt them.

I can't hurt her and I can't hurt our kid. I grew up in a big family. I can't stand how quiet the house gets. When Rain was with me… even as quiet as she is, she brought a type of life that reminded me of West Virginia. I didn't need drugs around Rain and I don't need them now… because what I need is to solve my fucking problems for once and stop being Mickey Ford, the world's biggest fuck up.

One more night. I can survive one more night in jail. At least if I tune out the sound of my cellmate jacking off. He's a heroin DUI and these guys are always fucked up. I close my eyes and wish I could close my ears instead of listening to him beating it like a baboon.

Rain, baby… I wish you were here.

Well, maybe not next to this overgrown masturbator. But somewhere else. With our kid. With our family. It's crazy how I miss her. It's crazy that I could have gone my whole life not knowing that the only reason I felt so numb was because I needed this… *Love.*

Despite my good neighbor's masturbation session, which continues far too long, I get some sleep and an answer to my prayers. Seb must have made peace with Meg Nigel and this far into the process, I've discovered that peace with Meg Nigel often costs more money.

Judging by the new Cartier bracelet on her stack, Seb must have shelled out a good check.

"Good morning, client," she says sweetly. Okay. Did Seb send himself bankrupt? Meg is *never* this cheerful.

"Did I finally get life in prison?" I grumble.

"Nope. I'm coming here to apologize."

"What?"

"Listen, Mickey," she says, her tone getting harsh and then quickly pulling back from the edge. "I will *kill* Keith if he gets anywhere near my cousin one more time. Right now, even if you are a pain in my ass, the thought of her getting back together with Keith is too painful. So I'm sorry for breaking you guys up and causing this mess but I need you out of jail and I need you to get Rain."

"Get Rain? What do you mean, get her? Where is she?"

"Seb and Angie tried to help her by showing her the place you got, but... she's run off... *with Keith*. And your dogs."

"What?!"

"We don't know how else to explain it! She won't answer her phone and I don't know what else to do. Mickey... I can always find her. But this time... she's gone."

"Gone..."

"Please, help. I love her scrappy ass more than anything. I know Rain thinks she isn't good enough for you or anything, but she is good enough. She has a good heart beneath all the lying and phone addiction."

"I know she does."

Meg sighs.

"I should have seen it earlier."

"What?"

"You two are perfect for each other."

"Oh, really?"

"Rain hasn't ever known real love, Mickey. Her parents don't care about her and Keith takes advantage of her. I try to protect her, but… I honestly suck at this stuff. This is why I don't *have* kids."

"Yeah. Can't say I've had real love either."

"You look after her. And she looked after you. At least she stopped you from breaking house arrest way earlier. Seb bet you'd only last 48 hours. Earl bet a week."

I try not to take it personally that my closest friends think so little of me. Then again, I can't exactly blame them. Maybe I can get out of these itchy prison rags sooner than I thought. It's easy to agree to help Meg.

"Okay. Okay. If you do your lawyering, I can get out of here and kick some ass."

"Do you know where she might be?"

"Not a fucking clue. But she's the woman I love, and she's carrying my child, so I'd damn well better find her."

Meg smiles.

"Thank you."

"Thank you… for your blessing."

"My blessing?"

"Well… uh… I hope I have it."

"Of course."

"Good. I want to look after her, Meg. You won't have to worry about Rain Wilson. I have a way of keeping her in line."

"Weirdly enough… you're right."

"What about the website?"

"There's a new owner, but *Celebz Leaked* has been silent for weeks. Charlene and her twin skipped town and… we don't know who owns it or what the hell is going to happen."

"But they're quiet. Maybe we need to wake them up."

"Are you suggesting we send the people who blackmailed you after the woman pregnant with your child?!"

"Listen… if the internet can find my ass hiding out in Ithaca, New York… they'll find Rain."

"This could get her hurt. It's too dangerous."

"Get me out of here, Meg and I promise you, I'll die before I let anyone hurt Rain Wilson."

"Promise."

"I promise."

"Swear on the Bible?"

"I swear on the Bible and my Meemaw's grave."

"Screw this up and I'm going to set Logan on you."

"Got it. How are the dogs?"

Meg scowls. "She took the damn dogs, Mickey."

"Right! She has the dogs. Yes. This is going to be a piece of cake."

"It will?"

"They're my dogs, Meg. I have GPS in them."

"You have GPS in your dogs?!"

"When I lived in Beverly Hills, they got out and knocked up several prize winning Beagles. After that, the court ordered the GPS chips."

"Your dogs are serial rapists?!" Meg says, clutching her purse in revulsion.

"Hey! Pippin and Sam were just following their instincts."

"Why aren't they neutered?!"

"They are now."

"I can't believe the court ordered your dogs to have a vasectomy for being sexual predators."

"Maybe that's what I remembered…"

"I'll see if I can have you out of here tonight. Try not to get into any knife fights."

"I'll do my best."

"Do better than your best. I'm worried about Rain."

"So am I."

29

RUNNING AWAY WITH KEITH

RAIN WILSON

Seb and Angie were too easy to escape from. I think they got it wrong. Everyone got it wrong. No one suspected that I'd run off with my worst nemeses — Sam and Pippin. But now, I have these mutts (sorry, Mickey) under my control because of the gas station beef jerky I stole from Seb's truck, and I am finally taking proper control of my life...

I pressed a gun against Keith's stomach and told him to drive off. Yup, I pretended I was getting back together with Keith, but... I kidnapped him.

Where'd I get the gun? It's Tennessee. It wasn't that hard. I knocked on my old neighbor's door and yes... I pushed my boobs together when I asked if I could borrow one of his weapons. Ivan sells drugs, so he has a lot of guns. He tried to get with me, but got turned off when I said I was only seventeen. Keith had dumped me for the week because his new girlfriend, who went off to Howard, was back in town and he didn't want me around.

"The serial number on this one is shaved off. Don't ask why," he said, handing it to me in a black plastic bag. *Cool.* I got my ass a gun and then I went to get my ass a Keith.

I didn't plan on asking any questions. I just planned on doing something smart for once and getting revenge on everyone who screwed with me and Mickey's life. Not just Keith.

I have about six months before this baby gets too big for me to haul around, so I have six months to get revenge on Charlene and Charlotte Bishop, too.

No more playing nice. No more acting all sweet and innocent. I have a baby to protect, and I can't have anyone coming after me.

Mickey's in jail right now and if he's buying me apartments in the city, he doesn't think he's getting out. I can't just sit there and take that. I have to do something. *Urgently.*

I can't just sit around crying about being the world's biggest loser. Hello. I could give my kid low self-esteem. The way my mom did to me. I wanted to shoot Keith so badly, but he was driving on his bad foot, so I resisted the urge and at least got to enjoy him wincing every time he stepped on the gas.

I made Keith drive me to a cheap, shitty motel 20 miles outside of Nashville. I didn't let him talk. I cranked my Shareen Richards tracks all the way to the motel. Ha. Then I got his ass out of the car, paid for the motel and took him to our room on the second floor where I finally handcuffed Keith to the radiator…

Pippin and Sam followed us into the room and the guy behind the counter was so busy staring at the large

Doberman Pinschers that he didn't notice the gun I had obviously pressed into Keith's back. Maybe he just didn't give a fuck. *Good.*

And here we are now... Right in that shitty motel.

"Listen, Rain... I don't know what you think I did to you—

"Shut the fuck up, Keith. You were always a gross old weirdo."

"Gross old weirdo? Bitch, you better..."

I cock the gun, and Keith falls silent. Ha! At least my baby can know that once in my life, I did something that made me a badass. My heart is racing though because I could go to jail for this. And I could send Keith to jail, too.

"That's right," I tell Keith, trying to sound more bad ass than I feel. "Quiet down."

"Where did you even get a gun?" He sneers, like he thinks I'm too stupid to get a gun. Well, guess what, you don't even have to be smart to get a gun. You just have to know a guy.

"That's none of your business."

"What are you going to do to me, Rain? You ain't built for jail."

"I'll worry about what I'm built for, Keith. You have bigger problems. *Much* bigger problems."

"Like a crazy dark bitch—OW!"

I throw a lamp at his head. I barely even touch him, but of course, Keith and his bitch ass has to make a scene. This man has *no shame.*

"HELP!" He whimpers. "What do you even want with me? You're crazy! You're obsessed with me!"

He rattles his handcuffs against the radiator. Poor Keith. It doesn't feel so good to be the one manipulated now, does it? I smirk.

"I need you to get Charlene and Charlotte down here."

"It's bad enough your cracker ass white boy shot me. Now you want to do the same thing. I've had enough of you tired black bitches holding a man ba — OW!"

"Haven't you learned your lesson?" I snap, fighting every urge in my body to shoot Keith.

"Rain, stop doing this. What we had was real. We can put all this mess behind us. I'll take you back."

He really doesn't get it, does he?

"What we had was about as real as Kylie Jenner's ass," I snarl. All my rage comes out. I hate Keith so much for what he took from me and it just all comes rushing to me in that moment. Now that I'm going to be a mom, I know the truth. I'd never let a crusty old asshole like Keith lay a hand on my baby. I should have been a normal teenager. I was just lonely and friendless, and he took advantage of that.

Now, none of that matters.

"Damn," Keith offers. Eloquent, as usual.

"You tried to rape me. You sold me out. And worst of all… you took advantage of me when I was sixteen and stupid. It took me getting pregnant to finally understand… *you ain't shit.*"

I have *always* wanted to tell Keith that. I can't smile too hard because I have to act tough, but I'm giddy as hell on the inside.

"I ain't shit?" He gasps, like the thought never crossed his mind.

"Yup. And I stuck around so long because I didn't have any self-esteem. Well, that's all going to change. I'm going to look after my baby and make sure none of you evil motherfuckers gets close to ruining my life again."

Keith stares at me, and I try to ignore my pounding heart. I don't know why I'm giving a speech like I'm an anime villain, but I feel like if I don't keep talking, I'll have to do something else and I didn't exactly plan *this* part out super well.

Pippin and Sam hang behind me in the motel room. I had to pay an extra $400 to get past their no pets policy. It's crazy to think, but this is probably the worst hotel Sam and Pippin have stayed at. Pippin put his paw on the bed when he entered the room and then wiped it aggressively on the floor for about five minutes.

Even Mickey's stupid dogs are more bougie than me. But that's okay. I don't need to be bougie right now. I need to get Keith to listen to what the fuck I'm saying and help me get revenge on the people behind *Celebz Leaked*.

"I'll put the phone to your ear and I need you to tell them that you have a scoop. Tell them that I'm here, pregnant with Mickey's baby and you've asked for a ransom."

"I can't lie like that."

I whack him across the head. Hard.

"But you can lie to cheat on me?"

"I didn't lie about that! You chose to stay with me."

"You *chose* to cheat on me!"

"A man can't choose who he cheats with."

"He could choose not to cheat!"

Hold on. Why am I yelling at Keith again? I pick the lamp up and toss it at his head again. This time it hits him. Hard.

"You are a crazy bitch!"

"Good! Now if you don't do what I say, I'll kill your ass for real."

I storm off into the motel hallway to give Keith's loser ass time to think about what I just said. Who am I kidding? I need to think too. I'm not exactly a kidnapper. Honestly, I can't even believe this plan is working. None of my plans work.

I didn't really think it through and now I might have to sleep in the same room as Keith. Ew. I'd rather sniff Pippin's ass the way Sam does — and trust me, he does a very gross and thorough sniff.

I pace in the hallway, hiding the gun in my sweatshirt and then I get thirsty, so I go down to get a *Diet Coke* from the vending machine. I drink half of it before I head back to the room. I hear two solid barks from the other side of the door. I push the door open and… scream.

"Pippin! Sam! What on Earth did you do?"

I hold on to the gun with a shaky hand and race over to Keith, lying slumped over the radiator. Maybe that lamp hit his head a little too hard or something. There's a little blood coming out of his ear. *Shit…*

"Keith? Keith, you idiot… wake up!"

30

CATCH HER IF YOU CAN

MICKEY FORD

"She spent two days at a shitty motel and then she took your dogs... where?!" Meg screams at me like she's going to rip my ears off.

"She skipped town, Meg. If she's with Keith, she ain't coming back."

"This makes no sense. Rain wouldn't take your dogs to move in with Keith."

"Then what the hell is going on? She won't answer her damn phone. You got me off the hook with a fine..."

"Only because my defense was that you're too much of an idiot for house arrest," Meg says. "And you paid a huge fine. 20% of your net worth."

"Thank you."

Honestly, I don't even know my net worth anymore, so it makes no difference if 20% is gone. I'll play more bass, write another album, I'll get it all back. For Rain.

Meg rolls her eyes. "We need to get my cousin's raggedy ass back to Nashville."

"Okay. How does a road trip sound?" I grin, shoving my hands in my pockets and imagining how many ways Meg would kill me if we had to sit behind the wheel together for several hours.

"Horrible," she sneers.

"You're right. This is a job for *Rebel Blood*."

Meg doesn't bother hiding her skepticism (or any of her emotions).

"Your band? Think you four can stop partying long enough to find my cousin?"

"We have a tour bus. We have GPS. We can find her without your help."

"Are you *sure*?"

"No. But maybe it's best you stay here in case *Celebz Leaked*… resurfaces. The Feds want the original owners."

"Let's pray they don't resurface," Meg answers, and for once, I agree with my lawyer.

Meg leaves me to sort out my band, threatening me several times over her cousin's life. Kara agrees on a road trip as long as there's plenty of weed for her to trip out on — and she wants to bring a new girl.

Earl Wayne Jr. agrees because he's just that agreeable — and going through yet another break up within his harem of crazed girlfriends. Nobody likes when Earl is single. He drinks more and if you aren't careful, he'll steal your girl. He stole Tati from me when we were younger, but I stole her back. Now, both of us are way too old for that. Earl's even older than we are, even if he doesn't look or act like it.

Seb agrees to the trip, but only if I promise I'm not using.

Sebastian just picked a wedding date with Angie and she's freaking out over being the other half of a celebrity wedding and practically kicking him out of the house so she can get some space from dealing with Daisy who now leads Seb's team now that the truth about Charlene is public information

For the first time, I can look Sebastian in the eye like a man and promise him sobriety. I don't want to use anymore. I want to put my family first. I want to be the man I always knew I could be.

I want to find my girl. Our team climbs onto the tour bus outside of Seb's house. Angie and Calypso wave goodbye to Seb, who suddenly looks devastated to leave them behind, even for an instant.

"She's on the move."

"How far?" Kara asks, hanging onto her newest fling for dear life. The red-headed woman with tanned skin and freckles across her face giggles and kisses Kara on the cheek.

"She has a 15 hour head start."

Earl stretches and yawns.

"I can catch her."

"What do you mean you can catch her?" Seb snarls. "I got Tito to drive."

"Tito can't catch her. I can catch her."

"How do you plan on working out a 15 hour headstart?"

"First, I've been sober for the past 24 hours, so I have a clear head. Second… NASCAR family. I've had my share of speeding tickets." Earl cracks his thick neck, long hair dusting his shoulders. "I can kick some serious ass."

"The point is to avoid getting speeding tickets so we can avoid sending Mickey Ford's ass to jail."

"He's already in jail," Earl grins. "The courts cleaned him out with that fine. He can't afford anything."

"Thanks, Earl. Real helpful."

"I'm just playing around, buddy. I'll get the keys from Tito."

Earl thumps me on the back with his giant hand, nearly putting a hole through my rib cage.

We get onto the bus, but by the time it pulls off the street, I wonder if we've made a huge mistake. I must have been higher than a kite the last time I let Earl Wayne Jr. drive me anywhere.

Even Seb's gone pale as Earl pushes the tour bus to its limit at 90 miles an hour.

"That colossal fool is going to kill us all," Seb snarls.

Kara and her girlfriend are kissing in the back of the bus with the smell of liquor permeating the air. Seb stiffens uncomfortably. Kara barely drinks, but when she does, it doesn't take much to get her and her gamine lady loves stinking drunk. We both notice the smell. That's the one thing you always notice when you're sober.

"So. How's sobriety," Seb asks me, stroking his chin and grinning, his tongue rolling around the bottom of his jaw. Ground him.

I give him an answer I think he'll understand. "Better with Rain."

Seb grins and nods. "I know that feeling. That love… it's something, isn't it?"

"It's what we write songs about."

"My songs were all bullshit," Seb mutters. "Until Angie."

There's still tension between us from my secrets. And it's about time we stop having secrets. "I have to come clean."

"About what?"

"Five years ago. Why all this started."

Seb is a soothing presence. He's like an older brother to me, although there ain't much difference in our ages. He's stern and old school Southern while I'm reckless from the outside, incapable of slowing down to Seb's natural blues rhythm pace of life.

"Talk, Mick. I want to know."

So I tell him. I think it will be hard, especially with Kara and her girl making out at the back of the bus. But I can't keep this a secret from anyone any longer.

By the time I'm done, Seb's red.

"I swear, I'll kill Brent."

"You can't kill Brent. You've read our contract. Brent owns us."

"Owns us… he ought to get a boot up his ass."

Seb mutters a bitter apology, realizing what he just said. I shrug. I numbed all my pain out years ago. And then I made it worse. Day by day, it's getting better, and I'd be lying if I said it wasn't because of Rain. She gave me something to take care of. Something to care for. A reason to be alive that means something, unlike money or cars or tattoos. Rain means something. At least to me.

"We can't do anything, Seb. You know it. We can't put our selfish needs on the line."

"Selfish? The man was involved in… a crime."

"A crime that most men in Hollywood get away with. We have one more album on our contract. We can make it one more album."

"And then I'll put that son of a bitch six feet under," Seb snarls. I know he means it.

Kara sits up and stops kissing her girl. "Can you two stop killing my buzz?"

Despite her harsh words, her gaze meets mine, and I notice the sad expression on her face. Kara doesn't talk much about her feelings and she seems to find men far too emotional, but I know she understands pain.

"Shut up, Kara," Seb mutters. "You want Brent dealt with more than any of us."

Before Kara can protest (or more likely, agree with Sebastian), Earl kicks the bus up a notch.

The bus speeds up to nearly 100 mph and we're all too white as sheets to say anything else. Earl might catch up to Rain, but he never promised we'd get there alive. Now I wish I had him promise that in writing.

We stop in the evening to stretch our legs, and so Earl can have a smoke. Kara and her girl smoke together too, blowing O-rings and then kissing until their lips turn red.

Earl needs to sleep, and Tito can take over behind the wheel. Rain's night stops are our best chance to make up the distance and by some miracle, we didn't catch a single State Trooper on the road North.

Rain's in Pennsylvania. At least I assume she's still with Pippin and Sam. I haven't considered the possibility that she might be nowhere near them and she could be in Keith's hands...

If he has his hands on her, I'll kill him this time. No more mercy shots. Seb told me not to bring my gun because my guns always make things worse, but I think Sebastian's picking up too many prissy notions from Angeline. A gun is a gun and sometimes, a man needs a gun.

"Where the hell do you think she's going?" Seb mutters as he kicks back on the bus, pulling his hat over his eyes so he can get some sleep.

"I don't know."

"Think Keith is giving her any trouble?"

"I don't know."

I don't want to think about what Keith could do to her. Ravaging her, probably. My hands clench into fists unconsciously. I try to relax. Rain wouldn't let him touch her. She knows how much I love her and how much it would kill me.

"Try to get some sleep," Kara says. "We'll monitor her GPS. Tito will drive while Earl rests. It'll be slower, but we'll catch her by morning."

"I don't know if I can sleep."

"You can," Kara says firmly. "You want her to see the real Mickey Ford when you step off this bus, not a jail zombie who needs a shower."

"Thanks for the self-esteem boost, Kara."

"Just being honest, Mick. Just being honest."

Her girlfriend drags her back to her bunk bed. It's been a long time since we've been on this bus together like this. Seb's right. It's time for the band to write a new album. It feels like we're on the verge of moving on. Growing up. The kid music we made about drugs and all that other bullshit seems so stupid.

I don't want to spend my whole life chasing girls. I just want this one. And damn it, I'll have Rain Wilson back. I swear. When I finally get her back, I won't let her go. I don't care what any stupid gossip column says or does. She's my girl. *Mine.*

31

MY PLAN TO BE A BADASS

RAIN WILSON

Okay, Rain. Calm down. It's fine that your plan to be a badass totally didn't work and Keith either died of natural causes or got mauled to death by Mickey Ford's dogs.

This is totally fine. Yup.

It's totally fine that I wrapped Keith in blankets and dragged his ass out the back of the hotel and somehow got him in the car. Yup. This is great. Everything is going **just fine.**

It's also fine that I drove back to Nashville and dropped him off at his apartment, right? Well, his mama's apartment. But the same thing. She hated me. His mama always said that I was fast and trying to trap Keith for his money. I didn't want to stick around and explain that I accidentally killed her son.

Don't ask how I got him up the stairs, but let's just say Mickey's dogs earned themselves a lot of beef jerky.

I killed Keith. I killed Keith. I repeat it to myself to accept the truth. I am officially a murderer.

I killed Keith. Holy shit. I killed Keith. This is definitely bad, right?

The cops probably found him already. That's why I took my accomplices and I hit the road north to freedom. My daddy used to say that we had family who went north to Detroit. I considered going there, but thought better of dragging my troubles there to someone else's doorstep. I have to look after myself now. I can't afford to hate Sam and Pippin anymore. These Dobermans are officially my family. We're going to ride or die to the Canadian border. Once we get into Canada, I'm going to take the last of my savings and get my act together.

I'll hide out in the boonies and start from scratch.

Canada's the perfect place to start fresh. I mean… they have lots of great things in Canada. Health care. Tim Horton's. Celine Dion. Caribana. Poutine. It's basically a dream world. In the winter, Sam and Pippin will keep me warm in our little cabin and if anyone gets near me from the outside world, I'll shoot them.

Thanks for the gun, Ivan…

At least if I shot Keith, I could have prepared for his stupid dead ass. He just… dropped dead. Who does that? I should have called an ambulance… I should have called a freaking ambulance!

By the time I make it to Pennsylvania, I get paranoid about stopping. Meg stopped blowing up my phone, which made me more suspicious than anything.

It doesn't matter how paranoid I am, I need to sleep and Sam and Pippin are whining, which makes me think they need to take one of their giant poops. I get them out of the car at some stupid highway truck stop and shove my gun into my bag as I walk them up to the park.

It's dark and creepy out here, but I'm the one who anyone should be afraid of. I'm armed. Dangerous. And I think I might have finally convinced Mickey's mutts to be loyal to me. He's in prison, so he'll probably be thankful someone's taking care of them.

When I get to Canada, I'll look up his case and contact him when he gets out. By then, he'll probably know that I'm a fugitive on the run from killing Keith. We can be criminals together. It's romantic. It makes me want to write a song. I still can't sing, but I read all of Mickey's songwriting books and I think I could write one for him.

For us. I'll have to write him letters too. Meg wrote her boyfriend letters when he was behind bars. They weren't together or anything, but that's not the point. They're together now... It's romantic.

Pippin scampers ahead, and I follow, urging Sam to hurry behind me. Pippin yaps at a tree and then squats, getting ready to plop down his giant daily dookie. Dogs are seriously gross.

Sam rushes Pippin and sticks his nose in the dumb dog's ass at precisely the worst time. Sam sticks his tongue out and then backs off rapidly as Pippin continues his poo. I try not to barf as I shoo Sam off and open a little baggie beneath Pippin's butt.

The smell is horrendous.

Sam doesn't squat and start doing his thing too like he usually does when he catches Pippin in the middle of a nice poo. He stands behind me and growls. It's a low growl in the depths of his throat that sends a shiver down my spine. I adjust the plastic bag and stand up straight.

I put my hand in my purse to grab my phone, but I wait just a moment too long. I feel a hard *thwack* on my cheek and then my knees buckle. All the breath exists my lungs in a hurricane whoosh and my knees hit the dirt. My face lands on the earth inches away from Pippin's pile of shit as I lose consciousness.

The rumbling wakes me up. I'm in a car. My car. The backseat, to be specific. I try sitting up, but I can't move. My eyes shoot open, a sudden spike of adrenaline surging through me as I realize my hands are restrained behind my back with rope or zip ties. I try to speak, but my mouth is gagged and *so* dry. I can smell the dogs and hear their breathing, so at least they're here. They're alive.

Pippin leans over and licks my cheek. I try to breathe through my nose, but I suddenly find it difficult to get air into my lungs. There is a *huge* difference between Mickey tying me up in a sexy way and this mess. I'm utterly trapped.

Knocked out and kidnapped. Again.

My gaze finally focuses on the people in the front seat, although I don't exactly need visual confirmation to guess who could be responsible for someone like this. I thought they were both gone, but they obviously aren't.

The biracial twin sisters behind *Celebz Leaked*. Char and Lottie.

Sweat beads on my brow as my eyes drift around the car. It's dark, so they probably can't tell I'm awake yet. If I'm careful, I can learn a lot before they notice me.

Unfortunately, they only grant me a few moments of peace. Charlene gives her twin sister sitting in the passenger seat a nudge. I didn't struggle to tell them apart. Their looks had probably diverged years ago despite their identical genetic origins.

"Thanks for the help, Rain," Lottie says gleefully. I hate that triumphant edge to her voice.

I keep breathing slowly through my nose. I just have to tune her out and think of a plan. I still have the dogs and I can still kick, even with my feet bound.

There has to be a way out. Char's suspiciously silent next to her sister. I guess that's how you get around, Lottie. She uses everything you say as fuel. **The Tyrant** chose her name well.

Lottie continues, "Keith told us you tried to kill him."

I killed him.

"Good job," Lottie says gleefully. "Unfortunately, we had to call in bigger guns. You'll still go to prison, though."

My stomach knots and I think they're going to take me to the police.

"What the hell are we going to do with her, Lottie? She has prize winning Dobermans that Mickey can track."

"You don't know he can track them," Lottie snaps.

"I worked for Seb Jefferson for years. Mickey loves those dogs, and she's an idiot."

Lottie gives me an annoyed glance and then turns back to her sister.

"That's easy. We'll make her shoot them."

"That's not funny, Lottie," Char says softly, glancing down at her phone again.

"Stop being such a bitch," Lottie snaps. "You lost your job, whatever. I sold the site for $2 million. You're getting your cut."

"I liked that job."

"Get a new job. You can come work for me."

Char shifts uncomfortably in the passenger seat. Not even The Tyrant's twin sister finds herself completely comfortable.

"We could film her shooting the dog," Lottie says. "That would make us some quick cash."

"That's sick."

"What? Maybe Seb Jefferson can take you back. Just blame it all on me. I don't care."

"You ruined that job for me. You ruin every job. It's not funny, Lottie."

"To you," Lottie corrected. "It isn't funny to you. To me, it's hilarious. Listen, I'm trying to make it up to you. Keith gave us a huge scoop. She's freaking pregnant, Char. Dream big. We can have a ransom."

"You're not going to get away with asking for a ransom." Char cast a pitiful look in my direction. "She looks like any basic Downtown hooker. Mickey Ford's famous. Why should he care about her?"

Maybe I was wrong to assume Char was any better than her sister.

32

WHAT THE HEART WANTS

MICKEY FORD

"Meg? What's going on?"

We're ninety minutes away from Rain's location and everyone else is sleeping except Tito, who keeps driving the bus at a reasonable speed so we can catch some shuteye and make up the distance between us and Rain.

"I don't know what my cousin is up to but... Keith's dead."

"What? Murdered?"

"He was apparently outside his mom's apartment, slumped against the wall, talking to someone on the phone. Someone came up to him and shot him. Four gunshots. The security cameras in his building were hacked so they don't know who it was, but... she was with him. It has to be her. All the footage is gone from the entire afternoon."

"Rain did that?"

"I don't know what she did! Listen, Mickey. I had Logan shake down a freaking cop to get this information. She shot him and skipped town. You need to find her. Now. If I have to defend my cousin, I'll do it, but I can't do that if she gets too far out of Nashville before the cops find her. I'm breaking laws, Mickey."

"I'm close. Don't worry. I'll find her."

"Get closer. Rain's pregnant, Mickey. She can't live her life on the run and she can't go to prison for a mistake. Keith's trash. If she shot him, she probably had a good reason. I can work with a good reason."

That's lawyer talk for "lying her ass off", but I keep that to myself.

"I want to find her just as much as you do. Trust me."

"She'll be fine. We're close, and Earl is about to take over at the wheel. Once he drives, we'll close whatever distance we've got between us. I promise I'll bring her home, Meg. I promise."

"Don't disappoint me, Mickey. Please."

"I won't. She's my girl, Meg. I'd do anything for her."

Kara's staring at the GPS screen.

"Mickey, something weird's happening."

"What?"

"The dogs are separating."

"What? By how far?"

"Ten miles. Ten and a half miles."

"Give me that…" I snatch it from them and look. They're right. Pippin's off in one direction and Sam's going in another direction. They're getting further apart and I don't know what that means.

"Which one is closest?" Seb asks, hurrying over and glancing at the screen.

"Sam."

"So the question is, where do you think Rain is?"

"I don't know."

"We should split up. We have about 90 minutes to catch her."

"I have to be the one to find her," I insist. I can't promise that she won't bolt if Kara or Seb show up without me.

"Then you'd better get good at guessing. I'll get Earl to stop the bus and get us a car. You make one good guess, Ford, and I'll get you to your girl."

"Thank you."

"You're my brother, Mick. I'd do anything for you. Anything."

"Thanks."

"While we're here… Angie told me I ought to ask you sooner rather than later… would you be the best man at my wedding?"

"What about Earl?"

"I think Earl wants to wear his turquoise belt buckle and denim to my wedding, so I want him far in the back," Seb says with a grin. "Plus, it's always been us against our demons. You and me. I want it to be you."

"Then I accept. Brother."

We give each other a big hug and Kara gags, whispering to her girlfriend, "See? They're so sensitive." Her girlfriend grabs her hips and Kara's cheeks flush a very sensitive shade of pink. I think she likes us sensitive. And we all like Kara just fine, too.

Seb works his magic and gets us a car. And by that, I mean he throws $30,000 in cash at a guy in a dealership to get a used Mustang.

"Why a Mustang?"

"I used to love 'em. Plus, it's lime green. That's bad ass."

I question Jefferson's tastes, but I ain't a car guy, so I slide into the passenger seat and kick my feet up.

"Any idea who we're chasing?"

"Pippin. She wouldn't be with Sam. She doesn't get along with Sam."

"Cool. I'll tell Earl and Kara. Are you sure?"

"I know her. She doesn't get along with Sam at all. It has to be Pippin."

"Then let's do it motherfucker."

"Let's do it."

We take off like a shot down the highway. Seb drives better than Earl, but he's still fast. He gleefully passes a family in a Honda Civic and waves at the kids in the back seat who proceed to have a meltdown, screaming at him and banging on the windows.

"That'll be in the news tonight."

"I fucking hope so."

"So Daisy's back?"

"Yup. Reluctantly. She's finally taken to Angie and I know Char set her up."

"Good."

"Maybe. If Daisy won't learn her place, I'll have to get rid of her. I know she's had her sentiments but... Angie."

Seb puts Angie and Calypso first. Always.

"Yeah. Angie."

"Rain's pregnant, Mick. You're out of jail. Providing we can keep her out of jail... you're going to be a dad."

He's getting the serious tone in his voice, like he's about to give me a lecture.

"Don't even say that. I can't imagine. What am I going to do with a kid?" He's the only one who can know how it scares me shitless. But I love Rain and I know I'll love our baby. I can take care of both of them. I have to. I can't afford to be America's fuckup anymore. It's time to grow up.

Seb glances over and shrugs, his jawline clenching nervously. "Don't miss the shit I missed. I'll never get it back. Callie's my everything, and I missed so much of her life. I don't want you to do that."

"I won't."

"Good. You know what that means, right?"

I shake my head. Seb knows that complicated thinking doesn't appeal to me.

"It means you marry her."

"Marry her? Rain?"

"You love her, don't you?" Seb snarls, ready to bite my head off.

"Yes. I love her. But… I'm not good enough to marry Rain."

Seb always looks at me like he wants to strangle me.

"What the fuck are you talking about?"

"She's beautiful, Seb. And I'm a racist guy. She thinks I'm ignorant."

"She loves you. Even if you are ignorant."

"I have to take of her. I want to take care of our kid. But when she gets older…"

"When she gets older, she'll be thankful you stuck around. Marry her."

I don't know why I'm arguing. Of course I want to marry Rain. I probably would have married her the night I met her. I have a way of being reckless.

"I want to. It's what my heart wants…"

"Then do it. We always have to think about other people in our line of work. We deserve love. Actual love."

"I'd have to tell my ma I'm marrying a black girl. She might not like that."

"She doesn't like you snorting coke out of groupies asses, either. Live for yourself. You can't care what other people think."

"Oh, I'm past that. I just don't want to hurt Rain. I've done too much to hurt her already."

"You won't. Once you get her from wherever she ran off to… keep a hold of her. You'll do fine. She's crazy about you for a reason I have yet to figure out."

"And the baby?"

"Try not to drop the baby. Don't repeat the same mistakes your ma made with you."

"My ma never dropped me."

"Right. I knew that," Seb mutters, flicking his fingernails.

We sit in silence for a while, but we're getting closer. My gun is in my pocket. Seb knows I have it by now. He can spot a gun. But he says nothing. I wonder if he thinks Rain is in danger. Real danger.

I'm coming for you, baby.

33

WHEN THE RAIN FALLS DOWN

RAIN WILSON

"How the hell did that stupid mutt get its ass out the window?"

"Maybe you should have tied the dog up too," Char says with all the enthusiasm of MTV's *Daria*.

"I don't have time to care about the stupid dog. I hope it gets hit by a tractor trailer."

"That's sick, Lottie. It's a dog. A living thing."

"Fine. I'll pull over in a bit, and you can cry over the stupid mutt. Is she still sleeping?"

"I think so."

I am not sleeping. I slowly worked my hands free for the past forty minutes and my wrists are rubbed red and raw. I nudged my least favorite dog out the window. I hate Sam, Mickey knows that. He'd never leave me trapped in a back-seat with him.

I might not be able to escape properly and they might kill me, but Mickey loves those dogs. He has to have them chipped. If someone finds an expensive dog roaming around and checks the chip... they might find me. It's a long shot, but it's only one part of my plan.

The next part is to get more mobility from my hands, so I finish untying myself. I have to pretend to sleep and move so slowly that neither of the twins in the front seat detects it.

I shift my hips a little, trying not to wince as my raw wrists rub against the rope. The car lurches forward. I hear Char scream, "SLOW DOWN!"

And then I feel the impact. We all catapult forward and my throat tightens as I realize... we're flipping through the air. The car lands with a thud almost too soon and I hear a crunch that's so loud I almost think I feel it. A rush of cold air bursts through the open window. Shattered glass. Flashing lights. I'm fine. I'm fine. I try to squirm forward, but I can't move.

Not at first.

"Pippin!" I scream. Mickey's dog is in this car. He should be in this car. "Pippin!"

I hear a low whine and my stomach balls into a knot. *No.*

"PIPPIN!"

I finally twist my body around enough to see that Pippin's trapped. There's a piece of the car pinning him in place and he's hurt. He's really hurt. *No. This is my fault.*

"Pippin, I'm sorry!"

His whining gets louder. My breathing grows more frantic as I struggle more to escape. I hear sirens. There might be other cars. And Pippin's stuck. My head feels foggy and I know I'm not thinking straight, but adrenaline rushes through me and makes me want to do something. I crawl through broken glass out of the window. I can't feel it in my arm at all.

I don't look at the front seat. I can't bear to look. The front of the car is completely crushed. I make it out the window. *My baby.*

If my baby makes it past the clump of cells stage, it'll be a miracle. I get my wrists free and stand outside the car. Rain. The Tyrant hydroplaned and flipped the car because there was too much of it and the road was slick with black oil. I can see the rainbow streaks on the road and the rain comes down faster. And faster. Water drips down my face and into my mouth. Ew. I probably need a shower. My hair and clothes stick to my skin. I glance at the car. Pippin's still trapped. He could die. He probably will. But I don't have a choice.

I try to get close to him, but I can't reach.

"I'm sorry!" I call to him. He lets out a soft, yielding whine. My chest tightens.

I have to run.

I don't know how my feet carry me as far as they do, but I end up at least a mile away from the accident. No cell phone. Nothing. And Pippin… he's dead. Tears prick my eyes and there's no way in hell Mickey will forgive me. I tried everything. I tried changing. I tried acting like a bad ass for once in my life, but everything still fell apart.

It's my fault for not accepting Seb and Angie's help, but they don't understand. I can't just sit around that beautiful house while Mickey's in jail and people who could hurt our baby are roaming about. I couldn't wait for the Feds to take their sweet time with Keith.

I don't think Char or Lottie will roam anywhere. I didn't have to look to know that they were… crushed. The cruel irony of the accident feels like iron nails driving into my temples. Mickey Ford had an accident, and Lottie laughed at him. Still, it's hard to feel gleeful about her dying.

I don't feel gleeful about Keith either.

And I definitely don't feel safe. I lost both of Mickey's dogs and I only have my debit car, cell phone and passport that I was going to use to get to Canada. I don't have a vehicle anymore, so if I plan on making it, I'll have to walk.

I'm no Harriet Tubman. I don't think I can walk North for freedom for days at a time. Especially not if it's this cold. I miss Nashville already. I walk for a long time. A really long time.

I get to this weird motel that looks even creepier than the place I took Keith. Even if I have no luggage and look like a mess, the lady working at the front desk gives me a room. The room smells like cigarettes even if it's a non-smoking room and when I lie on the bed, it makes an aggressively loud creak.

I lay back and put my hand on my stomach, and then it all hits me. I'm on the run with even less than I started with. Keith is dead. *Celebz Leaked* is dead. It's just me and my baby now. I don't want to cry. I can't cry. I just lie there for a bit and eventually, I fall asleep.

When I wake up, I half expect to find Meg Nigel standing over me, but it's just dark, quiet and I'm all alone without my phone. I turn on the television and direct the channel to local news.

It's the only way I can find out about the accident without asking the lady at the front desk and drawing attention to myself.

Two dead and a dog identified as a prize-winning Doberman belonging to Rebel Blood singer Mickey Ford. The news reel then shows about 25 minutes of highlights about Pippin. My stomach twists into an uncomfortable knot. I have to tell Mickey I killed his dog. And poor Pippin. Tears prick my eyes. That dog didn't deserve to die.

34
A DEATH IN THE FAMILY

MICKEY FORD

Seb walks out of the police station with a card. The details and information of my pup. The late Pippin Ford officially declared dead. Seb identified him. My heart aches, but not just because my prize-winning Doberman is gone.

"They'll send his body down to Nashville so you can bury him. Kara called. They found Sam and they're taking him home. Earl will take care of him. It'll be you and me and whatever the two of us can think of when we put our heads together."

Rain. We still need to find Rain. As we get closer, I can't help but feel like she's slipping through my grasp. If I'm too late, I might miss her. I might miss her for good and I can't accept that. I love Rain Wilson. More than anything.

"She wasn't in that crash. Celebz Leaked took Pippin and set Sam free. She's dead, Seb. I think she's dead," I whisper.

There's nothing easy about admitting my suspicions, but I can't help it. If she ain't dead, where is she?

"She isn't dead," Seb urges, but I can't shake the feeling he's only saying it to make me feel better. I don't feel better at all. I feel... lost.

My dog died. Pippin. How the hell is Sam going to go on without him?

"We should search the area around the crash. What if she was there? What if she escaped?"

"Escaped where? She's eighteen and she's... Rain's sensitive Seb. She acts all tough and keeps it quiet, but she's a sensitive girl."

"Is that why you like her?"

"It's more than that," I grumble. "But that's a part of it. Five years ago, men attacked me and they attacked another woman. I never forgave myself for not stopping them either time. With her... I can protect someone who needs it."

"Rain can weasel out of situations better than you think."

"If you and Angie weren't always distracted in the bedroom, perhaps it wouldn't have been so easy for her to get away."

"She's crafty," Seb counters. "Right now, that's a good thing. The car crash was a weather related accident. If she was there, she walked up and got away because they pulled bodies out of that crash and none of those bodies were hers."

"What do we do? Where do we find her?"

"Motels," Seb says. "Think about it. She'd get tired. She'd need rest. If she was nearby, she'd be at the cheapest, shittiest place you can find."

"I don't think so."

Pippin's gone. And I can't help but think that means she must be gone too. Seb smacks the back of my head.

"We have to try, Mickey. She's nearby, or she's on the road again. Either way, we'll find her."

"She wouldn't give up on me," I mutter. "Not in this situation."

"Exactly. So we can't give up on her. I'll call Angie and let her know I'll be up North a while longer."

"Fine. What the hell are we going to eat up here?"

"I don't know. The food is terrible. We'll try to find some hot chicken. I bet Rain will be hungry when we get her."

Hot chicken in Pennsylvania? That would be a trick. But I don't want to cloud Seb's Tennessee optimism with a reality check about the disturbing food profile in the North. I just keep thinking about her and my damned dog.

I loved that dog. But I can't even shed a tear over Pippin, knowing Rain may not be safe.

We never end up finding hot chicken, and we drive to four motels. Neither of them has any sign of the girl we're looking for.

"We've checked every motel in 10 miles. If someone hurt her, I'm going back to jail, Seb. I hope you know."

He nods with a mixture of stern acknowledgment and lingering disapproval.

"We'll find her. Maybe she walked a long, long way."

"Perhaps."

At around midnight, we come to a place fifteen miles away from the accident. It's the last motel available that's not way too far. She has to be here. This has to be the one. Seb stops his car, his blue eyes surrounded by bloodied veins. He needs sleep more than I do, I reckon.

"C'mon. If she ain't here, we're driving to the nearest Ritz Carlton. I'm sick of this."

By "this", Seb means all of rural Pennsylvania, which he's been cursing under his breath for the past several hours.

"I'll go in. You wait in the car. We haven't been lucky tonight. I don't see any reason that'll change."

Seb nods and reclines the chair, pulling his hat over his head and attempting to get what sleep he can while I crunch my Chuck Taylor's over the gravel toward the dingy motel entrance. There's no sign of a car or anything that could belong to her and it's cold. I hope she ain't sleeping outside. That would make finding her much more urgent.

I push the door open and the woman behind the counter recognizes me.

"Oh my God! Are you Mickey Ford?"

"Yes, ma'am."

"Oh my God! What are you doing in here in our hotel? Are there cameras? Is this reality TV?"

"No. I'm here on... personal business."

She turns red and then reaches into her pocket. She nearly takes the picture without asking when she catches herself.

"I'm sorry, do you mind if I take a picture with you?"

"Sure. No problem."

"My daughters will not believe this! What on Earth are you doing out here? Mickey Ford. Mickey Ford is at my hotel. Nobody is going to believe this without proof."

She rounds the counter excitedly and even if my bones ache and I miss Rain more than anything, I allow her to take the picture. Three times. Her hands shake so much with excitement that the first two come out blurry. Imagine all this over shitty Mickey, the runt of the Ford litter. I try my best to smile, but I think I look stupid.

She keeps beaming at me and I stare back, uncertain of what to say.

"Well? You mentioned personal business? Surely you can't be staying here. There are way better hotels up in Erie..."

"I'm looking for someone who might be a guest here? A girl?"

"What kind of girl?"

"She's black. Around eighteen years old. Have you seen anyone matching that description?"

"We don't get too many people who match that description around here."

"I'm sure you don't."

My heart pounds nervously. For the love of God, woman, I just took a picture with you when this is the worst I've looked since I spent my evenings puking all over West Hollywood. Can you please just give me a real answer?

35
SAFE

RAIN WILSON

I wish I still had my gun when the knock comes. I try to approach the door soundlessly and tell myself to calm down and that it's probably just the woman at the front desk.

I want to ask who it is, but then the door just opens on its own. It *is* the lady from the front desk, but she's not alone. Mickey towers over her the way he towers over me and when he sees me, the corners of his lips curve into a gentle smile.

"That's her," he says.

"Well, I'm sorry for intruding," she says gleefully, like she really isn't sorry at all. "It's just... Mr. Ford said he was worried about you and when you didn't answer right away—

"It's fine," I whisper, glancing from her to Mickey. She looks like she had a total freak out over meeting a member of *Rebel Blood*. Judging by the red and impatient flush on Mickey's face, I probably got that right.

"Come here, you," he says. But I'm frozen.

"Pippin…" I whisper, giving him a guilty look. Of all the ways I've hurt Mickey, this is the worst. But he just keeps looking at me like none of that bad shit matters anymore.

"I know," he says solemnly, his pants hanging low around his waist as he lifts his arms, outstretching them so I know there is an open invitation. "Now do what I say, little lady."

The lady at the front desk moves aside, but she doesn't stop staring. I'm just shocked she doesn't take out her phone and start filming. Despite everything, I can't resist Mickey's commands.

I hurry over to him and wrap my arms around him. Tightly. He wraps his arms back and his sweater smells amazing. Everything about him smells amazing and despite myself, I smile. Mickey isn't content to hug me. He grabs my cheeks and kisses me. One big kiss.

My heart races. I have so many questions, so many things I want to know, but then there's kissing. Mickey's lips push mine apart and he sticks his tongue in my mouth. The rush of emotion makes me light-headed and I stumble backward a step and find his large, warm palm on my lower back.

"Careful, Rain," he whispers.

I lean in and hug him again. The lady keeps grinning.

"Well. That was a joyous reunion."

Mickey clears his throat. "Yes. So far."

His hand travels about an inch lower down my back and I feel… safe.

"I'll square up her bill with a little extra if you promise not to tell anyone what you've seen?"

"Tell anyone? No way," she says. "This will stay between me and my girls. I don't want any rumors or any nasty bloggers ruining this for me. I freaking met my daughter's favorite singer. This is the best day at work, I've ever had."

Mickey pulls out a wad of bills and hands it to her. The woman almost cries as she hugs him and then wanders off with her phone glued to her ear, chatting excitedly.

Mickey slips his hand around my waist and pulls me close.

"You've been in a lot of trouble, little lady."

"I know," I tell him, only because I'm too tired to say anything else.

"I got out of prison to come find you."

"Don't you think that was a little too easy?"

"Trust me, I paid a pretty penny to your cousin."

Suddenly, I remember that this reunion can't possibly be perfectly happy. Pippin's dead. Keith's dead. And Celebz Leaked...

Mickey glances over at me and his face falls when he sees my concern.

"Baby, you're pregnant and you've been through a lot. Seb's out in the parking lot taking a nap. I want you in a proper hotel tonight."

My hands move to his and I squeeze them.

"But what about… everything?"

"Pippin. Sam. Keith. Char. Lottie. Celebz Leaked. Meg. Angie. Calypso. Seb. Kara. Earl Wayne Jr."

"Yes!"

"I don't want to worry about them tonight. Sam's fine. And you're with me. That's all I want to think about tonight."

I don't know if Mickey means that, but I'm too tired to argue. It's well after midnight and I was already close to falling asleep by the time he showed up. I don't want to say no. I'm too happy to see him again. Too happy to think that there may be an end to all our troubles.

We drive for a long time before we get somewhere Seb considers a proper hotel. Cranky and tired, Seb stalks out of the car to get our rooms. Mickey won't stop glancing back at me in the rearview mirror. I hate that I've made him worry about me.

Seb helps us all inside and whispers something to Mickey in hushed tones before leaving us. I'm too numb and tired to think about how fancy the place is. Mickey puts his hand on my lower back to guide me into the room. I wince when he touches me. I feel… broken down. Exhausted.

Once he shuts the door, I take in the giant king-sized bed with snacks everywhere and water. I can't remember the last time I had a drink. Mickey puts his arms around me more forcefully. A hug. I need one of those really badly. I hug him back and he squeezes me.

"Baby," he whispers. "I finally have you back."

Mickey talks about me like I'm precious. It makes me nervous, but I can't deny how good it feels to have him hold me like this.

I don't want him to let go and I press my head to his chest, allowing myself to feel his warmth. His presence.

"I killed Keith. I think."

"I know," he whispers. "You shot him…"

"What? No. I didn't shoot him."

"Rain… Meg told me Keith was outside his ma's apartment when someone shot him."

"I put him there, but I didn't shoot him. I swear."

Mickey's fingers tighten on my waist.

"You ain't lying?"

"Not to you. Not after all we've been through."

I mean that. It turns out Mickey was right. I can't lie to him. He considers me for a moment and then appears to accept my answer.

"I love you, little lady."

The words send a rush through me. It's like teenage dreams I never allowed myself to have are coming true. I grin and press my body against his. Mickey feels so safe.

"I love you too."

Mickey's finger caresses my lip, and he sighs. "You are… trouble."

"I know. Everything I do goes wrong."

Mickey grins, a response I find surprising. It's my fault his dog died. I feel tears welling in my eyes as his last moments cross my mind. Maybe I didn't hate those dogs as badly as I thought.

"Why are you smiling?" I ask him.

"Because. Everything I do goes wrong too. But we don't have to be screw ups forever. When we lived together… for a moment in time, everything looked right."

"Then I got knocked up."

"Hey, that was my fault," he says.

He pushes hair out of my face and then pulls me against him with a firm grasp. Mickey…

I don't want to let go of him. And I won't have to. Not anymore. I let him kiss me and then I stumble forward against his chest, pushing him backward against the wall to the hotel. Mickey chuckles.

"Wow," he whispers. "You *really* miss kissing me."

"Shut up."

"We'll worry about Keith in the morning. Right now you need to get some rest."

No. The thought is urgent and insistent. I don't need sleep right now. I need something else. My palm travels from Mickey's chest all the way down his stomach.

"I don't need sleep," I say, my hand pausing at the waist of his pants.

He chuckles and then kisses me hard. Then he pushes me against the wall and holds me there, pinning me with his hips as our kissing gets more intense.

"Bed," I whisper. "Let's get in the bed."

36

PUBLIC RELATIONS

MICKEY FORD

She sleeps next to me peacefully, her small breasts rising and falling with each breath. I watch her bare stomach and press my pale hand against her smooth, dark skin. She is *so* pretty. Too pretty. Seb's right. I totally want to marry her. If I could, I'd marry her now. First, I have to wake her, which means ruining my princess's sleep. Hm…

I don't want to wake her yet because there's trouble ahead and Rain's like me… she has a way of making her troubles worse. Better for her to sleep. For now.

I order coffee and breakfast to the room while she sleeps and crawl into bed next to her, promising myself I'll wait patiently. But she's warm. And snuggly. And Rain. I let her little butt nestle in my crotch.

I remember what it was like to be her age. So innocent and sweet. And Rain's like I was — full of mistakes. I don't judge her for them and she doesn't judge me for mine. Not really.

Her sharp tongue is just her self-defense. But there's nothing for her to fear. Not anymore.

I kiss her shoulder, and that does the trick. She makes a grumbling noise and hides from the light spilling from the floor-to-ceiling windows.

"Wake up, angel," I whisper. "Daddy ordered coffee. And breakfast."

Rain stirs slightly, her murmuring growing somewhat coherent as she nestles even deeper in my arms. As her butt presses into my crotch, containing my arousal grows harder.

When she feels the warm thud of my dick pressing against her butt, her eyes snap open. She glances over her shoulder with one eye closed, giving me a suspicious Rain Wilson look.

"You're hard."

"Yup."

"We had sex for hours last night," she groans, trying to hide the pleased smile on her face.

"I know," I whisper, tasting the delicious sweat that dried on Rain's shoulder.

"How…" she whispers, but it's too late. I roll on top of her and Rain instinctively spreads her legs as our hips rest together. A little smile teases across her face.

"You're really hard," she says.

"Uh huh."

"Tell me that's not the breakfast you ordered," she whispers.

"Nope. Eggs. Bacon. Texas toast. OJ."

Her stomach rumbles, and Rain nervously covers it with her hand.

"Stop, that's making me so hungry."

I kiss her stomach and press my hand to it. She makes me feel really pale. But she's so... cute. I run my fingers over her hips and then stop on her stomach again.

"Good. You could use some food after what you've been through."

I kiss her again, warmth spreading through me. She cups her hand around my butt and pulls me close.

"I could," she whispers. "But I think we have time before they get here."

"Five minutes? I can make you cum in five minutes..."

I make her cum *several* times in five minutes, and Rain is awake. Very awake. She rests her head on my chest and runs her fingers down my abs. The food still isn't here.

"Mickey?"

"Uh huh?"

"What's it like being famous?"

"Great. Incredible. Shitty."

"If we're together... I won't have a choice," she whispers, getting all serious and quiet. Rain is usually quiet, but her nose flares a little when she's serious. It's very cute. I like her nose. It's round and perfect to kiss.

"I suppose not," I answer. I don't like to think about being famous. It's just being seen all the time. It's uncomfortable.

I feel discomfort rising in me.

"Then I need to do something with my life," Rain says, sitting up and considering me seriously. "I don't want our baby to think I never got it together."

"Well, little lady, you're eighteen, I'm twenty-eight. You don't have to have it together. That's why you've got me."

"I can't just let you take care of me."

"How many years did you take care of Keith?"

"A lot."

I can tell she's thinking about Keith and what will happen to her when she leaves here. Rain doesn't have to worry about that.

"Then let me take care of you."

"No. I can't. Not forever. I want to do something with my life."

"What do you want to do?"

"I don't know."

Mickey grins. "See? That's sweet. That's what being eighteen is about. I like it."

I kiss her again, but she pulls away, more serious than I've ever seen her.

"It's time for me to grow up. Maybe... I should go to college."

"College? I didn't know you wanted to go."

"My ex-best friend went to college. She's at Vanderbilt."

"Wow. Fancy."

"She's really smart, but she's a year older. Still, I could study, take classes."

"And I could pay," I offer. Rain raises an eyebrow.

"I can take out loans," she counter-offers.

"Hell no. If you get into college, I'll pay."

"What about us?"

"Baby, what about us? I have my career already. Wherever you go, I'll follow. I might have to find the nearest mansion with acres of land, but... I want to be with you. College. No college. Whatever you want."

"I'd have to study a lot."

"I can help."

She gives me a look.

"You're right. Probably best I leave the studying to you and you leave the songwriting to me."

"I'd ask LaShawn stuff about how she got in but... she hasn't been replying to me."

I freeze.

"What did you say your best friend's name was?"

"LaShawn. She always used to say she knew someone famous but... I don't think she was serious. She'd never tell me who it was. She worked on Celebz Leaked for a while but then... she quit."

"LaShawn *who?*"

I can feel a strange sensation coursing through me, like fate brought me to this hotel, this bed, this exact spot with Rain, so I could hear a name I hadn't heard in years. The name of a fourteen-year-old girl I caught in a position that was beyond compromising. The ages match up, but it ain't exactly like LaShawn is an uncommon name amongst African Americans.

When I pulled her off that table, I'd asked for it.

"What's your name, sweetheart? Tell me your name and then... run like hell and get help."

She was covered in piss. Blood. Semen. Snot. She cried her name out — both first and last out of habit.

"LaShawn Plummer," Rain says. My head swims. I stare at my girlfriend with transformed cobalt eyes. The world spins around me and I want Rain to repeat the name, even if I heard her well enough the first time.

"LaShawn Plummer."

"Yes. Mickey? What's wrong? You just got like... really pale. Is this a Caucasian emergency?"

She bounces up and presses her palm against my head. Fuck, her hand feels hot. I grab hold of her wrist and Rain freezes, considering me with a confused look.

"Your best friend's name is LaShawn Plummer?"

"I just told you that she won't even talk to me, so why does it matter?"

"It matters because it's her... it's the girl I found five years ago."

"In LA?"

"Yes..."

Rain's hand falls from my face, and she edges back.

"What? No... That can't be true..."

"I wouldn't forget that name."

"What about a face? That can't be the girl. Why would she be looking for a job with the *Rebel Blood* manager?"

"Show me a picture."

"For once in my life, I don't have a phone."

"Does she have social media?"

"Not after she quit *Celebz Leaked*."

"Fuck, Rain... I need to know."

"Why? She never went to the cops. It was five years ago. And anyway, LaShawn doesn't even talk to me. We were close, but... I screwed that up. Because of Keith."

I take her hand in mind and squeeze it. This isn't over, but I need to think. I need to let this news

"Listen, baby. If anyone is a screw up, it's me. College. Let's worry about you and college. What do you want to study?"

Rain shrugs.

"I used to like social media and being on my phone, but… that's where my problems started. I want to do something real. Like Meg. Or Angie."

"Or me…"

"Well, I can't play an instrument. Or sing."

"But what about… public relations?"

"Public relations?"

"You did an excellent job spreading horrible rumors about me while you were underage. I'd hate to see what you could do with some polish," I tell her.

Rain grins. "Public relations… do you really think I could do it?"

"Little lady, if I can become the most successful bassist in the South, you can do anything."

"You're forgetting the part where you have talent," Rain protests.

"Trust me, little lady. You have nothing but talent…"

I give her another big kiss as a knock at the door announces our breakfast.

37

LASHAWN

RAIN WILSON

"You seriously don't want a new phone?" He asks.

"No. I'm switching back to a flip phone. At least until I need one for classes."

"University of Southern California. Are you really going to make me move back to LA?"

"Maybe. If I get in."

"You'll get in."

"It's either there or Syracuse."

I'd be lucky to get into any public relations program, but Angie helped with my essay and Meg sent her corrections to both of us.

"I own a place in Ithaca. I'd love to have you in Syracuse. I'd get you a little city apartment and on the weekends... we could hang."

Mickey moves closer to me and puts his arm around me. Getting my life together. This feels... good.

"And when I give birth, you can raise the baby while I get my paper."

"Maybe my first solo album will be about being a dad."

"Solo album?"

Mickey shrugs. "We've all been thinking about going solo. We just have... one more project. One more album together..."

Rain stops walking and I stop talking. She points at a small, dingy looking yellow brick building. Yikes.

"Okay. This is it. Her student apartment."

"How did you find this again?" Mickey scratches his head and I still think some of my secrets ought to stay that way.

I shrug. "Little tricks I picked up from Celebz Leaked. Forbidden knowledge I'm only using because you're my boyfriend."

I'm wearing a white shirt and denim overalls and I feel like we match. A lot. Mickey's wearing a white shirt and jeans. All his tattoos on his arms are exposed and they're so sexy. He shoves his hands in his pockets.

"She won't answer," Rain grumbles as we get closer to the apartment door.

"It's student housing. Of course she'll answer."

Mickey knocks on the door, which I'm too scared to do.

"She was only fourteen. She probably doesn't remember me."

"I think she'll remember seeing Mickey Ford on the worst day of her life."

Mickey would have an unforgettable face even if he wasn't famous. We had to work hard to get him to LaShawn's door with no one noticing. We're on a college campus in Tennessee. This place is crawling with Rebel Blood fans and the totally staged announcement we're dating will be there in three weeks.

Mickey's PR wants to claim I'm a "model" and they're working hard to make my social media seem like I've always been a model. Whatever. After everything that's happened, I'm done with social media. For good.

I'm going to stop gossiping, stop lying and make a real life for myself. Finally.

Mickey had a hoodie on pulled up over his face as we walked across campus. Now it's tied around his waist like a 90s kid, but I don't judge. Mickey *is* a nineties kid. He knocks again.

"LaShawn?" He calls.

I glare. Maybe a *female* voice would be less appalling considering what she's been through. I clear my throat, but I can't bring myself to say anything.

Suddenly I feel like I made the wrong choice coming here. LaShawn made it clear she wanted nothing to do with *Celebz Leaked* and she wanted even less to do with me.

The last time I tried reaching out to her, she didn't even reply. Now I'm showing up with my boyfriend, who thinks she's the girl he saw getting gang raped. I don't want to believe it's true, but...

LaShawn came to *Celebz Leaked* for a reason the way all of us did. When we became online friends, she was always mysterious. When we met up in person in Nashville, her hate for Rebel Blood was real.

"They tell this rags to riches story but… it's not even real."

I got involved with Celebz Leaked because I was bored with my life and wanted an escape. But why had LaShawn started digging up dirt? And why did she leave?

Maybe she had a reason for hating Rebel Blood. I always thought that the celebrity she knew had met one of the boys and said he was an asshole or something. That happens.

But now, I'm wondering if there was more to the story and if LaShawn lied to me. Finally, the door opens. But it isn't LaShawn. It's a white girl with scary green eyes and a short haircut.

"Who are you?" She barks at me, glaring at me up and down with a look of disgust on her face.

"We're looking for LaShawn Plummer?" I say, trying to sound as sweet, polite and collegiate as possible. Mickey hangs back, his hoodie and sunglasses quickly replaced once he realizes the girl isn't LaShawn.

"LaShawn's visiting her brother this weekend, she's not here. I think she's coming back tonight."

"Okay. Thanks."

The girl opens the door wider and finally notices Mickey. She shrieks. Loudly.

"OH MY GOD. THAT'S MICKEY FORD. AHHHHHHHH!"

Doors fling open instantly down the hall. Mickey grabs my hand tightly.

"We'd better get going…" he mumbles.

We hurry down the side exit as the pounding of footsteps down the dorm hallway follows us.

"Faster!"

We barely make it out in time and we have to hide behind the bushes as the hordes of Vanderbilt girls tear LaShawn's roommate a new one for lying to them about Mickey Ford. Rebel Blood is serious business on a campus like Vanderbilt's. We're about to give up when I spot her. She walks through the gates of campus and I freeze, suddenly too scared to go through the plan. I grab Mickey's hand and point to her.

"That's her," I whisper. He freezes next to me, as if he's lost the courage to go forward.

"Well?" I ask him, the suspense killing me. If it's the girl, I want him to tell me. She was fourteen five years ago, which makes her nineteen years old, just like my LaShawn Plummer.

"It's her," Mickey says. "I'll be damned. It's her."

Then something strange happens. LaShawn stops on the path and glances over her shoulder. She doesn't notice us several yards away. A man comes down the path after her jogging.

"I'll be damned," Mickey whispers. "That's Earl?"

Both of us are surprised.

Earl Wayne Jr. stops LaShawn, tapping her on the shoulder. She flings her body around and then yells at him. Not like they're strangers. Like they're... friends? Family? She pushes him and then storms off toward the dorms, her face scrunched in rage.

"We'd better go," Mickey whispers. "I don't know what we just saw, but... we'd best get going.

We sit in Mickey's new car — a basic black sedan — drinking bubble tea and staring out at nothing.

"So Earl knows your best friend LaShawn," Mickey says with the enthusiasm of a real detective. I suck three of the tapioca balls into my mouth at once. Yum.

"Uh huh."

"And your best friend LaShawn is the same girl I saw."

"Uh huh."

"Do you think Earl knows?"

"I don't know. He's your friend."

"He's Earl. He knows so many women it's difficult to keep track of all of them."

"I guess he has his secrets too," I tell Mickey. "But LaShawn? What are the chances?"

"We'd better ask him," Mickey says.

Hello, Mickey, rule number one of stalking is you keep it a secret.

"We can't ask him now! Maybe we should... you know... follow him."

"Follow him? Is that how you got all your dirt on me?"

"Well, we lived 2,000 miles apart for most of the time I worked on the blog... so no."

"Fine. Just this once, we — shit... where'd he go?"

And just like that, we lost him. So much for our detective work.

38

EARL WAYNE JR.

MICKEY FORD

"Why are you afraid of Earl again?"

"He's big."

"Seb's big."

"Seb's scary too!"

"My friends are cool and they like you. Now come on... we need to grill him. I need my little detective on the case."

Rain protests again, which is funny because I just made her cum twice. You think she'd get a little more compliant, but who am I kidding? Rain has always been just as difficult as I am.

"C'mon baby," I whisper, running my lips over her neck. "Let's go find out what that big old redneck is hiding and maybe… your friend will change her mind."

"I doubt it. LaShawn hates me. I did something unforgivable."

"Like what?"

"I sold her out."

I raise an eyebrow. "The way you sold me out?"

"Yes," Rain says. "But I want to make it up to her. It was like the worst friend break up ever."

"What if I talk to her for you?"

"You always say the wrong thing."

"The wrong thing worked on you…" I reminder her.

Rain smiles. I'll never get tired of that innocent smile. She's incredible. I kiss her again and grab onto her waist. She giggles as my hardness presses into her.

"Again?"

"You get me hard *all* the time."

"I think it's your natural state."

"Maybe it is…"

Her lips are perfectly soft around mine and I want to enter her again, but then there's a bark and a whine outside the door. Rain pushes me off.

"We have to go to him. He isn't handling the grief well."

Sam…

Rain throws on my white t-shirt which looks like a dress on her as she pads across the floor to let me Doberman into the room. He whines as she pats his head and throws her arm around him.

"I'm sorry big guy... why don't you get into bed with us."

Okay, now I'm paying attention.

"I thought you didn't like him in the bed?"

"That was before. Now he's grieving. He needs us."

Sam gives me a triumphant look before nudging me aside with his nose and nuzzling against Rain who throws her arms around him dramatically.

"The two of you are..."

"Perfectly happy," Rain finishes, grinning and nuzzling the dog's neck.

Screw it, Earl can wait. My girl and my dog are curled up in my bed and it's only right I lie with them. We wake up a few hours later. Earl's still at his place and it's getting dark out. Rain and Sam are curled up together at the foot of the bed.

I kiss my little lady on the cheek and get out of bed to put on a shirt. Sam follows and I grab one of the guitars off the wall, sitting next to Rain as I sing her awake. She moves her head to my lap first, her tight braids falling around her cheeks as I play. When she wakes up, she wraps her arms around my neck and kisses me.

"That was beautiful."

"We could still work on that album together. Maybe that's what we can do after my last one with the band."

"I still can't sing."

"So what? Neither can half the singers out there. I can teach you. And anyway, you could be my muse. That's good enough."

We make love again until it's properly dark and we're properly late to meeting Earl. He said we could stop by anytime, so I ain't too worried about it, but Rain's nervous, I can tell.

Earl ain't like me and Seb. He's had plenty of time in large country homes. He always stays right downtown in the thick of the action. He has a small studio he keeps empty above one of the old Honky-Tonk bars and another penthouse a block away from the Hilton.

We're going to the penthouse. I text Earl several reminders to get his girls out of there if he has any staying over. I don't need Rain stumbling upon Earl's sex den. He likes drinking almost as much as he likes fucking and I can hear my ma's voice in the back of my head chiding me for bringing my girl to what she'd call a den of sin.

Rain seems more nervous about the sinner than the sins, anyway.

"If he hates me as much as Seb, I need an escape route."

"He'll be fine. Earl's untouchable."

"Lottie always said that."

Rain never brings up the girls behind Celebz Leaked, and she never brings up the fact that she watched them die. I still don't know what she saw that night, but I slip my hand in hers when I see her expression. Don't worry, woman... I'll protect you.

She allows me to take her hand and sighs.

"He's untouchable because, unlike the rest of us scumbags, Earl Wayne Jr. was born rich. His mother's family owns a NASCAR team and his father's family owns thirteen plantations and distilleries across the south. Rum money. That's what Earl comes from."

"Is that supposed to make him less terrifying?" Rain grumbles.

"He's more humble than his upbringing makes him sound. He spent most of his time raised by the maid, playing with her kids. That's all I know. He doesn't talk much about his family but… his name in the paper means their name in the paper so they sue anyone who publishes something negative."

"That explains a lot."

"Like I said, he's untouchable."

I greet the doorman and walk to the elevator. My fingerprint works on the P button that will shoot us 10 floors up to Earl's downtown palace. The doors open and the thick smell of rum permeates instantly.

We step out and the doors close with a final thud. Rain squeezes my hand and glances around at Earl's house. It's not what you'd expect, given the way he dresses. Earl dresses like a rich guy's idea of a cowboy, but his house looks like a vampire lives inside it. Everything is black, red and made of leather, like the world's bacheloriest bachelor pad.

"MICK DID YOU FINALLY GET YOUR ASS DOWN HERE."

Rain freezes and squeezes my hand. Earl's booming voice is enough to scare her, but then again, he has that effect on everyone. He emerges from his kitchen half naked with wet hair and a towel slung low around his waist. He puts his hands on his hips and looks us up and down at her. He has a big American flag tattooed on his chest and a short cropped blond beard.

"Finally. I thought you were scared to let her meet me or something," he says, his gaze fixing on Rain, who meets his eye but still looks terrified.

"Rain right?" Earl says, sticking out his hand to shake hers and crossing the room with a single step. Rain nods nervously and takes his hand.

"Y-yes… Nice to meet you Earl."

He guffaws and clutches her hand in both of his, shaking Rain's entire body like she's made of feathers. She winces as he finally releases her tiny hand from the grasp of his enormous paws.

"Welcome. Make yourself at home. I won't bother offering either of you a drink. Congrats on the baby, Rain."

"T-thanks," Rain stammers, sticking to my side.

"She's nervous," I explain to Earl. "So try not to scare her."

"Nervous? What's there to be nervous about? I don't bite."

He flashes her a smile, which doesn't exactly calm Rain down. He's still shirtless, the tattoo on his chest exposed as well as the rest of his hairy redneck body.

"Can you get dressed? Rain doesn't need to see you in your damned birthday suit."

"Are you sure?" he asks, winking at her.

"Out."

He leaves to get dressed for a moment and Rain relaxes.

"Okay. I just need to spit it out and ask him if he knows LaShawn."

"I can do that," I tell her, rushing to help.

"No. I need to do it," Rain says. "I can let you protect me when I actually need it. But I have to learn to face up to awkward stuff. Seriously. Leave it to me."

"How have you grown up so much?" I murmur, pulling her against me.

"Because," Rain whispers. "When you're in love with the right person... you have room to grow. Duh."

"You are ten times wiser than I was at your age."

We kiss and we don't stop until Rain realizes that Earl has been leaning in his doorway for about five minutes. Watching.

"Don't stop on my account. It looked like she enjoyed that."

Rain makes a little squeak and then fights her instinct to hide her body behind me.

"Earl, I have a question."

"Ask away!" Earl says, flopping down onto the couch and letting his long blond hair flow behind him.

"Do you know a girl named LaShawn Plummer?"

Earl sits up. Instantly.

"How do you know LaShawn? Is this a blackmail thing?"

"No!" Rain says, but then she seems to forget what to say and stumbles over her words as Earl gets red and clearly angry.

"What do you know about LaShawn?"

I step between them and scowl at Earl.

"Calm down, she only asked a question. LaShawn Plummer was Rain's best friend. And… she's the girl."

"What girl!?" Earl yells.

Shit…

39

WEIRD DREAM WORLD

RAIN WILSON

Of course, Mickey "forgot" to tell Earl about his ordeal. Sigh, we are both so spacey. He never had the same relationship with Earl he had with Seb. Earl was always older, wealthier, and just different, according to Mickey at least. He had his own life and his own situation before Rebel Blood.

But that doesn't mean he's a bad friend. I see him going through the emotional journey as Mickey tells his story. I am desperate to know the truth about how he knows LaShawn. It all adds up now. LaShawn actually knew someone in Rebel Blood. She was so good at keeping secrets. Better than me.

When Mickey finishes, Earl scowls. His hair floating around his head in a blond cloud, destabilized by Nashville humidity, makes him look like a lion or a Greek God.

"LaShawn's like a sister to me," he says. "You don't understand what this means."

"What does it mean?!" I blurt out. The suspense is literally killing me, and Earl Wayne Jr. moves as slow as molasses. When you're rich, all you have is time. Earl raises an eyebrow in my direction and then smiles.

"Five years ago, I offered to help LaShawn. I gave her a phone number, bought her a plane ticket, and while I worked on some business of my own, I gave her a contact and I told her... I told her they'd help her. Which means... this is my fault. Fuck. Fuck..."

Earl blanches as the realization hits him, and he buries his face in his hands.

"I'm going to kill Brent," Earl snarls. "He helped cover this up?"

"Listen, you can't kill Brent. Not yet," Mickey says, a statement that Earl doesn't take kindly to judging by the raging expression on his face.

"You don't understand, Mick. LaShawn's brother's in prison. She has no one to protect her. And now you're telling me that the girl I've known since she was... damn it! I need you two out of here."

Earl's mood shifts and my instincts tell me exactly what to do when a gigantic white man gets pissed off. I keep my eye on the elevator and then grab Mickey when I remember I need his fingerprint to get it to work. Mickey, like every white man ever, views all signs of danger as a challenge.

"We ain't leaving. If you know that girl and if she's hanging around you—

"Who said she was hanging around me?"

"Mickey..."

"We saw you," Mickey blurts out.

"Saw me? Are you stalking me? Or is it you?"

Earl's eyes fix on me, and I suddenly feel small and terrified. Mickey puffs his chest out.

"Don't look at her like that unless you want trouble."

"I'll look at her however I please."

"I'm warning you Earl, don't mess around," Mickey snarls.

"Mickey, let's go!" I scream, dragging on his sweater. Mickey's not listening because Earl just had to throw out another jab.

"You sure liked messing around when it was time to knock up a teenager."

"I told you not to talk about her like that," Mickey snarls.

"I thought you said not to look at her," Earl says. "I can talk about her however I want."

"You ignorant motherfucker..."

"Mickey... no!" I scream, but it's too late because my boneheaded rockstar boyfriend punches his band mate in the face. Hard. Earl stumbles backward, shocked, but he doesn't wait a minute before returning with another swing that Mickey barely dodges.

"Stop fighting!" I screech.

But they don't listen. Mickey grabs a chair and swings it at Earl, who groans as it hits him hard in the back. Shit...

"How could you wait this long before telling me?" Earl yells, grabbing a piece of his broken chair and swinging for Mickey's head. I shriek and throw a pillow at them, hoping to get them to stop fighting. If this doesn't work, I'll have to do the unthinkable... call another equally terrifying *Rebel Blood* band member to get in the middle. Great. The last thing I want to do is face Seb Jefferson, who I'm pretty sure could crunch my bones for breakfast like the giant he is.

Instead of calling Seb, I leap between them and stick my palms out.

"Stop! Or you'll be abusing a pregnant lady, which would be horrible if I leaked it to the press."

They both stop. Mickey stares at me, dumbfounded.

"You wouldn't do that, babe," he says calmly. Earl drops his weapon.

"I would never hit you. I'm sorry. 'Fraid I lost control of myself."

"Yes. You did. Both of you did. Now, whatever happened to LaShawn five years ago was a tragedy. Yes, Mickey should have spoken up earlier and Earl... maybe you should be more respectful. But you are best friends. America looks up to the Rebel Blood friendship. So talk things out. Please."

Earl sighs and shakes out his blond hair.

"She's right."

"I know," Mickey says proudly. "She's really smart. Soon, my girl will be going to college."

"College?" Earl says, raising an eyebrow. "Well, look at you. If you need me to put in a good word anywhere... I did a couple years at USC before I dropped out."

I can't deny that my ears perk up, but I have to solve this situation first.

"Thank you, Earl. Right now, we have more pressing concerns than my university admissions."

"Right. LaShawn. Well, neither of you has to worry. I'll talk to her."

His jaw tightens and beneath his cool exterior, I sense troubling emotions that he probably doesn't want to talk about with a stranger.

"That's it?" Mickey says.

"I've known her since she was a baby. Hearing this is like hearing something happened to my sister. I'm sorry I blamed you, Mick. It's just... it's my fault. I thought I was helping her. I thought..."

He trails off and then I notice that he's upset, fighting back painful tears. His fists clench and the tears disappear.

"I'm going to kill Brent."

"You can't kill Brent."

"Are you sure?" Earl snarls. "Because if he's responsible for this..."

"He could still end all of us. Yes, he has dirt on me from that night, but he had dirt on everyone else, too. I don't see how we'll get out of this.

"Listen, Mick…" Earl says. "I don't care what dirt he has. LaShawn is…"

"She's a good person," I chime in.

"Yeah. She is. And you were her best friend?"

"Yes," I answer sheepishly. "I ruined that with all the Celebz Leaked stuff."

"Maybe I'll talk to her for you. After all, she'll have you to thank."

"Um… for what?"

"LaShawn's in trouble. She refused to tell me what it was, but now I know. I'll take care of her."

"Not in like the mafia way, right?"

Earl guffaws. "She's funny, Mickey."

I use a line straight out of the Meg Nigel playbook.

"Confirm or deny, can you keep her safe?"

"Confirm. And I can tell her who she has to thank. Whatever you've done, Rain, I can tell you're a good friend."

"I wasn't though," I say, taking responsibility for my past. "I just want to be different now. I'm going to be a mom. It's time for me to grow up."

Earl grins.

"She's a keeper, Mick."

"Don't I know it." Then Mickey squeezes me tightly and I get the deep sense that everything will work out for us in the end. We love each other too much to let anything get between us.

"If LaShawn needs anything, please ask. I owe her so much so… if there's any way I can help, please tell me," I say.

"I will. Now if you don't mind, I'd like to call her."

"Sure. By the way… did you get Seb's invite?"

This is the first time I'm hearing of this invite so my ears perk up. Earl nods.

"Uh huh. I was thinking of bringing Lara."

"It's Angie's baby shower. Are you sure Lara's the best choice?"

"Do you even know Lara?"

"I know you have horrible taste in women," Mickey grumbles.

"She'll be fine. All my girls are fine."

Mickey gives him a doubtful look.

"Are we going?" I chime in.

"Of course. It's a Rebel Blood party at Seb's mansion. You'll finally get to see me rock some bass."

"I watch you play guitar every day."

"It's different in the band," Earl assures me. "Trust me, you'll like it."

Then he flashes me a mischievous wink. I can't believe it. Before I met Mickey, I was a total outsider, a curious creature on the outskirts of the Rebel Blood world. Now Earl Wayne Jr. is *winking at me.*

It feels like a weird dream world, but it's real. And it's my life. I have to start living it.

40

PLAIN AS A PINK DIAMOND

MICKEY FORD

Rain collapses on my bed against a heap of new clothes.

"None of these look good!" she moans. "I'm going to a celebrity event, Mickey and I'm normal. I'm plain!"

Her distress is apparent, but Rain is crazy. Plain? She's about as plain as a pink diamond.

"Babe, you'd look gorgeous in a potato sack."

This is apparently the wrong answer.

"Your ex-girlfriend is going to be there!"

"She's bringing a date. Don't worry about it. We're going to have a kid together. You don't have to worry about my ex."

"That's easy for you to say! My ex is a dead man, and yours is some skinny super model."

"I think I've moved on from super models. I prefer super Nashville girls with nice butts who understand guns and… you know. Stuff."

"So you like me because I used an illegal weapon and have a big butt?!"

"You're great at cuddling."

"That's not helping as much as you think," Rain grumbles.

"What about this dress?"

It's pink and tight. Very cute.

"Don't you think it's too slutty?"

"You could never be slutty," I tell her. "And anyway, you'd look cute in pink."

"Thank you," she relents, smiling and holding the dress against her body. Still no sign of our baby, but… he's in there. And I can't help but smile every time my eyes meet hers. Our big change is coming and I'm grateful for it.

"I can help zip you up."

"Is this just a cheap ploy to see me naked, Ford?"

"You bet your ass it is."

Rain smiles, which never fails to brighten my mood. See, Rain doesn't know that I have a surprise for her tonight. It's not just the night of Angie's baby shower. I have a little something special planned for her.

My girl…

She strips down to her skivvies, and naturally, I steal a glance at her body. She still has flawless skin. She still looks young and innocent beneath it all, but she acts older. She ain't the young woman who stole her way into my mansion all those months ago. I touch her, trying to remind myself that she can't break. She's strong. I kiss her shoulder.

"C'mere."

"Shouldn't I be getting that dress on?" She protests, but she already dropped the dress and she has her arms wrapped around me.

"Uh huh. After we make sure that we arrive fashionably late."

"And how are we going to do that, Mr. Ford," she teases, running her fingers down my chest. I inhale sharply, her soft fingernails scraping down my chest get me instantly hard. I pull her body closer to mine, yearning for more than just her warmth. I want to be closer. I want us to join.

I cup her buttocks with a firm grasp and pull her against me.

"I have some ideas that will make us very late. And if I remember correctly, I still owe you punishment."

"Yup. I think I owe you at least a year of sex."

"A lifetime, even." I lean in and kiss her. I love that feeling of kissing her and the way she melts in my arms. She makes me want to be strong. No more drinking. Nothing.

She pulls away and I press my lips against hers again. No. Tonight, the only tyrant she has to worry about is me and I plan to take her to bed and show her a thing or two. We stumble backward, kissing as we fall into bed for the third time that day.

Why can't I get enough of her?

She's already half naked, so it's my turn to join her. She practically rips off my shirt, savoring my muscles with her small hands running all over my body, touching and appreciating every inch of my physique. I'm not the athlete Seb is, so I'm more lean without the bulging muscles that America likes on our leading man.

Rain seems to like my leanness. She reaches for my belt, desperate to undo my buckle. There's a mischievous grin on her soft face. I'm hard. Naturally. This appears to be my permanent state around Rain.

"Go on," I urge her. "Take it off."

My buckle pops, and I feel a familiar surge of desire for her. My girl. She hurries my pants off and then strips me down to nothing. There isn't a single layer between us anymore, just the smooth, warm skin of our bodies pressed together.

"I love you," she whispers.

"I love you too," I murmur. "You're my summer rain… washing away everything bad that's happened to me."

"Isn't that a little corny?"

"I feel way more than a little corny around you…"

I kiss her neck and then her collarbone. She's everything to me. As I'm kissing her, Rain gets all squirmy and withdrawn.

She blurts out in her characteristic whisper, "I'm sorry."

"For what?"

"For everything. For being a bad person."

"If you judged me for all the bad shit I've done, how the hell would this work out?"

"But I judged you. I helped run a hate blog."

"Are you doing it now?"

"No."

"Exactly. And I'm not drinking. So stop fussing and come here..."

I grab her hips and pull her to me, kissing my way down her stomach until I can finally come to her spread thighs. They're practically glued together with desire already, but it's nothing compared to what Rain is about to experience.

I tease her tiny crop top over her stomach and expose her sweet stomach. Rain whimpers as my tongue runs over her navel. Her skin is so beautiful. I like touching it. I like teasing it. I can't believe I resisted for so long.

A low growl in my throat forces her to spread her lower legs apart. Rain whimpers as my tongue slides between her lower lips, teasing her flower open and exposing the tiny pink nub.

Her fingers rush to my hair — she likes my hair, and she especially likes digging her small fingers into the brown shaggy tangles. Rain pushes me closer to her wetness and my tongue darts out in a slow, teasing lick.

"Mickey..."

"I think you deserve *some* teasing tonight..."

She squirms in mock complaint, but we both know she likes good, long, teasing foreplay. I spread her lower lips again and Rain buckles, edging her hips forward as she desperately tries to convince me to quit my teasing.

No, ma'am... That won't work.

I rub my tongue around her lower lips, avoiding her clit but sucking on her pussy like an ice pop in summer. Rain bucks her hips up again, moving her soft little pussy over my face and running her lips along mine.

I chuckle and give her a deep kiss, which makes her moan... *loud.*

"That wasn't funny," she gasps as I pull my tongue away and laugh.

"Yes, it was. I like teasing you, little lady."

I pull her closer to me and lick her pussy again, more furiously. She cries out as I edge her close to a climax, focusing attention now on that tiny, hardened nub. *Oh, yes... that feels good.*

Rain's moans get louder and I drive my tongue deeper, spreading her apart with two fingers, which I slide slowly into her tightness. Her butt is like a pillow against my hands as I cup her cheeks, sliding my fingers inside her and working my tongue against her clit.

"Cum for me baby..." I whisper before I return my attention to her and Rain obeys. All the teasing gets her nice and warm, so when I push her over the edge, her cum gushes out of her, sticking to her thighs. She's soaked and my tongue slips out over her bared thighs, ready to lick every drop as I pull her close to my face.

Mine. She's finally all mine.

41

LITTLE LADY

RAIN WILSON

"Mickey... we're going to be late. We should go."

"No," he growls, kissing his way up my stomach impatiently and then pinning my hands over my head. "I want you now."

"You're just all horny because it's a baby shower and I'm... you know..."

"Pregnant with one of my sons?"

"We don't know if it'll be a boy."

"Hm... I'm guessing it will be."

"I wanted a daughter though so I could do her hair in those cute styles from YouTube."

Mickey laughs. "I've got long hair. You can put some of them corn rows in our son's hair."

"Corn rows? What do you know about corn rows?"

"I know they look nice on you," he whispers, touching the top of my braids, which are corn-rowed to my head. Mickey's never touched my hair so confidently and for the first time I don't flinch and I don't expect some weird comment like Keith always made about my hair.

"Thanks," I whisper. "Your hair looks pretty good too."

Mickey shakes his hair out, doing that American heartthrob thing, and I giggle, pulling him close to me and kissing him. Hard. I'm kissing Mickey Ford and if I'm honest with myself? It's a dream come true. He stops pinning my hands to the bed, which is perfect, because we roll over together intertwined and I get on top of him.

Mickey has a great dick for getting on top, and these pregnancy hormones aren't a joke. He gets this mischievous grin on his face like he can read my mind.

"I like the way you think, little lady."

"Pretty sure I'm a grown lady now," I whisper, leaning forward and kissing him. "So there…"

His hands rush to my hips, and the thrill of Mickey touching me never gets old. I don't think it ever will. I grab his big dick and place it at my entrance. It's not just big, it has this great curve that means when I ride him, he touches the clit with each deep stroke. I want that… I *need* that.

"C'mon," he whispers. "Take it all in, babe."

Guiding my hips, Mickey slowly lowers me onto his giant staff, which is so big and heavy that it leans off to the side. I bite my lower lip to prepare for the initial pain of getting Mickey's big dick inside me.

"Yes…" I whisper, balancing my weight on my palms, which press mercilessly into Mickey's bare chest, enjoying the feeling of his muscles and the visual of the tattoos covering his skin.

We moan together as I take the rest of him into me. I'm full and it feels so fucking good to have Mickey Ford inside me. I move my hips, but his dick is so big that just moving sends this wave of pleasure and pain through me.

"Easy baby," he whispers as I ride him. His voice is gorgeous. Everything about Mickey is gorgeous. My hips swivel and then bounce and Mickey groans, hair falling away from his face as he gives in to our mutual pleasure.

Our hips move together, mine rocking faster as I feel myself climaxing all over Mickey's hardness.

"Mickey… Oh my god… Mickey…"

And then the explosion overwhelms me. It's crazy how good it feels to cum and then I get all filled with giggles, which Mickey loves.

"You came really hard, huh?"

I gasp as his dick moves inside me.

"Yeah."

"I think we can make that happen again…"

Then Mickey grabs me and flips me on my back, edging his hips forward so he's even deeper inside me than before. Oh God…

He has so many ways to punish me and filling me with his big, hard cock is my favorite. He runs his lips over my neck and then teases my nipples awake as he makes love to me slowly.

I want to cum again. I need it. But again, Mickey slows down and engages in his habit of painful teasing. He hikes my thigh up around his tattooed torso as he makes love to me. I keep kissing him and holding him and wishing that we didn't have to go anywhere at all.

But Mickey's thrusting increases in place, and as I approach another orgasm, I can tell he's close. My nails dig into his taut muscles as we move together. Our bodies synchronize and our breathing becomes a single pulse until we finish in explosive climax, intertwined beneath the sheets of Mickey's enormous rock star bed.

His cum gushes out of him, coating my wetness with a thick spray of white seed as Mickey groans with pleasure. His muscles tighten and he kisses me as a final spurt erupts from his staff, spreading his thick juices on my inner walls.

He groans with pleasure and presses his hips into me deeper.

"I love cumming inside you," he whispers. "Is that bad?"

"No. Not bad… but it definitely got us into trouble."

"Don't you worry, little lady. This ain't more trouble than I can handle."

He kisses me again, and I feel torn. I have the urge to embrace Mickey's stamina and make love to him again, but I want to be fashionably late, not make a grand entrance that seems impolite.

"No," I whisper. "We should go."

"Look at you being all responsible."

"It's the new me. Like it?"

"I love it," Mickey whispers. "And I love you, baby. So let's get your sexy ass in that dress and hit the town. I couldn't be happier that you're my girl."

Mickey. He claims that he always says the wrong thing, but that can't be true, because when it comes to me, Mickey definitely always says the right thing.

Maybe meeting his ex-girlfriend won't be so bad. Maybe everything will end up okay in the end. Even the Keith situation worked itself out. Sort of. Char and Lottie apparently shot him in the end, according to the cops. I don't know if it's true, but I'm glad my name is out of the muck. Yes, I thought I killed Keith, but I didn't. So maybe I'm not a loser, or a screw up. Maybe I just made a lot of mistakes and if I don't start cleaning them up, I'll end up like Keith. Or Char. Or Lottie.

I don't want to be a loser. I want to be a girl who can hang with Mickey Ford. I want to be his girl.

Mickey leads me out of bed and tosses the dress at me.

"Let me see you put that on, little lady. I'm taking you out tonight."

I grin and press the dress against my body again. Yup, it's totally going to look amazing. And I have nothing to worry about.

42
THE TIFFANY'S ACCOUNT

MICKEY FORD

I park in the back and let myself in. Seb and Angie's fancy system announce me as I walk up the back staircase with Rain to find a very pregnant Angie with a very fussy Meg standing next to her.

"Rain!" Meg says, surprised. "Holy shit, you look... like a supermodel."

"Are you serious?" Rain asks, glancing back at her butt. "Are you sure my butt isn't too big in this?"

Her butt jiggles, looking more delicious than a peach cobbler.

"Does Mickey look like he's complaining?" Angie teases, throwing a wink in my direction that makes me turn redder than a summer tomato.

Meg notices my red face and cackles.

"What do you think, Mickey? How do you like Rain's butt in that dress?"

Damn, they're all looking at me now, especially Rain, and I don't want to tell them all the things I'd like to do to that butt.

"I like it. I like it."

It's shockingly easy to make me turn red and get all shy.

"You two are adorable together," Angie says. "Go on upstairs. But um… Seb told me to warn you that Tati's there."

Rain gives me a worried look that makes me want to kiss her, but I just squeeze her hand to let her know it's okay. We're here, it's a baby shower. There won't be any drama at all.

At least… not until I propose. Seb and Angie talked about this before. Angie doesn't want her baby shower getting in the press too much, so they want me to get down on one knee for Rain at the baby shower so my thing overshadows theirs and Angie can maintain her privacy.

"It's much easier to hide a baby shower beneath an engagement. And by the time you two have a baby… maybe Earl will get engaged!" She told me.

Good plan. Before tonight, I put my internet sleuth skills to use and dug up Rain's social media profiles. After scrolling through hundreds of her old comments and hate posts about me, I finally found the gold mine. Her "vision boards" from when she was fifteen years old.

Fifteen wasn't as long ago for her as it was for me and it was all I had to go on, so I hoped I made the right choice. I just want her to say yes to this crazy life of mine so she can go to college. I can record another album and we can retire together. We don't need much money, we just need each other and the kids — the shit that makes life worth living.

She's all I care about.

When we're upstairs, it's hard to miss Tati laughing loudly and leaning on Earl's shoulder while telling a story — probably one of her several stories involving old rich guys and yachts. Rain sticks close to me and appears to warm up a little when she sees Earl.

She might still want to talk about LaShawn. Earl notices her and sticks his arms out for a hug.

"Rain Wilson, I'll be damned. You're the reason they made pink."

Tati falls away from him as Rain trots forward, allowing the big old blond to give her a bear hug. When he finally lets her go, Rain immediately asks about LaShawn. Earl's smile fades into worry.

"I'm looking after her. Don't you worry."

"Do you think she'd talk to me?"

"I can make sure she does," Earl says. "Trust me."

Tati bounces forward, grabbing onto Earl's arm and giving me a big Hollywood smile.

"Mickey! Aren't you going to introduce me?"

"Hey, Tati. Um... this is Rain. Rain, this is Tati."

"His ex-girlfriend," Tati says, sticking her hand out for Rain to shake. Rain shakes it, looking petrified.

Tati glimmers at Rain.

"So... who are you then?"

"She's my girlfriend."

"Oh?" Tati says, wrinkling her nose. "That's new."

"Not really," I say, grinning. "Just private."

"I can see why you'd want to keep it private," Tati says. "She's gorgeous."

But she says the last part with a strange tone to her voice.

"Nice running into you."

I pat Earl on the back and take Rain's hand. I don't know if Tati means to be passive aggressive or anything, but I don't feel the need to force Rain to stand around listening to it.

"That was nice…" Rain says. "I think."

"Don't let her get to you. Kara's in the main room with the cast of *Nashville Summer*. *We* can go in there."

"The cast of Nashville Summer?! Do you think I could meet Rodrigo?" Rain whispers excitedly.

"Sure. Why don't you go on in, I'll get Seb to help me bring the baby gift upstairs."

"It's enormous," Rain says. "Sure you don't want my help?"

"You're gorgeous. Go mingle, little lady. I'll be right back."

It's torture to be away from her for any meaningful measure of time, especially when she looks like this and especially considering what we were doing earlier. I find Seb hiding from the drinks in the kitchen with a sad wine glass filled with chocolate milk. He shoves it across the counter as I walk in.

"Were you just…"

"Shut up," he grumbles.

"Parties are hard."

"Yes," Seb snarls at me, embarrassed that I walked in on his weird sobriety trick. "They're hard. But I'm doing this for Angie and our baby. Callie's with her gran for the night for the first time. It's hard."

"Your mom?"

"Uh huh. They fell in love with each other. And I thought my ma would be… I don't know. Different. Racist, I guess."

Seb glances wistfully at his chocolate milk, but then appears to change his mind.

"Let's get the gift inside, Mick."

We grab the giant pink wrapped box from the car, even if we could have assistants do it. We need to have a little talk in private.

"Think she'll say yes?" Seb asks.

"Yeah. I hope so."

"Tati's been asking strange questions. Did you warn her?" Seb says in a hushed tone.

"Why would I warn her?"

"I don't know… because she's crazy about you? And I mean… you didn't exactly end on the best of terms."

"I don't remember that being my fault."

"You were using. You don't remember anything being your fault."

"I just saw her. She was fine."

"Just be careful, that's all," Seb grumbles. "Women get funny around marriage."

"Didn't you just hire a backup wedding planner for Angie when she specifically told you not to?"

Seb glares. "Shut. Up."

We get the gift to the foot of the stairs when we hear a loud shrieking sound coming from upstairs. Not just one person screaming. Several.

"What the fuck is happening up there?"

Seb runs up the stairs, taking them three at a time. I bound after him as fast as I can. He pushes the door open and runs out into the main room for entertainment to find everyone's backs against the wall and Rain Wilson in the middle of the room, with a gun pressed to her head.

I know Seb's eyes are darting around the room for Angie, but my eyes fix on Rain and my ex-girlfriend… Tati. Last I checked, tiny handguns weren't part of the baby shower dress code, but damn it, Tennessee will do this to you.

Everyone is scared out of their fucking minds that Tati is going to shoot someone, but I know she won't hurt Rain. That wouldn't exactly look good to her online following.

"Tati! What are you doing?"

Everyone, especially Seb, looks at me like I'm crazy. I'm just surprised Earl doesn't also have a gun and that he doesn't have it pressed to Tati's back. My eyes scan the room for a split second and Earl isn't even there…

"I know you're going to propose to her, you idiot!" Tati screams. "We still share a Tiffany's account."

Fuck. This has to be the worst way this could have ever gone done.

43

CAPTIVE

RAIN WILSON

It's me again, captive. Again. This time, I don't even care that there's a gun to my head because my soon-to-be-murderer will probably kill me, anyway. I need to react to this.

"Propose to me?! And who shares a Tiffany's account?"

"You made me share that account!" Mickey snaps at his ex. "And I forgot."

She scowls at him and presses the gun harder into my head like she's trying to use it as a drill. I freeze, forgetting my indignation as well as the mixture of several other emotions brewing inside me.

"That's not all, you idiot," Tati snaps. "You leaked my nudes."

"What? Tati, I'd never do something like that?"

"Oh yeah? Then explain to me how there was a new *Celebz Leaked* post two hours ago with a picture of my boobs from our vacation to Santorini that only you could have?"

"Tati, I swear I had nothing to do with it."

"Really? Because I got a letter in the mail that was all creepy that told me you and this woman were to blame."

"It's not true… and did you have to do this at a damned baby shower? You have my number."

"I didn't have to do this at the baby shower, Mickey. I had to do *this* at the baby shower to give all those freaks something much more exciting to talk about than my damned boob job."

Then, Tati points the gun at Mickey's chest and shoots. I scream instantly as Mickey pauses for a moment before stumbling backward. He falls to the ground slowly, but it still looks like it hurts.

Half the room runs away and only a few stick around to try to undo the terrifying scene unfolding before us. I think Meg got Angie out — thank goodness. She's way too pregnant to remain in the middle of a shootout.

"Those were totally supposed to be blanks!" Tati screams, her Russian accent getting thicker as her emotions bubble to the surface.

This woman is irking me! I push her out of the way when she goes into hysterics. She shot Mickey. Fuck. She shot him right in front of me and now…

Seb already has his phone out and two of the guys who play country singers on *Nashville Summer* restrain Tati and take her gun.

But there's a lot of blood and it's coming from Mickey's chest. I'm no expert, but it looks like it's way too much blood. My heart quickens and I hold his hand.

"I don't have much time, do I?" He whispers.

"Stop it, you idiot," I whisper. "Don't say that. Seb's calling someone."

"I'm sorry, baby."

"Rain, get away from him," Seb says. "Don't look. He'll be fine."

I glance at Seb, and I can tell he doesn't believe that. But what choice do I have?

"No!" I scream at Seb. "I'm not leaving him. I'm never leaving him."

So when the EMTs come, I fight and end up in the back of the ambulance with Seb and Mickey. It doesn't matter how rich you are back here. It's still terrifying. And there's still blood. I still want Mickey to open his eyes, but he hasn't opened them since we left the house.

Then it hits me... I killed him. I killed Mickey Ford, and this is a punishment for everything bad I've done. Because this is the last time Mickey will end up in the back of an ambulance, it'll be all my fault, and the worst part is... I love him. I love him so much more than I thought I could love anyone.

I don't want Mickey to die. But it's too late, isn't it? You don't survive a shot to the chest. Tati's going to prison, I imagine, but that doesn't even matter. I don't care about punishing people or revenge anymore. I'm going to be a mom. It's time for me to grow up...

When they take Mickey out of the ambulance at the hospital, they have to separate us and take him to an operating room to get the bullet out. I ask if he's still alive, but no one cares to answer my questions, or they don't want to tell me he's dead.

I guess this is how my great love ends. All I can do is sit in the waiting room with Seb, who's all big and angry until Angie and Meg show up, both worried, both shaken from the baby shower gone wrong, and both ready to fight.

"Rain!" Meg calls to me, rushing me and wrapping her arms around me. "Don't worry. They'll help him. They'll get the bullet out. He'll be fine."

"He won't be fine," I whisper. "And it's all my fault… I'm going to be a broke single mom, just like my mom said I would be…"

I sniffle and bury my face in her shoulder. Meg stiffens her back. She's one of those people who always tries to be the strong one. I can't deny that she's always been there for me.

"No," Meg says. "Don't you say that. He'll be fine. You'll get into college and ten years from now, you'll look back at this and you'll be so proud of yourself for getting through it."

I want to let go of her, but I can't. Angie and Seb hold each other tightly. Seb whispers to her in a deep voice, keeping a hushed tone so only Angie can hear. And then she falls against him, her large pregnant stomach pressing into Sebastian. There's a flutter in my chest. I'll never have that again with Mickey if he doesn't wake up.

And what about our baby? My heart feels like it's already broken. Meg notices the change in my expression and slips her hand into mine.

"Come on. Let's go for a walk."

"I don't want to leave."

"You need fresh air. So come."

Reluctantly, I follow Meg. She's the sort of person who commands attention everywhere she goes, especially with her new neon yellow Jimmy Choo pumps and her white tweed Chanel suit — very sorority girl meets law firm, meets afrocentric sista. (Meg also wraps her hair in a yellow pattered fabric that matches her shoes).

Once we're outside, she exhales and leans against the door, giving me a once over.

"Finally," she whispers.

"What?"

"We need to talk. As a family."

"What happened?"

"Nothing. It's just... Mickey will make it and then you'll be pregnant and then... I just want to make sure you don't end up with another Keith."

"Mickey's not like that."

Keith would have never taken a bullet for me.

"I know. But I want you to know that if anyone ever fucks with you again, I will send Logan after them and I'm not responsible for what he does."

"You two are still…"

"Together. Yes. It's complicated but… we love each other."

"Yeah."

"Listen, Rain… The *Celebz Leaked* stuff might appear to be over, but I've been looking into it and someone just moved the server. Let's assume that whoever did that just wants to archive the website but… it's impossible to trace who owns it and that worries me."

"Do you think they're still going to… you know… have everything *Celebz Leaked* did?"

"No. The cops have Charlene and Charlotte's hard drive. The dirt is gone. But they're rock stars. They always have more dirt. You're more than capable of looking after yourself but… I have your back."

I nod politely and Meg giggles.

"I don't know how you worked one over on Mickey Ford. Care to share advice?"

I shrug. Meg doesn't need to know all the dirty details of how we got together.

"Go after what you want, Rain. You deserve all of it. Remember that."

"What about Mickey?" I whisper. I can't bear the thought of what might come… next.

Meg offers me a sad expression.

"We'll go back in. Come on."

Her hand squeezes mine and I realize that she's putting on a pleasant face for me, but Meg isn't sure Mickey will make it either. That scares the crap out of me.

44

SEB'S UGLY MUG

MICKEY FORD

Fuck. When I finally open my eyes, it only takes me a few minutes to adjust. The doctors and nurses stand over me and I half expect to see Seb's ugly mug knocking my lights out for instigating a shoot out at his baby shower.

Shit.

"Mr. Ford?" A gruff-voiced doctor intones.

I make a sound that feels like speaking, but isn't. At all.

"Put him on a drip. Let me know how he's doing in a few hours."

The doctor wanders off, but the nurses stand around whispering in hushed voices. They probably all had to sign NDAs just to get in here if Seb Jefferson has anything to do with my accommodations, which he probably does. This is Seb's work through and through.

One nurse approaches me and touches my forehead with a cool hand. My eyes flutter toward her and she steps back like she just put her hands on a painting in a museum.

"I'm sorry."

"My name's Nereida," she says. "I just moved to Tennessee with my husband and kids. I'll be looking after you for a while. Do you remember what happened?"

"Yeah."

"Do you remember your name?"

"Mickey Ford, last I checked."

I flash her a smile and Nereida takes a step back. She's pretty. But now, pretty women just make me think about the only pretty woman I want to put my hands on.

"Rain."

"No, it's sunny out. Typical Nashville, it'll probably rain later."

"No… I mean… my girlfriend. Is she here?"

"Oh! Her name is Rain. That makes sense. She's outside. The nurse is talking to her. We can't allow her in yet."

"Okay."

"You were legally dead for a minute and a half. You've been out for a few hours since they revived you. The doctor just wants to make sure you're fine."

"Dead?"

"Sorry. Some of the others don't agree but… it's better to be honest, isn't it?"

"Yes, nurse. I agree."

"I'll see if I can pull some strings. If she's the first thing on your mind, she must be really important to you."

"She's beyond important to me," I say. "She's everything."

Nurse Kelly looks like she wants to melt in the ground. I was being honest, but I would have said anything to get her to bring Rain in here.

The next person to burst into my hospital room is the opposite of Rain Wilson. Instead of a short, sexy black girl, Seb's mean mug peers around the door, his platinum hair sticking up in spikes around his exhausted, angular face.

"You fucker," he grumbles, looking right past Nereida Kelly at me like he's going to kill me. He strides into the room and the nurse hurriedly evaporates. Seb could strike the fear of God into a moose or a bear if he tried.

"Can you stop fucking dying on me?"

"I'm alive. I made it."

"Made it? Until I have to pull your scrawny little neck out of trouble again."

Before Seb can make good on his threats, the door opens again and instead of the nurse, it's her. Rain.

"You won't have to do that, Seb. I'll take care of him."

Seb glances over his shoulder at Rain suspiciously.

"Rain? Are you allowed in here?"

"No. But I have my ways. And I had to see Mickey."

I grin. But then Rain walks up to me and slaps me. Hard.

"OW!"

"I thought I killed you!"

"Why?! You didn't even shoot me!"

I rub my face and Rain looks at her hand as if the damned thing acted against her will.

"It's my fault Tati shot you."

"Actually, Tati's in prison and Mick never told you why they broke up," Seb says.

"Seb!" I grumble. "I don't need her worrying about Tati."

"Not anymore," Seb says. "But she's always been a little dangerous around Mickey. It comes with the territory. You know... using."

"I'm not going back to that," I insist, touching Rain's hand as she slips closer to my bed. I'm not going anywhere I can't have Rain Wilson.

"That's not what I'm worried about. I bring drama!"

Seb scoffs.

"Are you serious? Believe it or not, this is the *least* amount of time Mickey's spent in a hospital annually since I've met him. Somehow, you have a way of keeping him out of trouble."

"I just overheard that he was legally dead for ninety seconds!"

"Overheard?" Seb grumbles, raising a suspicious eyebrow.

"I might have escaped from Angie and Meg to come up here. But I don't care about that. I just had to make sure you were okay."

I grip down on her wrist. Tightly. I'll be okay as long as Rain doesn't leave me. My chest hurts as I hold on to her, but with the painkillers or just the relief from holding her, all I feel is pleasure.

"I still want to marry you, if you'll have me," I tell her, kissing her cheek. "I don't know where the ring ended up."

"I have the ring," Seb says. "Tati had pocketed it before the cops came, but I er... I have my ways."

Seb's "ways" usually involve threats and his imposing physique. He drops the ring in my hand and I hold it up against Rain's.

"Will you say yes, little lady?"

"You took a bullet for me, Mickey. I said yes before you hit the ground. I love you. I love you more than I've ever loved anything and..."

"Stop," I say gruffly. Rain doesn't need to spill her heart out to me for me to know what's in it.

"I love you. And I'm the one who owes you, Rain. I might have gone back to drugs if you didn't keep me on my damned toes."

"That's not true."

"Oh, it is true. From the moment I saw you, I knew it would be you and me, kid."

"Kid?" Rain says, folding her arms and popping her hips with just the right amount of sass.

"Not anymore, I suppose. Now come, give me a kiss. I can hardly move."

She kisses me and despite my lack of movement, I slip the ring on her finger and my hand over her butt. Rain squeals and then climbs on the bed with me, apparently oblivious to Seb. It's not like Seb hasn't watched me kiss girls before — among other things.

He clears his throat, but Rain doesn't stop. She grabs my cheeks and carefully avoids pressing down on me as she straddles me and kisses me like it's the last night we'll have together.

"I love you, Mickey."

"I love you too, little lady."

"I'll give you two some time alone," Seb says. "And er... I'll make sure none of the nurses come up. You might want to take that finger off the heart monitor before you set it off."

Seb casts a nervous glance at the heart monitor, racing with proof of my love for Rain Wilson, the girl who nearly killed me. The girl about to have my baby.

My true love.

45

RAIN & MICKEY

Three months later...

RAIN

Angie gave birth three hours ago. Meg sent me a text message with a picture of a little blob shaped like a potato and wrapped in blankets with a little blue hat on his head. *Jacob Jamaica Jefferson.* It's a very celebrity name. I don't know if that's Angie's fault or Seb's.

The blogs are going crazy with speculation, but no pictures of little Jacob have leaked yet. I hope none ever will. He's adorable, and he deserves to stay far away from the mess. I feel a weird flutter in my stomach. Soon, I'll be the one with a tiny little potato. I wonder if he'll have Mickey's eyes. Or she.

I look at another picture from Meg which is even cuter than the first.

Callie's in another picture, glancing at her new baby brother curiously. At least Mickey and I created enough of a stir that Angie got exactly what she wanted from the press at her baby shower, and our engagement news was extremely well received.

I still have to wait to hear back from USC in the spring, but that means Christmas with Mickey and our baby, who isn't enormous or anything, but who I can now feel like a real entity in my belly. It's weird. No one prepares you for motherhood — at least my mom didn't.

Ugh... my mom.

I finally have to let her meet Mickey. Tonight. This is going to be... wild? Stupid? My parents were still mourning Keith a month ago. I probably shouldn't have let them find out about my marriage and baby via a gossip website — less controversial than Celebz Leaked, but still a gossip site — but I couldn't bear the thought of going back to them and explaining everything.

As far as they were concerned, Keith and I only broke up because he was killed in a tragic robbery gone wrong outside his mama's place. My parents are definitely not going to be chill about Mickey Ford. The best part? Mickey made this much, much worse by inviting his West Virginia family to a dinner party that was already going to be a nightmare.

Listen, I know Mickey's a good guy, but he had a freaking confederate flag tattooed on his thigh before we met. I can't imagine what his *family* might have tattooed. A thin blue line flag on their butt cheek? Donald Trump's face as a tramp stamp?

Mickey's reassurance isn't that helpful.

"Don't worry. They're religious. They hate tattoos."

"Wait, what do you mean, religious? Like Christian or something?"

Has Mickey forgotten the fact that we aren't married? The engagement ring is perfect, and I don't want to get married with a baby bump. But if his parents are religious, won't that be a problem?

Mickey explains how religious he means exactly. "I mean… no sex before marriage, no alcohol, no smoking, no drinking, no tattoos, no vices, no gambling, no usury."

"Usury? Mickey, is that even a word?"

"Yes, it is a word. A church word."

"What does it mean, then?"

Next thing you know, we're sitting on Mickey's new couch — black leather, which Sam loves — hunched over his phone to look up the word. We're going to get a new dog soon. Sam's too lonely and we're worried about how he'll handle the baby. Mickey wants another Doberman, but I love pits.

"See. I told you it was a word," Mickey says triumphantly, taking my phone and tossing it across the room.

"Mickey!"

"Ha. I knew something."

He puts his hand on my stomach and pushes me back so he can kiss me.

"Mickey!" I whisper. "Our parents are going to be here soon and there's staff in the kitchen."

His hand moves eagerly to my thigh.

"I can't help it. You smell… pregnant. It's hot."

"I am pregnant. But thanks for saying I smell."

Mickey's not listening. At all. He slides his hand up my thigh and then squeezes.

"Please…" he whispers. "Don't deny me access to your cunt when we're about to have the most uncomfortable dinner of all time."

I sit up straight.

"I thought you said it would be fine!?"

"Well… that was a lie to make you feel better babe."

I could slap Mickey Ford in his face. But my heart still does that weird little flutter when I look in Mickey Ford's eyes.

"Mickey!"

I try to get off the couch, but Mickey pulls me against him and when my hands press to his chest I feel abs. Hot abs. Mickey's hot abs. I already have an insane mental picture of those gorgeous abs covered in tattoos and I find it *very* difficult to pull away. I don't want to stop touching him. Ever.

"Okay. Sorry I lied but… my mom thinks we're married so we're going to have to… you know… pretend."

"But my parents know we aren't married. This is the worst lie ever."

"No, it isn't. It's simple. We got married at the hospital. We can say that."

"You get a certificate when you get married! They could easily verify this, Mickey. Your every move is in the press."

"What? You get a certificate?"

"Mickey!" I plead with him. His cheeks turn *really* red.

"Okay. We can fix this. I'll simply die on the spot," I grumble.

Mickey laughs.

"Stop."

"Stop?! I'm going to turn nineteen in three days and your parents are going to kill me for being black, knocked up, not Christian, jobless and unmarried."

"Well, they won't kill you."

"Thanks, Mickey. Thanks."

"Don't worry, little lady. I'll look after you. Now come here."

I lean forward and let him kiss me because... he's Mickey Ford. I never stood a chance, did I? From the moment his crazy blue eyes met mine, I had to have been smitten. My fingers rush to his hair. I love grabbing onto the shaggy strands and I especially love his tattoos. He has a new one on his wrist. *Rain.*

I run my fingers over it and Mickey chuckles, pulling me onto his lap.

"We can be quick," he whispers. "I know we can."

"This has to be one of our worst ideas yet."

"Oh, yeah?" Mickey says. "I think I have a way we can make it worse."

"How?"

"We could try… anal."

"Mickey!" I squeal, smacking him again. Mickey laughs uproariously.

"I'm just playing, little lady. Take those clothes off. I need a little something before dinner…"

His large biceps wrap around my waist, and I lean against Mickey, kissing him hard. Yes, yes, yes.

46

THE HISTORY WE HAVE

EARL WAYNE JR.

LaShawn. I finally see her coming back to her room. She knows I'm onto her and she's gone out of her way to avoid me. I normally wouldn't have time for things like hunting down LaShawn but… I'm newly and permanently single.

My best friend Mickey told me something that shocked me and everything I thought about Hollywood. I loved LA. I love Nashville. I love every damned place I put my boots. But there's someone I love more than any of that, someone who I hurt. She's like a sister to me. LaShawn.

I have to make amends for what happened. I have to talk to her about what I did.

I wait for her to walk into the building and I glance at my watch. She'll be back in her room in one minute which means I have one minute to justify why I broke into a college student's bedroom at eight in the evening. This ain't exactly my best plan.

I start tossing my baseball to calm down. It's always helped with my ADHD. I can catch it even in the dark. I love the feeling of the smooth leather. It reminds me of the drums. I can always hear a beat. 24/7. And now, I can hear the beat of LaShawn's footsteps coming down the hall. She's had the same walk since she was a kid, believe it or not.

She'll probably shriek like a banshee when she opens the door and finds me in her bed. Yup, I know LaShawn like the back of my hand. Her feet stop in front of the door and I catch my baseball, preparing for death.

LaShawn opens her door and screams bloody murder when she sees me on her bed. After a few seconds, she realizes its me, pulls her backpack off her back and flings it at me.

"Earl, you idiot!"

I try not to laugh at her. She's really scared and since I know what she's been through, it's not exactly a laughing matter. I just had to see her. It didn't matter how I got here.

"Hey."

"What the hell are you doing here?!" LaShawn yells, her chest fluttering like a hummingbird. Damn. I must've really scared her.

"I'm tired of you avoiding me."

"You are so arrogant. I'm not avoiding you."

"Oh yeah? Then why did you scream when you saw me?"

"You broke into my fucking bedroom!"

"It wasn't that hard."

She makes a little growling noise and tries to leave the room, but I am way faster than LaShawn. And bigger. And I know her far too well. Touching her wrist was the wrong move. She flings me off with surprising force for a girl that size.

"Don't touch me, Earl. What do you think Devonte would think if he knew you were in my room in the middle of the night?"

"I already told you that Devonte wants me to protect you."

"That is a joke," she snarls. "A big fucking joke."

"We love you, LaShawn."

Three months since I've seen her and she still looks at me like she wants to kill me. I've given her space but I can't stand it anymore.

"Don't you dare!" She screams. This time, I can tell she's actually angry. I held her in my arms when she was a toddler. I know what she looks like angry. "Don't you dare pull that shit with me. It might work on Devonte, but we are not your siblings, Earl. We were the maid's kids. You got everything in your life handed to you but Devonte got jail. And I got a student loan so big, I don't know if I'll ever be able to pay it off. So stop. We don't want your help and I don't want you in my life."

I bristle. It's not like there isn't an element of truth in what she's saying. Yes, LaShawn was *the maid's* kid. *The maid* has a name. *The maid* remembered my birthday. My father never did.

"I'm sorry about what happened to your mom."

"Your dad raped her," LaShawn snaps. "He's disgusting and your entire family is disgusting. Why do you even go visit Devonte? Do you get some sick thrill seeing a black man behind bars?"

LaShawn knows me as well as I know her. I was one of the first boys she knew. Our fifteen year age difference made me seem like a man to her far before I was one. And now... she's all grown up. And hates me. She doesn't understand how much I love her family. How sorry I am for what happened.

"Because... he's like a brother to me. I don't hold it against him what he did," I tell her. And I mean it. I visit Devonte because I love him and when he gets out, I will take care of my brother. For life.

LaShawn continues speaking, her voice quaking with rage. "Maybe you should hold it against him. He put your father in the hospital and he'll do it again when he gets out. Stick with your kind, Earl. We'll stick with ours."

"You are my kind," I tell her, grabbing her hand again. This time, I won't let get get away. "I watched you grow up."

"Let go of me."

"I don't want to."

She pushes me. Hard.

"I don't have time for this, Earl. I have to go to Rain's house."

"Rain?"

"She says she's sorry and I'm going to forgive her. Now that bitch is dead, I don't have anything to worry about."

"Little harsh."

"No. It's not harsh," LaShawn snaps.

My chest tightens. It's my fault she became like this. She used to be sweet. Gentle, even. But LaShawn had to toughen up and that's my fault.

"I'll take you. I know the way to Mickey Ford's."

"You aren't invited. It's a family thing."

"Rain's your family?"

"Her mom and I mom went to the same church when we were kids and I'm giving her a chance."

"Oh."

"Whatever, I don't have time. I'm just here to change. I'm already running late."

She glares at me like that's going to get me to leave. Oh, LaShawn... I fold my arms and glare back.

"Stop it," she snaps.

"What?"

"Stop glaring back. Just leave."

"I'm coming with you."

"I'm not bringing *you* as a date to Mickey Ford's private dinner party. I don't even want people knowing that I know celebrities."

"Ouch."

"It's awkward and embarrassing. I'd rather focus on my studies."

"I still want to take you out."

"Do you understand the word 'no' Earl?"

"Yes."

She glares harder.

"Please," I tell her. "Can we just talk tonight? It's not a date. I'm fifteen years older than you."

"Right. Like you Hollywood people don't all date kids," she snaps.

"Is that a yes?"

"Did it sound like a yes?"

"Okay. I think you'd look good in something… blue. To match my jeans jacket."

"Earl, I'm going to kill you."

"I know."

"You aren't coming."

"I'll give you a ride."

"Earl!"

"Your brother told me to protect you. I don't know what you need protecting from since you have all the charm of a wolverine, but I care about Devonte. Can't you at least give him peace of mind?"

Weaponizing her brother is low but… it's all I've got. We both love him. That's the only reason she hasn't truly ripped my head off.

"You left me alone for three months. I thought you gave that up."

I shrug. I definitely didn't leave her alone. I just watched from a distance. I think better than to admit all this to her.

"Fine," she says. "But you'd better go mingle the entire time."

"Are you going to wear blue?"

"No," she snaps. "I'm not doing anything you want."

"Except going to the party with me."

LaShawn gives me a bitter glare.

"This is why I hate you."

I thought it was the other reason. You know… the fact that nearly six years ago, I gave LaShawn a contact in Hollywood who flew her out to LA promising her dreams would come true and had her raped.

I never knew until recently. Not until Mickey Ford told me the details and I pieced together all the half-truths and the clues. Six years, she never told me.

I never knew how the meeting went, just that she wanted nothing to do with me. I didn't know what would happen. I can see on her face that she blames me. She thinks I set her up.

I don't blame her. My father touched women. Lots of women. He never quite made it to prison.

But I'm nothing like him. I won't hurt LaShawn. No one will ever hurt her again without going through me first.

"Let's go to Mickey's. I promise you can call me every name in the book on the way there."

"I'm in college, so I know a lot of names now."

"Good. I'd like to hear you call me every single one of them," I say to her.

"Good, big head. Now *leave*. I need to change into a dress that looks half decent."

"Something blue," I tell her, with a cheeky grin.

Click here to order the next book.
THE END

EPILOGUE

Hey motherfuckers.
I killed someone.
I know, I probably shouldn't admit this on the internet, right?
Let's call it satire.
I just had to get my hands on this blog.
I needed to share my big scoop with all of you.
So yes, I stole *Celebz Leaked*.
I killed for it.

<u>This tired little website has gone on too long with half-truths and dumb celebrity gossip.</u>
That's going to change.
I'm going to get the truth about everyone from the closest sources.
Leakers, you're the best at digging up dirt, but let's be real... you need someone who doesn't just dig things up.
You need someone willing to get dirty.

I'll need to lay low for a while collecting dirt and making sure my sources are right where I need them.

I'll be back.

And when I return, my big scoop will shock you and everyone in America...

Kisses,

Celebz Leaked

PROLOGUE

Several months earlier

EARL WAYNE JR.

"You called me up here. After telling me you never want to see me again and now you don't want to tell me."

"You can't tell LaShawn I spoke to you."

"I don't talk to LaShawn," I tell him, shifting uncomfortably as I admit it. He doesn't know what's gone down between us since he went to prison and I prefer to keep it that way.

The truth is, LaShawn doesn't talk to me. She grew up with one of the most famous men in America and she doesn't care. Yup, LaShawn isn't your typical teenage girl…

Devonte gives me a suspicious look. "You don't talk to her?"

This shouldn't surprise him. It's not like we've ever been close. She was fifteen years younger than me and my best friend. Even if she's all grown up now, I'm still 6'7", the only man who can make Seb Jefferson feel like a shrimp.

"She's your kid sister and she's terrified of me."

"She's a huge fan of your music."

LaShawn likes all music. She wanted to be a singer but something happened when she was in high school and she stopped caring. Stopped singing. I bet she still listens to the band, not like anyone gives a damn about the *drummer*. I play guitar, but not as well as Seb. Drums are my shit. Loud. Crazy. Just like me.

I sing a couple of the songs but I prefer country to rock. When I go solo, I'll only do country albums. But we're a long ways away from solo album territory.

"What do you want, Devonte?"

"You *owe* me. How could you not be talking to her? With everything going on…"

"What's going on?"

Devonte gives me one of his irritated little side-eyes, the whites of his eyes taking up most of the space on his bald head. He's giving me one of those *I'm tired of you, white boy* looks that he thinks I don't know.

"LaShawn wouldn't want me to tell you about what happened but… I'm worried for her."

"Why? What's going on? Is she finally breaking hearts up at Vanderbilt?" I say, hoping its something light and breezy, hoping that after my family, she'd found some happiness.

Devonte shakes his head, scowling.

"No. Not that. Something happened a long time ago and... whoever hurt LaShawn is back. She's scared. I tried to tell her to get a gun but she's still pissed at me. I don't know what's going on with her and it's killing me in here, man. I have 3 more months. 3 months. And she's my kid sister. I don't want anything to happen to her."

"What are you asking?'

"Go to her. She finishes college in a week. On the day she leaves, get her and take her somewhere safe."

"I'm not leaving Nashville until Seb's wedding."

Devonte snickers.

"Really? Did he even ask you to be the best man."

"Shut up. I'm saving that for your wedding."

Devonte laughs, but it's a sad laugh. He ought to be married already but his girl left when he went into prison. I visit my childhood best friend every week and put money in his commissary. Not too much, because it's already a hassle to keep my identity secret when I visit. I don't want to make things worse than they've already been the past five years.

"She's scared, Earl."

"LaShawn? What the hell could scare LaShawn?"

"She's more sensitive than you think," Devonte snaps protectively. "And nobody in this world looks after black women. She's my sister. I need you to just... get her off that campus and get her safe. I'll be there at the end of the summer and I'll take her off your hands."

"Take her off my hands? Are you asking me to kidnap her?"

"Yes."

"Devonte… It's LaShawn. Can't I just… talk to her."

"Devonte won't want to spend the summer with you."

"Why not? I practically watched her grow up."

"Exactly. And you're famous. She won't want you involved with her problems. But that doesn't matter. She's my sister and she's in trouble."

My stomach twists into a firm knot. LaShawn in trouble? She's the furthest thing from trouble. Devonte's kid sister always has been.

"Fine. I'll do it."

"Thank you."

Devonte sighs and raises his hands exposing the scar on his bicep. I try not to wince. He always made fun of me for being soft when we were kids. Maybe I ain't soft anymore, but I'll never get used to seeing the wounds Devonte has picked up in prison.

"She's hurting Earl. Be careful with her. I just need to make sure that nothing bad happens to her."

"Fine. I can handle that."

"Are you okay?" Devonte asks.

"How the hell can you ask about me?"

"Because. I have three months left. I'm bored. I need something to hold onto."

"I'm fine. Working on the last album and then… that's it. I guess we're done."

START SEDUCING THE SADIST...

"No special lady in your life?"

"Lots of ladies, none of them special."

"Damn, man. I respect that. You can't let these gold digging bitches hold you back."

"Exactly," I say to Devonte, reminding myself that I'm the one who has changed over the years, not him.

"Keep them in line. And keep LaShawn in line. She needs somebody looking after her. And she needs someone to keep guys away."

"Keep guys away?"

"She's been through a lot, Earl. I don't need any men around my little sister screwing with her head. She needs to finish Vanderbilt. She's on an academic scholarship. I just need you to keep her out of trouble."

"Fine. I don't even know how to get in touch with her."

"She lives in student housing. You can find the place and knock on her door. Get her out of there, whatever you have to do."

"Fine. I can handle that."

"No. You don't understand. LaShawn isn't the little girl running behind my mama's skirts. She's bad as hell. Don't be afraid to get rough with her but... not too rough. Hurt her and when I get out of here, I'll kill you."

"Mind telling me what's going on?"

"Not today, Earl. Just please... do me this favor. I owe you when I get out."

"Right. A good beat for my rap album."

Devonte laughs. "Middle America will shit themselves if you put out a rap album."

"Why? Don't think I can rap?"

"No, white boy. I do not. And don't let anybody in here catch you rapping or it's my ass that'll have to pay."

"Yeah. I get it. We don't have much time so… I'll head out. I'll find her and whatever's happening, I'll sort out."

"Thank you."

"You're my brother. I mean that."

"Yeah, white boy. I know."

We don't get much more sentimental than that. I leave the pen incognito — no flashy outfits for once, just a white t-shirt, a leather jacket, my hair tossed up in a dreadful man bun that my dad would hate. I don't want to make more trouble for Devonte. My past isn't a secret, it's just boring so nobody cares. I'm a rich boy on both sides, as white as clouds over North Carolina and easygoing as they come. My parents never had the time of day for me so I ended up spending all my time with *the maid*.

"The maid" as society calls the woman who was more of a mother to me than mine ever was has a name. Eloise Plummer. She immigrated from a small island in the Caribbean with her children — Devonte, who was exactly my age, and LaShawn. The baby. Devonte moved to America at fifteen when LaShawn was only one year old. She doesn't remember immigrating, but he does.

She doesn't remember her first days in America. But I do. We were all raised together and we always looked after each other. Always. LaShawn hasn't spoken to me since she was fourteen. I was already starting with the band back then and I thought she'd be crazy about the whole teen icon thing, but she didn't appear to give a damn. Too bad. It would have been nice to show her how far I'd come since our days playing to together with the horses or the goats.

I don't know why our friendship fell apart. Maybe it's just because I'm a guy and that makes things complicated. I don't know. But now her brother wants me to step in and he says LaShawn's in trouble. If she's in trouble, I owe her. If she's in trouble, I have to do something.

THE HISTORY BETWEEN US

EARL WAYNE JR.

LaShawn. I finally see her coming back to her room. She knows I'm onto her and she's gone out of her way to avoid me. I normally wouldn't have time for things like hunting down LaShawn but… I'm newly and permanently single.

My best friend Mickey told me something that shocked me and everything I thought about Hollywood. I loved LA. I love Nashville. I love every damned place I put my boots. But there's someone I love more than any of that, someone who I hurt. She's like a sister to me. LaShawn.

I have to make amends for what happened. I have to talk to her about what I did.

I wait for her to walk into the building and I glance at my watch. She'll be back in her room in one minute which means I have one minute to justify why I broke into a college student's bedroom at eight in the evening. This ain't exactly my best plan.

I start tossing my baseball to calm down. It's always helped with my ADHD. I can catch it even in the dark. I love the feeling of the smooth leather. It reminds me of the drums. I can always hear a beat. 24/7. And now, I can hear the beat of LaShawn's footsteps coming down the hall. She's had the same walk since she was a kid, believe it or not.

She'll probably shriek like a banshee when she opens the door and finds me in her bed. Yup, I know LaShawn like the back of my hand. Her feet stop in front of the door and I catch my baseball, preparing for death.

LaShawn opens her door and screams bloody murder when she sees me on her bed. After a few seconds, she realizes its me, pulls her backpack off her back and flings it at me.

"Earl, you idiot!"

I try not to laugh at her. She's really scared and since I know what she's been through, it's not exactly a laughing matter. I just had to see her. It didn't matter how I got here.

"Hey."

"What the hell are you doing here?!" LaShawn yells, her chest fluttering like a hummingbird. Damn. I must've really scared her.

"I'm tired of you avoiding me."

"You are so arrogant. I'm not avoiding you."

"Oh yeah? Then why did you scream when you saw me?"

"You broke into my fucking bedroom!"

"It wasn't that hard."

She makes a little growling noise and tries to leave the room, but I am way faster than LaShawn. And bigger. And I know her far too well. Touching her wrist was the wrong move. She flings me off with surprising force for a girl that size.

"Don't touch me, Earl. What do you think Devonte would think if he knew you were in my room in the middle of the night?"

"I already told you that Devonte wants me to protect you."

"That is a joke," she snarls. "A big fucking joke."

"We love you, LaShawn."

"Don't you dare!" She screams. This time, I can tell she's actually angry. I held her in my arms when she was a toddler. I know what she looks like angry. "Don't you dare pull that shit with me. It might work on Devonte, but we are not your siblings, Earl. We were the maid's kids. You got everything in your life handed to you but Devonte got jail. And I got a student loan so big, I don't know if I'll ever be able to pay it off. So stop. We don't want your help and I don't want you in my life."

I bristle. It's not like there isn't an element of truth in what she's saying. Yes, LaShawn was *the maid's* kid. *The maid* has a name. *The maid* remembered my birthday. My father never did.

"I'm sorry about what happened to your mom."

"Your dad raped her," LaShawn snaps. "He's disgusting and your entire family is disgusting. Why do you even go visit

Devonte? Do you get some sick thrill seeing a black man behind bars?"

LaShawn knows me as well as I know her. I was one of the first boys she knew. Our fifteen year age difference made me seem like a man to her far before I was one. And now... she's all grown up. And hates me. She doesn't understand how much I love her family. How sorry I am for what happened.

"Because... he's like a brother to me. I don't hold it against him what he did," I tell her. And I mean it. I visit Devonte because I love him and when he gets out, I will take care of my brother. For life.

LaShawn continues speaking, her voice quaking with rage. "Maybe you should hold it against him. He put your father in the hospital and he'll do it again when he gets out. Stick with your kind, Earl. We'll stick with ours."

"You are my kind," I tell her, grabbing her hand again. This time, I won't let get get away. "I watched you grow up."

"Let go of me."

"I don't want to."

She pushes me. Hard.

"I don't have time for this, Earl. I have to go to Rain's house."

"Rain?"

"She says she's sorry and I'm going to forgive her. Now that bitch is dead, I don't have anything to worry about."

"Little harsh."

"No. It's not harsh," LaShawn snaps.

My chest tightens. It's my fault she became like this. She used to be sweet. Gentle, even. But LaShawn had to toughen up and that's my fault.

"I'll take you. I know the way to Mickey Ford's."

"You aren't invited. It's a family thing."

"Rain's your family?"

"Her mom and I mom went to the same church when we were kids."

"Oh."

"Whatever, I don't have time. I'm just here to change. I'm already running late."

She glares at me like that's going to get me to leave. Oh, LaShawn… I fold my arms and glare back.

"Stop it," she snaps.

"What?"

"Stop glaring back. Just leave."

"I'm coming with you."

"I'm not bringing *you* as a date to Mickey Ford's private dinner party. I don't even want people knowing that I know celebrities."

"Ouch."

"It's awkward and embarrassing. I'd rather focus on my studies."

"I still want to take you out."

"Do you understand the word 'no' Earl?"

"Yes."

She glares harder.

"Please," I tell her. "Can we just talk tonight? It's not a date. I'm fifteen years older than you."

"Right. Like you Hollywood people don't all date kids," she snaps.

"Is that a yes?"

"Did it sound like a yes?"

"Okay. I think you'd look good in something... blue. To match my jeans jacket."

"Earl, I'm going to kill you."

"I know."

"You aren't coming."

"I'll give you a ride."

"Earl!"

"Your brother told me to protect you. I don't know what you need protecting from since you have all the charm of a wolverine, but I care about Devonte. Can't you at least give him peace of mind?"

Weaponizing her brother is low but... it's all I've got. We both love him. That's the only reason she hasn't truly ripped my head off.

"Fine," she says. "But you'd better go mingle the entire time."

"Are you going to wear blue?"

"No," she snaps. "I'm not doing anything you want."

"Except going to the party with me."

LaShawn gives me a bitter glare.

"This is why I hate you."

I thought it was the other reason. You know… the fact that nearly six years ago, I gave LaShawn a contact in Hollywood who flew her out to LA promising her dreams would come true and had her raped.

I never knew until recently. Not until Mickey Ford told me the details and I pieced together all the half-truths and the clues. Six years, she never told me.

I never knew how the meeting went, just that she wanted nothing to do with me. I didn't know what would happen. I can see on her face that she blames me. She thinks I set her up.

I don't blame her. My father touched women. Lots of women. He never quite made it to prison.

But I'm nothing like him. I won't hurt LaShawn. No one will ever hurt her again without going through me first.

"Let's go to Mickey's. I promise you can call me every name in the book on the way there."

"I'm in college, so I know a lot of names now."

"Good. I'd like to hear you call me every single one of them."

"Good, big head. Now *leave*. I need to change into a dress that looks half decent."

"Something blue," I tell her, with a cheeky grin.

1

BLUE.

LASHAWN

I can't believe I'm wearing blue. I hate Earl, but the only dress nice enough to see my ex-best friend with her new celebrity boyfriend is blue. This is just like Rain. She's one of those people who life always works out for. Seriously.

I had to claw my way into Vanderbilt and now that I'm here… I hate it.

I just finished paying off my dorm supplies from freshman year and my roommate's dad just got her a new car. There wasn't even anything wrong with her old car. She just *wanted a change*.

Earl would be better off taking my roommate to this stupid soiree. I don't even know why I'm going. I already forgive Rain for what happened. That's not why I haven't replied to her. I can't tell her the real reason until I meet up with her. Tonight.

Earl definitely gets in the way of this stupid plan, but I can't get rid of him. Not yet. I don't know why he keeps clinging to our stupid past together. We aren't really relatives and we definitely aren't friends.

"You look nice," he says, bending so he can re-enter my room. I glare at him. Just seeing Earl in here makes me want to throttle him.

"Whatever."

"You always wore blue as a kid."

"I always wore your sister's hand me downs, actually."

"I don't remember it like that."

"Of course you don't," she snaps. "Whatever, if you're driving me, let's go. I don't want to be late."

"Late? It's Mickey. If anyone will be late, it's him."

"Whatever."

"Want to drive my car?"

He dangles the keys in front of me like whatever stupid luxury vehicle he has is going to impress me. He's driven luxury cars his entire life. What's the big deal?

I roll my eyes. Earl is always doing this dumb big brother thing. It was cute when I was actually a kid but I haven't been a kid since… let's just say I haven't been a real kid for a long time.

"I don't care about your stupid car."

"Oh yeah? Even if it's your favorite."

"I don't have a favorite car."

"The LaShawn Plummer I remember *loved* taking rides in my Benz. What if I told you this car is just like the Benz but quieter. Sexier. Better backseat."

"I'd tell you to tell your girlfriend."

"I'm single, actually. For a while."

Earl? Single? I don't remember a time in my life when Earl didn't have a harem of women surrounding him.

"I don't believe you."

"Believe it. I'm 100% single."

"Have you gone crazy yet?"

"I don't need a relationship to be sane. Now are you going to get in the car?"

"Quit bugging me. I'm ready."

"You look great."

I hate that after all this time Earl saying those words has an effect on me. But I can't help it. I could never help any of this. I never stood a chance. I grew up at his feet and then I grew up fetching things for his daddy, brushing his sister's hair before school, helping my mama work around the house. I never understood how fucked up everything was until later.

But how could I have grown up without crushing on Earl? He was my first crush. My first crush was my first mistake. But still, there's an unmistakable pleasure I feel with his compliment.

I follow him to his car. Under the cover of night, it's easier for him to avoid detection although I don't think Earl cares about detection or he wouldn't wear that stupid cowboy hat or these absurd belt buckles all the time.

This one says *Blonds Do It Better* with a half-naked woman posing suggestively on it. It's so hideous that I bet it's custom.

"How've you been?"

"Don't make conversation. Just get me there."

I try not to act like his stupid car impresses me. It's orange, of course, that's just like Earl, and the seats are comfortable. It does remind me of the car he got when he turned twenty-one. I was just a kid when he'd take me for ice-cream or to the grocery store. I feel so old but Earl barely looks like he's aged except for the beard.

I feel guilty when he listens to me and for once in his life, stops trying to make conversation. When he finally stops the car in front of Mickey and Rain's place, I know I can't keep it all in. I have to say something.

"Sorry for being a bitch."

"You are not a bitch," he says, deliberating over each word. "Never."

"I am."

"No. You're not."

"Whatever."

"Are we ever going to talk about what happened?"

I glare at him. Seriously, Earl? I have way more important things to worry about tonight than the fact that Earl set me up to get gang-raped when I was fourteen.

"No."

"It wasn't a setup. I promise. I didn't know."

"But you weren't there," I whisper. "They raped me and you weren't even there to answer for it."

My cheeks feel really hot and I want to burst out of Earl's car and run. I don't even want to go toward Rain's place or see Earl's Rebel Blood band mate Mickey Ford. I want to sink into the ground and forget that I never had a choice in the matter of Earl Wayne Jr.

He's been in my life since I was a baby. Since before he became famous — when he was just rich, without all the problems. I didn't even want Earl to know that anyone raped me. The last thing I wanted was to be here, talking to him about it. Remembering.

"I can answer for it now. Anything you want. Anything you need."

"I don't need anything from you," she snaps. "Not everyone's after your family's stupid money."

"LaShawn!" He calls after me once I burst from his car and flee. I end up going toward the house, against my better judgment. I'm already here and since nothing is going right, I have to make something go right. I need to talk to Rain about what I've been doing during college instead of making friends with the stuck up rich kids of Vanderbilt.

But Earl won't just let me go. He won't leave me alone. I feel his hand on my wrist and a surge of terror rushes me. I whip around, my instincts forcing me to press my hands to his chest to push him away. I want him gone. But when my hands touch his chest, they bump up against something firm and solid.

My tongue hangs in my mouth like a cotton ball. Earl's white t-shirt is the type of cotton so soft it feels like silk and my polyester dress feels itchy and cheap in comparison. He holds my hands to his chest, tightening his grip so I can't move.

"LaShawn… stop."

"Let me go, Earl."

"Don't fight me."

"Let. Me. Go."

"I'm worried about you."

"I'm fine."

"You were such a happy kid. It's my fault that's gone."

"Yes. It is your fault. Thanks for the ride but I don't need to stand here talking to you anymore."

He lets me go, but he follows, keeping pace a few steps behind even if it would be easy for him to catch up to me and even easier for him to overpower me. When I get to the door, I'm about to knock when Earl juts his hand out and touches the keypad with elongated fingers.

"Don't worry. I have the code."

"Or I could ring the doorbell like a normal person."

He just has to flex. Earl punches in the code and pushes the front door open. This place is swanky. I'm not even jealous of Rain, I'm impressed. This place is crazy and Mickey Ford got it all for her. We take a few steps forward into the large foyer when I hear a strange noise.

"Do you hear that?" I whisper to Earl, who stands behind me, even if it's annoying. "Yeah. I do. Kitchen's that way, probably where the staff is. Come on, let's go this way."

Toward the noise? I guess I don't have a choice.

2

HER BUTT IN THE DRESS

EARL

Try not to think about her butt in the dress. Try not to think about her butt in the dress.

She's like a sister to me, but the second LaShawn steps forward toward the noise in the other room, my eyes are glued to her ass. I've never had anything like this happen before. And with LaShawn? It feels downright seedy. But there's a butt in front of Earl. A big, round, juicy bubble butt. With jiggle.

I bite down hard enough to make my lower lip bleed. But as I dab my lower lip with my thumb and glance down, I miss the exact scene that makes LaShawn yelp in surprise.

"OH MY GOD!" Rain yells, attempting to climb her naked body off of Mickey Ford's on their couch. Mickey grabs onto her, misinterpreting her moves and causing Rain to sail backward, her nude body splaying wildly as Mickey covers her breasts.

"You're early!" Rain squeaks, reaching for a cute pink dress.

"Sorry," LaShawn says, glancing at me awkwardly.

"We apologize. We'll just uh… head into the other room."

I grab LaShawn and pull her away toward's Mickey's dinning table, which is set for once. He barely eats. Certainly he doesn't eat as much as I do. We can smell dinner and hear staff from the kitchen but LaShawn looks distressed.

"Fuck. That was so awkward. I should leave."

"No! It's fine. Stuff like that happens to Mickey all the time."

"That doesn't make me feel better."

I want to reach out and touch her, but I think better of it. LaShawn would probably kick me in the balls if I tried anything she didn't want. I peek around the corner. Rain and Mickey are arguing now as they both dress.

"Uh… best stay here for a minute."

"Great. This is already ten times more awkward than I wanted it to be."

She folds her arms over her chest and I feel a strange flutter in my chest. Protect her. That's what Devonte wanted me to do, right?

"Listen, kid—

"Don't call me kid."

"I always call you kid."

LaShawn glares. This glare makes her look exactly like her mama — the woman who taught me how to trim my beard and tie my shoelaces. The woman who raised me more than my parents ever did.

"Stop it."

"Stop what?"

"I already told you. We aren't related, Earl. You aren't my big brother. We aren't even friends. If you want to help Devonte, good for you, but I don't want your help."

"Not even with the situation out there?"

Now LaShawn is definitely going to kill me.

"Name one way you could possibly make that any better."

I don't get a chance because Rain ambles around the corner wide-eyed and very slightly pregnant.

"Sorry," she says. "Everyone in our family is always late so we set the time early and didn't think anyone would show up."

"Hi," LaShawn says. "I'm here."

Rain hugs her and LaShawn tries to hug her back, but I sense her reluctance. Mickey appears behind Rain. He's the band's bassist and just got himself a new fiancée. A new *pregnant* fiancée who happens to know LaShawn, but I don't know the details of how.

Rain breaks away and sighs.

"I'm so sorry."

"You were only doing what you had to do. We both know that Lottie could ruin lives."

"Yeah. We do."

LaShawn's eyes flitter awkwardly from Mickey to Rain.

"Rain? Can I talk to you alone?"

Rain nods and that leaves me and Mick together for a spell. I pat him on the back with a large hand and Mickey doesn't buckle under the weight of it. Since he entered treatment, he's been getting stronger.

"Everything cool?" He asks, an oddly suspicious tone in his voice.

"Why wouldn't it be cool?"

"You've never talked about that girl but... you know her. Really well."

"I don't talk about her because there's nothing to talk about. She's family, that's all."

"Your daddy messed around?"

Yes, my father messed around, but LaShawn isn't my biological sister. I hate hearing questions about my personal life, even if it's from someone like Mickey who has bared himself to me more times than I can count. I still feel weak telling him. I still feel... shame.

"No. It's not like that. I've known her since she was a baby. I'm protective, that's all."

Mickey smiles, one of his obnoxious smiles that usually means he's going to say something dumb.

"If it's not like that, why were you checking out her ass?"

Fuck. I seriously hate Mickey Ford.

"Watch the way you talk about LaShawn," I snap. "She's not like that. She's not a girl like that. She's nineteen."

"Damn. I know. I know what she's been through."

"Then keep your mouth shut around her," I grumble.

"Easy, big guy. Want a drink?"

"Thought you were sober."

"I meant orange juice. You can mix it with whatever demonic concoction you have in that flask of yours."

I put my hand on my jacket pocket. Fuck. Where on earth is my flask? Mickey laughs when he notices me searching desperately for it. He peers around the door and starts laughing louder.

"What?"

"She's got your flask."

"What?"

I follow him and we both quietly look around the corner to see Rain and LaShawn talking, LaShawn sipping from my flask. How the hell did she get that from my pocket? Sigh.

She might not forgive me now, but ironically I take her stealing from me as some sign that there might be hope. While Devonte's in prison, someone has to keep her safe. I don't know from what yet, but I know something's going on.

Mickey puts his hand on my shoulder.

"So. Going to explain why you were looking at her ass?"

I throw his hand off me.

"Shut up, Ford."

"You like her?"

"No. I don't like her. I told you, she's like a sister to me. If you caught me looking at her ass it was only because… blue's my favorite color."

Mickey looks at me skeptically.

"Is that why your car is orange?"

"Shut up."

"Why don't you go for it, man?"

"Go for it?" I snap. "Didn't I already tell you not to talk about her like that."

"I mean a relationship. You're single, aren't you."

"I've known her since she was a baby and she's 15 years younger than me. I'd be better off dating Tati."

Mickey rolls my eyes.

"Please tell me you haven't gone there recently."

"No. I haven't gone anywhere recently. I'm backed up. That's probably why I'm looking at her ass."

"So you're single single. Not three or four backups single."

"Can you stop fucking reminding me?"

"Sorry."

"Aren't your family members coming to this dinner?"

"Yup."

"Do they know you aren't married?"

"Nope."

"Won't that be a nightmare?"

"Yup?"

"Then why did you invite LaShawn?"

Mickey shrugs. "I dunno. The more the merrier. I can smell something good in the kitchen. We should go steal a piece. I'm famished."

"You look famished," I mutter under my breath, following Mickey to the kitchen. I'm surprised he doesn't have Seb sprawled out on the couch, but I have to remember that Seb has his own family now and Mickey's about to do the same. Settle down. The thought makes me uncomfortable. Earl Wayne Sr settled down and look at how that turned out. Four unhappy wives. Several mistresses. And then his victims.

I'm better off alone, but it's hard not to feel a pang of something watching a guy like Mickey Ford act like a grown up. Act like... *a father*.

I'm here with a girl who doesn't even want me here. Maybe I should *date*. But I can't... not when it's my priority to look after LaShawn Plummer. Devonte doesn't ask much of me and I owe him so much more than this.

3

SHEZ BACK

LASHAWN

Rain has always had stupidly big eyes. They draw you into her round face. Because she's so dark, you don't even notice her other features until you get sucked in.

I'm the other way around. My skin is brown, like medium leather, and my nose and lips are a different shade from everything so it's the first thing people notice about me. I've always wished I had eyes like Rain's.

I feel oddly guilty beneath her gaze, even if she's the one apologizing. We had a falling out years ago, when we were both selling information to a celebrity gossip blog. I got out, Rain didn't, but somehow, her life worked out and she ended up engaged to Mickey Ford, the *Rebel Blood* bassist.

I can't believe she's apologizing to me when I'm the one who ghosted her all those years ago. I just wanted out and I didn't care who I hurt.

"I never held it against you," I tell her. "I swear."

"How did you hide that you *knew* Earl Wayne Jr. like... the entire time I knew you?" She asks, still the investigator.

"My family life has always been a mess. You know that," I explain. Rain definitely knows all about that. Her parents don't care about her and only want to marry her off so they can get back to their church social calendar.

"But *how*?"

"My mom's a maid," I tell her. "I didn't tell anybody at school because they were already roasting me for my relaxer, my off brand sneakers, my big nose and everything else. So no, I didn't tell them that I basically grew up a house slave to the richest family in the South."

Rain doesn't look judgmental or disbelieving, but she's one of those people who always has to know somebody's business. It made her a great gossip blogger and it makes her a good friend — if she's on your side.

"A house slave? Earl had slaves?"

I can hear the excited pitch in her voice go up. Even if she's changed, there's probably still a part of her writing the gossip blog headline in her head.

Crusty Earl Wayne Jr's SLAVE speaks out. Or something.

"My mama lived there in a little guest house and it was basically a shack where she stayed with me and Devonte. That was only when they were in the city. They mostly spent the summers in Nashville and my mom would just clean the house and stuff when they weren't there. A few times they'd come during the school year."

"That's crazy. So he was really really rich before the band."

"Yup."

Rain shifts uncomfortably and then she seems to muster up the courage to say something.

"I want us to be friends, LaShawn. I know I betrayed you and I know you have your own stuff going on but... it's almost over. *Celebz Leaked* is gone and I can make it up to you now."

Really? Almost over? I hesitate. Rain might have appeared naive, but when it came to Celebz Leaked — the gossip blog — she was usually the furthest thing from naive. She bordered on paranoid.

"It's not over," I say bluntly. "Three months ago, Tati's nudes leaked."

"There's been nothing since. It must have been old content that was scheduled. The new owners took the pics down."

"So you haven't seen it?"

"Seen what? I got rid of my smartphone."

"The new *Celebz Leaked* post..."

Hey motherfuckers.
I killed someone.
I know, I probably shouldn't admit this on the internet, right?
Let's call it satire.
I just had to get my hands on this blog.
I needed to share my big scoop with all of you.
So yes, I stole *Celebz Leaked*.
I killed for it.

This tired little website has gone on too long with half-truths and dumb celebrity gossip.

That's going to change.

I'm going to get the truth about everyone from the closest sources.

Leakers, you're the best at digging up dirt, but let's be real… you need someone who doesn't just dig things up.

You need someone willing to get dirty.

I'll need to lay low for a while collecting dirt and making sure my sources are right where I need them.

I'll be back.

And when I return, my big scoop will shock you and everyone in America…

Kisses,

Celebz Leaked

Finally, the expression I expect appears on Rain's face.

"When did this go up?"

"Last week. But that's not all… Someone's blackmailing me."

"Blackmailing you? About what?"

Before I can answer, we both hear the rest of Rain's guests arriving.

"We'll talk about this later," she says. "Have you told Earl?"

"No. And I don't think you should tell Mickey. We can work this out in secret."

"I don't like keeping secrets from Mickey," Rain says, glancing over her shoulder guiltily. "But I want to help you. If anything gets too real, I have to tell him, okay?"

"Fine. I get it. But I still want to keep Earl out of this."

"RAIN!" Her mother yells across the house. "Damn, baby girl, this place is amazing!"

I think Rain ended up so quiet because her mom is so loud. I close one of my eyes to adjust to the ringing in my ear. Rain runs off to greet her family and before I can make an appearance, I hear Earl stalking up behind me with his giant boots.

"Someone has to clean up the mud you track everywhere with these things," I tell him, without turning around.

"Uh huh. What were you two whispering about?"

"None of your business."

"My flask?"

I smirk. Pickpocketing Earl is honestly too easy. I spent most of my childhood getting my lunch money that way. One summer I'd saved up $276.45 in spare change I found at the bottom of his car.

"What's in it? It's nasty as hell."

"A little family whiskey. A little Caribbean rum. A couple caffeine pills."

"How are you even alive?"

"I chase it down with OJ. Want some?"

"No thanks."

"Everything good between the two of you?"

"That's none of your business."

"LaShawn…"

"What?"

"I'm trying. Please." I almost want to feel something when I look at Earl. He's always been larger than life to me. Seriously, he looks like he stepped off the page of an old Gap ad, except he insists on dressing like a crazed cowboy now. When he was a kid it was all Nantucket reds and bright polo shirts.

I hate that he's trying. I hate that he thinks we're a family when nothing could be further from the truth.

"I don't care."

"Fine. If we have to put up with each other the entire night, we might as well get drunk."

I snatch the flask. Good point. I got through most of the hard part with Rain and I need to face Aunty Kirsten (not my real aunty) who is a church aunty in every sense of the word. Apparently, Mickey Ford has a religious family too. Bottoms up.

I wince as I choke down Earl's nasty concoction.

"It's seriously disgusting."

"Next time I'll bring chardonnay."

"There won't be a next time. I don't want to talk to you."

"I gave you space for three months. Three months, LaShawn. Do you know how that killed me?"

START SEDUCING THE SADIST...

4
THE ACCIDENT

EARL

She never answers my question. She just tips more of my liquor down her throat and hands it back to me. Yes, I'll need a lot of this to get through the night. LaShawn wants nothing to do with me but I'm not letting her go back to that shitty dorm tonight.

I might not have overheard everything, but I heard that she's in trouble and if that damned blog is involved again... I swear... I'll have to do something about it.

We sit through dinner mostly ignoring each other. It's awkward. Very awkward. Then it turns into a screaming match. Then Rain confesses she and Mickey aren't married. Then the screaming match gets louder. LaShawn gives me an uncomfortable look. Mickey's mom calls him a sinner. He lifts his shirt and shows her a tattoo of an upside down cross. Now, she doesn't know Mickey got it by accident, because he's an idiot, and she starts praying.

Loudly.

LaShawn looks at me pleadingly. Yeah... She's right. Maybe it's time to go. Before the blessing/exorcism proceeds any further, we flee out the back door. LaShawn giggles the entire way down the elevator and then stumbles into me. Holy shit. She's drunk. I'm better at holding my liquor but clearly not much.

"Careful," I chuckle, stumbling back and doing a horrible job of holding her up. She leans back, falling away from me and slams into the emergency stop. We both laugh and lean against the walls.

"Wait..." she gasps between laughter. "Why is it stopped?"

"I don't know," I say. "I don't have a fucking clue."

We laugh more. Again. When you're drunk, the stupidest shit seems funny and right then, the stopped elevator between Mickey and Rain's new penthouse and the ground floor seems to be hilarious.

"I'll press the button LaShawn says triumphantly. Then she smiles and pushes it. Nothing happens."

"Here. I think it's this."

I lean over to push the emergency stop again but the elevator lurches and I fall against her, pushing her against the buttons. My body rests uncomfortable against hers, pinning her to the wall of the elevator. Before I can push away from LaShawn, our eyes meet. *No.*

My throat tightens and something I've been avoiding for months, probably years, swells within me. My voice comes out hoarse and desperate.

"Sorry."

"Get off me, Earl," she says.

"Yeah."

I step away from her but our eyes haven't moved away from each other. LaShawn's tongue juts out of her mouth, wetting her lower lips. I hate that I'm looking at her lips.

"I think the elevator's broken," she says.

"No. It's the button."

"The button doesn't work. See."

She slams the button and then the elevator jostles again, but doesn't move.

"Fuck," I whisper. "Fuck."

"It's okay, just use your phone."

We both whip our phones out. No signal. No wifi. Nothing.

"This is useless," LaShawn says. "Shit. Like my life couldn't get any more annoying."

"What's annoying about your life?"

"I don't want to do this, Earl," she snaps, an edge returning. "I just don't!"

She's drunk, I remind myself. Over emotional. But that doesn't stop my heart from beating a million miles a minute.

"I missed you."

I cross the little distance between us in the elevator.

"I mean it. I missed you. Devonte's gone and I have the band, I get that. But it's not home."

I can see her chest heaving rapidly. She's nervous. Or maybe just drunk. And I'm drunk. I must be. Because I start getting stupid and the next stupid idea that pops into my head I act on.

"You don't want to talk. Fine. I don't either."

I kiss her. For the first time. Ever. I swear I never had before and that I never wanted to. I tell myself it's the way the butt looked in that blue dress or the liquor coursing through me, but it doesn't matter. The need for her is urgent. And I take her lower lips between mine ignoring the urge to bite. Fighting the urge to hurt her.

I expect her to push me off any second but when her hands rush to my chest, she grabs the fringe on my buckskin jacket and pulls me against her. LaShawn kisses me back. She giggles and then pulls away, wiping her mouth.

"That. Was. So. Stupid."

Okay. Not exactly what I expect.

"Thanks."

"You have no idea," she says, now giggling and rambling. "I've had a crush on you since I was like… five."

"I was *twenty* back then," I remind her. I know, I kissed her first, but I still have a sense of right and wrong. It was one drunken kiss. It doesn't mean anything.

"I'm almost twenty," she says, giggling. "So that makes this 100% legal."

What the fuck is happening? I thought she wanted to rip my head off. LaShawn pounces. Grabbing my shirt again and then kissing me. She's a little messy but it's cute and I slow her down with my lips, savoring her. Tasting her. A crush?

Her hands slide under my shirt and I stumble with her against the wall as she kisses me. I love the way her hand feels and even if every part of me wants her now... *I can't.*

"LaShawn... stop."

"Why?" She whispers. "I know the men in your family like black women."

The hair on the back of my neck stands up. I'm nothing like Earl Wayne Sr. Nothing.

"Stop," I whisper. "It's just... we can't."

"You kissed me," she says, offended, stumbling back as all her emotions get magnified through drunkenness. "You kissed me like a pervert I might add."

"LaShawn..."

"I mean... what are you even doing here?"

"I'm here to look after you."

She's against the wall of the elevator again and I lean forward, pushing her into it. Hating the conflict surging through me. Have her. Fuck her. Own her. Stop her. Save her. Protect her. Our eyes can't stop boring into each other. We've never looked at each other like this before.

"I get it," she whispers. "You won't do it because of Devonte."

"He would kill us."

"He's in jail. It doesn't matter."

"It matters."

Then her brow crinkles with worry.

"It's the rape thing, isn't it?"

"It's not that. Fuck that. I'm going to kill those guys."

"Great, maybe you and Devonte will share a jail cell."

"I'm serious, LaShawn. I didn't know."

And finally, she relents, giving just the smallest part of herself.

"Of course you didn't know," she says. "But that doesn't make it easy to face you."

"Why not?"

She doesn't answer again. She just grabs my cheeks, raking her fingers through the blond stubble as she tiptoes to kiss me. She can hardly reach. She'll need me to lift her. I grab LaShawn and press her against the walls of the elevator, lifting her effortlessly.

"Why not?" I repeat, hoping this time, she'll answer.

5

GODS & MORTALS

LASHAWN

I grab onto Earl's blond hair. I've never touched it like this. I've never touched him. He was always like a God to me. Mortals don't touch gods. He presses his hips against me.

"Why not?"

"You wouldn't get it."

He peels the strap of my dress off my shoulder and kisses it gently. Lovingly.

"I need you," he whispers. "I know... I shouldn't..."

I push his dumb buckskin jacket off over his shoulders. This would be much easier if we were just naked. If we just got it over with. I'm not sober enough to stop myself from careening into this bad decision, but I'm the one who wants it. His jacket hits the elevator floor with a thud.

His shirt already sticks to his torso with sweat. It reminds me of the summers I grew up watching him toss a football around with Devonte and then tackling my brother to the ground. Now my hands grasp his sweaty shirt and I can only make myself say two words.

"Fuck me."

Earl pulls away from me for a moment, the words coming out of my mouth stunning him. He takes my lower lip between his teeth and squeezes slightly. It hurts. It hurts a lot. But kissing him will hurt anyway once I'm sober. Now, I'm drunk. And he's hot. His shoulders are even more broad than I remember and he hasn't aged in about a decade.

His hands rush to his belt buckle, but he's too drunk to get it open properly. I help him, lacing my fingers against his as I pry it open and get his pants down. He's hard. Really hard. And… *HUGE*.

"Oh my God!" I gasp as his dick unfolds out of his pants, uncoiling like an anaconda and hanging nearly down to his knees. It's not just that the monstrous thing is long, it's thick. Thicker than a coke can. Earl presses his hips into me again and this time when I gasp, it's terror.

"You can change your mind," he slurs drunkenly.

"No…" I whisper, because I'm too drunk to do any better. "I can take it."

"Are you sure?"

"Yes…"

Earl spreads my thighs apart and then presses his fingers between them, touching my basic white underwear beneath my dress. He moans.

"LaShawn… you're wet."

"Stop talking," I whisper, just in case Earl says too much and knocks me into sobriety. He grunts in response, obedient at least to this single request. Earl guides the head of his rigid member to my entrance and my thighs tremble as I have second thoughts. How long is this thing!?

His dick is so big it looks almost alien. I squeeze my thighs around his hips. Earl runs a finger over my lips.

"Scared?"

"No," I whisper, but then I scream *loudly* when he slides his length into me. Earl grins and then takes my lower lip between his teeth, biting hard. I can feel the blood coming out of my lip but I don't respond with anything except a loud moan from Earl burying his cock deep inside me.

He holds himself into me, grunting.

"I'm in," he whispers. "Holy fuck, you're tight."

I rip his shirt open and run my hands over his chest. Then his biceps. Earl has always had some of the nicest arms ever. He moves his hips faster as I grab onto his torso. With only two strokes, I cum… hard. He's enormous. His dick is so big that the slightest movement rubs *every* inch of me.

It's basically a giant walking cum stick. Each time I cum, Earl only moves his hips faster. His large body grunts against mine as he pins me to the wall, keeping me beneath his absolute control. Earl spreads my thighs wider, his finger finding my clit and delivering more pleasure than I think I can handle.

As I cum again, I squeeze my thighs tighter around him and then I feel him practically collapsing against me. His orgasmic groan sounds more like an animal roaring as he erupts inside me. The earth-shattering force of his thick cock bursting within me pushes me to the edge again and we both come to a very drunken simultaneous orgasm.

My fingers tangle with his blond hair as our lips meet. He's still inside me, his cum filling me as we kiss. Earl's kisses get more aggressive. I kiss back harder too. I hate him. I've hated him for so long. I blamed him. But this release feels... better than it should.

He eases me onto the elevator floor, helping me adjust my dress. Then he stumbles backward, putting his hand to his forehead.

"Fuck," he groans. "Fuck..."

His cock still hangs out of his pants. I'm still drunk enough to find it funny. I giggle and then the elevator starts moving as Earl begins the project of trying to roll his dick up the right way to get it in his pants before the elevator hits the ground floor.

"A little help here," he grunts. I stumble forward and by the time the elevator doors open we look *extremely* disheveled and my hands are inside Earl's pants. Oops. The elevator attendants apologize profusely for the delay and say a bunch of other stuff, but I don't even care or notice.

"I'm too drunk to drive," Earl says. "C'mon."

He throws his arm around me and if he's too drunk to drive, I'm too drunk to protest.

"Where are we going?"

"Calling my private car. I'm taking you to my place."

"Where do you even live in this city?"

I bet it's somewhere insanely tacky — like a bachelor pad on steroids. That's just Earl. I get it. He grew up in a house where all the walls and all the clothes were plain white. He wanted to be normal. He throws his giant arm over me and pulls me against him. I hate that the buckskin jacket smells so much like him and how that makes my thighs feel like they're glued together.

"A mile away from Mickey's place. Not far."

He ushers me into the back of the private car and puts the partition up. Earl leans over and grins at me.

"So. We're drunk."

"Yes."

"Very drunk," he says.

"Yes."

"How?!"

"Um, pretty sure that's your fault."

"No way," he whispers. "I had to drink to make it through the night without doing this."

Earl touches my cheek gently and then draws it to his. We're kissing again and it feels amazing. He pushes me back slightly and then he's on top of me.

"We have five minutes," he whispers. "Five minutes is a long time, LaShawn."

He lifts my dress again, kissing his way down my stomach. I close my eyes and let myself just feel him kissing me all the way down to my thighs. He pushes his nose between my breath first and I moan when his nose touches my underwear. I clamp my hand over my mouth. There's a *driver* here. I might be drunk but I don't need to do the most.

Earl's tongue darts out of his mouth and he licks juices off my thighs. *Fuck.* I moan even louder and he peels my underwear off again, pressing his fully flattened tongue against my opening. The pleasure is indescribable…

My fingers grab onto a handful of his blond hair and I stop thinking about anything except Earl's perfect tongue.

Click here to order.

FREE DARK ROMANCE BOOK

This month's kinky kinda-dark but not too crazy biker romance freebie 👇

READ FREE HERE 👇:
https://dl.bookfunnel.com/mn31wrohe8

EXTREMELY IMPORTANT LINKS

ALL BOOKS BY JAMILA JASPER
https://linktr.ee/JamilaJasper
SIGN UP FOR EMAIL UPDATES
Bit.ly/jamilajasperromance
SOCIAL MEDIA LINKS
https://www.jamilajasperromance.com/
GET MERCH
https://www.redbubble.com/people/jamilajasper/shop
GET FREEBIE (VIA TEXT)
https://slkt.io/qMk8
READ SERIAL (NEW CHAPTERS WEEKLY)
www.patreon.com/jamilajasper

JAMILA JASPER

Diverse Romance For Black Women

MORE JAMILA JASPER ROMANCE

Pick your poison... Delicious interracial romance novels for all tastes. Long novels, short stories, audiobooks and more. Hit the link to experience my full catalog:

FULL CATALOG BY JAMILA JASPER:
https://www.jamilajasperromance.com/books

MORE DISCOUNTED BUNDLES

PATREON

7 SEASONS OF SERIAL CHAPTERS

NEW serial chapters published WEEKLY on my Patreon.

Read all six seasons of *Unfuckable* (Ben & Libby's story)...

For a small monthly fee, you get exclusive access to over 375 episodes of my first completed serial as well as access to the current ongoing serial, *Despicable*.

PATREON

PATREON HAS MORE THAN THE ONGOING SERIAL...

⚡ INSTANT ACCESS ⚡

- NEW merchandise tiers with **t-shirts, totes, mugs,** stickers and MORE!
- **FREE paperback** with all new tiers
- **FREE short story audiobooks** and audiobook samples when they're ready
- #FirstDraftLeaks of Prologues and first chapters **weeks** before I hit publish
- Behind the scenes notes
- Polls and story contribution
- Comments & LIVELY community discussion with likeminded interracial romance readers.

LEARN MORE ABOUT SUPPORTING A DIVERSE ROMANCE AUTHOR
www.patreon.com/jamilajasper

ABOUT JAMILA JASPER

Jamila Jasper is an Amazon bestselling author of African American women's fiction and romance novels. She writes contemporary interracial romance novels with gut-wrenching plots, titillating alpha male bad boys, and strong female main characters from diverse backgrounds — from London, to Atlanta, to Kampala. In her free time, Jamila enjoys hiking, spending time with her cat and salsa dancing. Use the icons below to find Jamila Jasper on social media. Use the hashtag #JamilaBWWM and post the Jamila Jasper book you read online for a social media shoutout!

- facebook.com/bwwmjamila
- twitter.com/jamilajasper
- instagram.com/bwwmjamila
- amazon.com/author/jamilajasper
- bookbub.com/authors/jamilajasper

THANK YOU KINDLY

Thank you to all my readers, new and old for your support with this new year. I look forward to making 2021 an INCREDIBLE year for interracial romance novels. I want to thank you all for joining along on the journey.

Thank you to my most supportive readers:
Sydney, Phia, Sharon, Charlotte, Assiatu, Regina, Romanda, Catherine, Gaynor, BF, Tasha, Henri, Sara, skkent, Rosalyn, Danielle, Deborah, Kirsten, Ana, Taylor, Charlene Louanna, Michelle, Tamika, Lauren, RoHyde, Natasha, Shekynah, Cassie, Dreama, Nick, Gennifer, Rayna, Jaleda, Anton, Kimvodkna, Jatonn, Anoushka, Audrey, Valeria, Courtney, Donna, Jenetha, Ayana, Kristy, FreyaJo, Grace, Kisha, Stephanie E., Amber, Denice, Marty, LaKisha, Latoya, Natasha, Monifa, Alisa, Daveena, Desiree, Gerry, Kimberly, Stephanie M., Tarah, Yolanda, Kristy, Gary, Janet, Kathy, Phyllis, Susan

Join the Patreon Community.

Made in the USA
Middletown, DE
14 June 2023